MACKENZY FOX

AXTON

BRACKEN RIDGE REBELS MC

BOOK 7

DEDICATION

For my readers. I cherish all of you,
thank you for your continued support x

AUTHOR NOTE

CONTENT WARNING: Axton is a steamy romance for readers 18+ it contains mature themes that may make some readers uncomfortable. It includes violence, possible triggers such as prison, guns, kidnapping and as always….LOTS of steamy love scenes!

BLURB

Bracken Ridge Arizona, where the Rebels M.C. rule and the only thing they ride or die for more than their club is their women, this is Axton's story

AXTON:

I'm supposed to feel elated, on top of the world; ten years of hell and now I'm free.

I want to make amends, right the wrongs and let go of the past.

Yet, the fire still rages within.

The time I lost, the family that moved on, the friends that let go.

The one thing I didn't expect, was her.

She's my new boss, the one I answer to, she's off limits. And I've gotta toe the line or I'll end up back in jail.

I fight every instinct that tells me to take her, screw the consequences.

I thought there couldn't be anything worse than a prison cell, but I was wrong.

My own personal brand of purgatory is taunting me, testing me and this is one fight I cannot fail.

For everyone's sakes.

STEVIE:

I don't know what I expected from my new employee, but *this* isn't it.

He's everything that spells ex-con.

Rough round the edges, covered in tattoos and eyes that burn like wildfire.

I'm meant to live and work beside him, be his boss, show him the ropes.

But all of that goes out the window the minute we're alone together.

I didn't expect my insides to ignite every time I see him.

The skeletons in his closet hang over him like a dark cloud, one that draws me in no matter how I try to fight it.

And fight I will.

I can't fall for the resident bad boy.

I know he's not good for me, no matter how much my wildest desires crave him.

NOTE: This book is book 7 in a series but is written as a stand-alone with no cliff hanger and a HEA. Recommended for mature readers only, it has adult content.

Bracken Ridge Rebels rule...enter at own risk!

BRACKEN RIDGE
REBELS
ARIZONA
M · C

CHAPTER 7

AXTON

It feels surreal to be walking these halls for the last time. While it feels like a lifetime, I know I've got so much to make up for; I came in at nineteen years old, now I'm twenty-nine.

The one thing I did right was get my eight thousand hours in electrical contracting completed once I was moved out of maximum security. Now I just have to apply for my license so I can practice legally.

I snort at the notion. *Legally.*

So much has changed since I was on the outside.

Some talk about how hard it is tryin' to get back into society, others say it's easy. Just gotta put your mind to it and keep outta trouble. That's easier said than done.

I've lost count of the number of guys that I've seen leave, then come back within a couple of years or even months. It's like a revolving door, and that's what fucks with my head the most.

I don't ever wanna be back in this place ever again.

Maximum was no fun.

Minimum was no picnic either.

I've been caged for so long that I don't even remember what it's like to feel simple enjoyment anymore. The only thing anyone can look forward to in the joint is the day you leave.

Sure, I kept myself busy. I kept in shape. Lucky for me, I was already fairly solid when I came in here — even at nineteen — but that don't mean shit when you're new.

I don't like to recall some of the bad stuff that took place when I first arrived. I never got fucked, though. Thank Christ. Only reason being was Brock, my brother, knew people on the inside, and for that I'm forever grateful. There're some bad apples in here.

Don't swing that way, never will, but I can hardly fuckin' wait to sink my dick into pussy again.
I'd only been with a couple of chicks in my lifetime, had no one steady before I got locked up, but then again I was more into drugs and runnin' my mouth off than chasin' skirt. Girls back then came and went, but there was no one special, nobody that I even remember.

I've forgotten what it's like to even be around a woman. Things have changed in ten years.

Chicks are different now, and I can't wait to reacquaint myself in their arms and between their legs.

I walk toward the next door as the warden unlocks it, and I step through to my final destination: the reception area. I've just got to sign my paperwork, take my belongings – which are no use to me now – and head the fuck on outta here.

The best thing of all; my brother Brock will be waiting.

He's the best brother anyone could ask for. I'm lucky; he's always had my back, even when I got locked up the first time. Son-of-a-bitch said he was gonna get locked up too, just to protect me. That broke me. Somewhere deep inside me, I knew he'd do it, but I had to talk him out of it. There was no point in us both going down.

I did all right, better than most. I didn't take any shit or show any weakness, and people respect that, even if it makes you a target for the first few weeks until the next fish arrives. And they always arrive, in droves.

I don't like to think about the night I got locked up very much. Truth is, I barely remember. I was so high and out of it on cocaine and alcohol that I could've done anything.

I got sent away for armed robbery. Yeah, I robbed a convenience store in downtown Phoenix in order to get initiated into a gang, except I wasn't exactly stealthy or as clever as I thought I was. The sawed-off shot gun wasn't loaded, but the pistol in the back of my jeans was.

It was the worst day of my life, when I woke up in county in handcuffs. I could've killed someone in my drug-hazed stupor and that would've haunted me for the rest of my life.

Even though being locked up for the better part of ten years was no fairy tale, at least I'm not on death row. I always try to look on the bright side. One thing about being in prison is you learn to believe in miracles and pray that you'll get out of the snake pit alive.

I was one of the lucky ones… the shit I've seen…

The door buzzes as we step through.

My heart races in my chest, chills running through my body as goose bumps raise on my skin.

This is it.

Then I see my brother.

Don't fuck this up. You've got one chance.

We stare at each other through the glass.

He looks like me except he's got more of a tan, and I'm taller by just a little bit. My lips turn up at the corners as I give him a nod. He nods back, his eyes bright fuckin' blue, also like mine. *I once got told I had pretty eyes.* That thought has me snorting as I shake my head. Ain't nothin' pretty about the Altman brothers.

I sign a couple of forms, grab my gear, and give the clerk a nod.

It's obvious from the "good luck" I get from her that she thinks she's gonna be seeing me again. *Not on your life, sugar.* No way in hell I'm coming back in here ever again.

They walk me to the final set of doors, and as I turn, the warden leaves me and locks the door behind him.

And… I'm free.

It feels odd, not having one of them standing beside me watching my every move. Alone time isn't something I'm used to.

I stand in front of my brother as we face off.

"You got shorter since the last time I saw you?" I jibe.

"Speak for yourself. Looks like you need a fuckin' haircut." He gives me a slap upside the head, even that gesture brings back memories of us as kids. Brock's signature move.

"Yeah, didn't wanna be too pretty. Ain't nobody's bitch, and I kept it that way."

He smirks. "Good to see you, brother."

We clasp hands. I swallow hard. My brother's not an emotional man, never has been, but having kids has changed him, and finding his ol' lady. Though I always knew he and Angel were gonna be together, back when I was a kid.

"Now you get to see my ugly mug every day."

"Every day?" He frowns. "Didn't sign up for that shit."

I grin and he pulls me in for a hug, slapping me on the back. "Not gonna get all sappy on me, are you, bro?"

He slings an arm round my neck as we walk off together, leavin' this shit hole behind me once and for all.

"Things are gonna be different this time. We're gonna do things right, you and me. You hear me?"

"You make it sound like you missed me." I laugh. "I guess ten years can do that to a person. You just forgot how annoying I am."

"You got that right."

He lets go of me and we walk toward his truck. I can tell it's his before we even get there.

It's a bright red and black Toyota Raptor with all the modifications, brand new tires, and a menacing-looking exhaust.

It seems some things never change.

I try not to be fascinated by every single fuckin' thing. The air feels different already.

The air of a free man. There ain't no greater feeling.

Brock unlocks his truck, and I climb into the passenger seat.

"You must be doin' all right to be drivin' this, though I thought the kidmobile may be a little more child friendly."

Brock snorts. "Angel drives the mini-van."

"And you don't?"

"Rawlings likes the truck." That's his daughter.

"Chip off the old block, huh?"

"Yup. Proud to say she's daddy's little girl. You're gonna love her. She's seven going on twenty-five, smarter than me too. That's gonna be fun when she starts dating at forty-five."

I snort a laugh. "How's the old ball and chain?"

"Things are good, man," he replies, starting the beast up. "Couldn't be better. Ethan's barely two weeks old. Kids change everythin', dude, lack of sleep bein' one of them."

"And here I was thinkin' you were gonna be a bachelor

forever. Angel always was a good woman. Liked her a lot."

"She's excited to see you, bro." He turns to look at me. "How you doin', like, really?"

I smile. "I'm good."

He frowns. "I know you just got out, but if there's anything you wanna get off your chest –"

It broke him that I got locked up, and it kills me that I did that to him, that I did it to all of my family and the people I hurt. But it's my trauma, my wrongs, not his. I don't want him to carry that burden anymore.

"I'm good, brother, maybe in time, but I did okay. I'm not off the rails, not gonna be either. Got no intention of goin' back to that shit box. Gonna keep my nose clean. Know that's easy to say; I've been out five minutes, but prison gives you a lot of time to think. Sometimes I feel like that's all I fuckin' did. My brain never stopped thinkin'. I'm not gonna be a statistic, bro. I'm never goin' back inside."

The words hang between us as I look out the window and Brock pulls out of the lot.

"Glad to hear it. Shit's not gonna be a picnic, but you've got all the support in the world. For one, you're not homeless or destitute, but I mean it when I say don't fuck this up, Ax." He turns to look at me. "You gotta help yourself. You're gonna be workin' long hours, prospectin' too. You'll be doin' whatever the club wants you to do, no questions asked. We got a strong brotherhood, so the only way this is gonna work is if you toe the line. When you're patched in and makin' it on your own, then we'll talk."

"I got it. Last thing I wanna do is let you down again. I'm not afraid of hard work."

He grunts. "That's good 'cause we got plenty to do."

I sit back with my hands behind my head. I can't describe how I feel. Elation just doesn't cut it.

I feel like the luckiest son of a bitch there ever was.

"You know how much I appreciate it, you helpin' me get back on my feet," I say as he pulls onto the road. "I won't let you down. That's a promise."

It's all words, he knows that. Of course, I'll say it now, I'm free, but he needs to see it where it counts.

"Perfect. You start first thing Monday."

"Monday's my lucky day, then."

He snorts as I grin.

The big house fades away in the distance behind us. Soon, the slate will be wiped clean. I may never quite get over the experience, but I'm where I need to be now, with the world at my feet. A new beginning.
I don't look back. There's nothing left there for me, just pain and misery, and they are two things I don't intend to take into my new life.

Not now. Not ever.

I climb the stairs up to my room at church, palming the back of my neck. It's only temporary until I move over to the apartment above the Stone Crow tomorrow.

I've had a few drinks, but the party got interrupted with Steel's ol' lady and Bone's lawyer getting kidnapped. Steel is the Sergeant at Arms, and Bones is the Road Captain who organizes all the club bike rides. I even apprehended one of the heavies who came onto our turf. Felt so fuckin' good.

I know Brock said I had to keep my nose clean, but this shit's a little heavier than I first thought. The Bracken Ridge Rebels aren't a one percent club, but they clearly still have some enemies.

Shrugging off my jacket, I stumble into my room. It's small, neat, and has its own bathroom. I don't need much; anything is like a palace compared to where I've been. Showering alone is going to be an interesting experience.

I kick off my boots and rip my shirt over my head. I'm about to shrug my jeans off too, when I see movement out of the corner of my eye.

I'm over there in a second flat, my hand around whoever's throat it is as she squeals. I immediately let go.

"Who the fuck are you?" I say, as she corners herself against the wall. It's then I notice she's in her underwear.

"Bambi."

I blink once, twice, then a smile tugs at my lips. "Yeah?"

My eyes flick down to her ample rack. *Holy fuck.*

"Yep."

"What you doin' up here, in my bedroom?"

She runs a hand along my collarbone, down one pec, and traces the Eagle tattoo clutching a skull that splays across the entire expanse of my chest.

She's pretty, but let's face it, I'd fuck a mailbox after ten years.

"Thought I'd come up here and keep you company," she purrs, her eyes flicking down my body, and I know she likes what she sees. She keeps her hand movin' down my stomach through the small smattering of hair at my naval. Then she runs her palm over my already hard cock.

I don't suppress the groan that leaves my throat. I reach out and cup one tit as the other reaches for her hair. She's dark-haired, has pretty eyes, and a plush mouth that I want to claim, if only for tonight.

"Been waitin' for you, baby girl," I mumble, my lips hovering over hers as her palm squeezes me.

Fuck. The women here are damn straightforward. Nothin' wrong with that, but I haven't been around a woman since I was nineteen, and prison wardens don't count. The last female encounter I had was a roll in the hay with one of the chicks from school whose name I don't even remember. I haven't had a whole lot of experience, truth be told, but my cock still works just fine.

"You have?" She continues strokin' me as I glance down at her hand.

I nod. My lips move over hers softly, testing how it feels, as she makes a moaning sound that makes my dick grow harder. Our tongues collide, and I pull back.

"You okay?" She's already breathing hard.

I swallow hard. "Been in the joint ten years, babe."

She smiles. "It's okay. I'm good with newbies."

I give her a chin lift. "You gonna unzip me, beautiful?"

She grins, her other hand grabbing my ass and giving it a squeeze.

So fuckin' grabby. I like it.

She does just that and then tugs them down. My cock springs out, and she grasps it with one hand as I stare down at her in awe. *She's gonna blow me off.*

Again, another first. I hope I don't shoot my fuckin' load too quick. That will be embarrassing.

This girl knows what she's doin', and right now, I don't fuckin' care who she is or the fact she's probably been with everyone in the club. I've got enough condoms to see me through another long decade, so that ain't gonna be an issue.

She starts to lick the end of my dick as I groan, moving my hands into her hair. *Yeah, I'm not gonna last.*

"Your cock is so big," she says in between licks as she grasps it and squeezes harder. *Fuck.* They talk dirty too.

"Yeah, definitely been waitin' for you, baby," I reply

as she takes my entire length into her mouth, and I know I've arrived in Heaven as I start to move my hips and fuck her mouth. She takes it all, like a good little girl, moanin' and groanin' as she reaches a hand inside her panties to rub herself.

The feeling of a woman's touch… that right there tells me I'm never going back, as if that were ever an option. I swore I'm not gonna be a statistic, and I meant it. I'm clean. Didn't do any drugs in prison, and I cleaned my act up when I started school behind bars.

This is my chance and I'm gonna take it, startin' with this chick… Bambi.

I snort a laugh as she looks up at me.

"We're good, babe," I say, pushing her head back down on me.

I'm right where I need to be, and I plan on not getting a whole lotta sleep until Monday morning. Sleep is overrated anyway.

Axton

BRACKEN RIDGE
REBELS
ARIZONA
M · C

CHAPTER 2
STEVIE

I check the time on the wall for about the hundredth time this morning.

Today is the day Axton starts work.

He moved in yesterday. But being my day off, I was at the hospital, visiting my sister, Kennedy. She's been recovering from being kidnapped and assaulted, along with Steel's ol' lady, Sienna.

I'm shaken up from seeing her like that, all battered and bruised. I'd be lying if I said I haven't questioned my position here with the club and the danger that it brings.

Bones was stabbed a few months ago when Lucy and Rubble – another couple from the club – were in trouble with shit that came back to haunt them from his old club in Phoenix.

It has made me wonder what the hell I'm doing more than once.

But, I also can't deny the fact that the club's President, Richie Hutchinson, also known as Hutch, has been good to me. He's given me a promotion, is letting me live rent free with free meals, and pays me well. Hutch is not an asshole or a creep. It's the main reason I haven't quit already, especially now after Kennedy's ordeal.

When she's feeling up to it, I'm going to have a long chat with her. Not that Bones is leaving her side. He doesn't even go home to shower, which is kind of sweet, but I may have to intervene soon.

I never imagined, fresh out of college, with a degree in business management, that I'd be working for a motorcycle club in a small town where everyone knows everyone.

I grew up in Cali with my sister and a single, working mom. We never knew our father and that has had its difficulties, with him wanting to reconnect over the years.

I moved to Phoenix to be with my boyfriend, Lukas.

I stare at the wall.

Lukas.

He got a job in the armed forces and then was deployed shortly after graduation. I've seen him five times in the six years he has been gone. Things have been rocky for the last year and while I've always been supportive, Lukas is my first and only boyfriend out of high school. We were each other's best friends long before we became a couple.

I haven't told Kennedy yet, but Lukas ended things.

The last time he was home, things were different. He's changed so much in the six years he's been away and, to be perfectly honest, I don't know how to be in a relationship with him anymore. I've never been a super needy person, but lately I've been feeling the lack of support and the things we both wanted have changed.

I shouldn't be relying on my sister for pep talks and career advice; it should be him rooting me on, as I have for him. I've always had his back, and I get it's difficult being deployed. I don't envy anyone who is serving. It's a completely selfless thing to do, and that's why my heart aches.

I still love him, maybe I always will, but I also feel guilty over the relief I feel that he's finally said it. It's not even about intimacy, which is obviously a problem in any long-distance relationship, but I've always been loyal. I never cheated on Lukas, even when I got offers while working the bar or out with friends. I could never lie to him.

Tying my hair up in a high ponytail, I swipe on some lip balm and apply some bronzer. I don't wear a lot of makeup and don't like to fuss too much with my appearance. Unlike my sister, who's pale and has red hair and freckles, I'm blonde and tan. She wears suits and pencil skirts, and I wear cut-off shorts, jeans, and chucks. I guess you could say we're chalk and cheese.

I stare in the mirror and give myself another pep talk.

"It's going to be all right," I say out loud. "He's going to be nice and funny, easy to train, and great to work with. I won't have any problems with him…" *Even though he's an ex-con.*

I try this law of attraction shit all the time. I can't say whether it has an affect or not, but I haven't fallen on my ass yet.

"He's nice and funny, easy to train, and great to work with," I say again, like it's my walking mantra.

I take one last look and grab my coffee mug, then head out the door to start the day… running right into Axton Altman. Well, I think it's him. He is coming out of the apartment opposite mine across the landing, so I don't know who else it would be.

I don't know what I expected, but as he turns around to face me, my eyes go wide.

He's big, wide set, tall – *massively tall* – and has short, blonde cropped hair, ear discs in each ear, with a healthy blondish beard that's not so disheveled that it covers his face, but it's decent. But that's not what grabs my attention… oh no. It's his eyes.

They're bright blue, like the sky on a cloudless day. Except they're beautiful, piercing and completely unnerving all rolled into one.

His heavy, darker brows turn down in a frown as he takes me in.

"Uh, hey," I say, rubbing one hand down my side to wipe it, then I hold it out. "Assuming you're Axton, I'm

Stevie, your new…" I trail off, but saying "your new boss" seems a little silly.

He looks down at my hand as a small smile plays on his lips, then he shakes it. As expected, his hand is large, rough, and warm.

He looks kind of scary. I can see tattoos peeking out the top of his shirt.

Nobody told me he was going to be this good looking either…

"You can say it. You're my new boss." He gives me a chin lift. "Reporting for duty, ma'am."

My eyes go wide. "Uh, you can just call me Stevie. It's totally fine. So now is probably a good time to clear up a couple of things before we start."

He's still holding my hand.

"All right." He finally lets go, and though the polite thing to do would be to step back into his space, he stays in mine instead.

"I obviously know that you just got released and all." I go on, my eyes hitting the ground at least three times as I speak. "And that things are different, you know, on the outside, and I'm… well, I'm happy to have you on board. With me. You have a clean slate, and I don't judge." *Do I sound like a complete moron?*

His lips twitch, but he stays completely still. "Thanks for saying that."

"I take it that you don't take issue with me being your boss?" I go on.

"I don't have anything against you, no."

"I mean..." *What do I mean?*

"With you bein' a woman?" He finishes as I look up to meet his gaze. His expression is one of amusement.

"Uh, I guess, yeah."

He leans closer to me. "Just because I haven't been around a woman in a decade, doesn't mean I've got anythin' against 'em. Far from it, actually. You won't have any problems. Just show me what you want me to do, and I'll do it."

Glad we got that out of the way.

I clear my throat. "Well, I'll start by showing you around."

"Sounds good." He sweeps his hand toward the stairs. "Ladies first."

I scurry past him, descending the stairs as fast as possible.

I know it's been a while since I had a man's hands on me, and it was *just* a handshake, but his touch sent little butterflies buzzing around in my stomach. The sheer size of him alone...

Brock and the club wouldn't put me in danger. Hutch respects me... he gave me all this responsibility... he wouldn't send Axton here unless he was sure...

"…good coffee around here?" Axton's asking behind me.

Shit.

I turn around. "Sorry?"

His lips twitch again. "Just asked who makes good coffee around here." He nods down at my cup. "Aside from your place."

I unlock the door that leads toward the bar, and he follows behind me. I switch the lights on as I pass by the hallway.

"This is instant, unfortunately, but the Coffee Bean makes great coffee, and we have a Keurig machine here in the restaurant. You can use that whenever you want."

"A what?"

I smile, taking a sip. "It's a fancy name for a coffee pod machine."

"Right."

We walk into the bar. It's closed, as we don't open for three more hours, but I wanted to get a head start on showing Axton everything, and we have deliveries coming in later today.

"So, this is the bar," I say stupidly. "I've done a little bit of a job description and a checklist, so you can have a read through it, if you like. If there's anything you're not sure of, then we can work through it. Then, I can give you a grand tour."

"No problem."

"I'll need to get your social security and bank account details." I hand him the forms and the paperwork.

"Brock's takin' care of it. Sortin' it out this week. You probably think this is a little pathetic."

I look up at him as he leans against the bar.

"Think what's pathetic?"

"I'm almost thirty-years old, and I don't even have a bank account." He's wistful, and it makes me feel a little like I'm intruding.

"Not at all. You've been inside. It's not like you can just pop on down to the bank…"

His eyes flick up to mine, and I slap my hand over my mouth.

Great, now he thinks I'm taking the piss out of him.

"I'm sorry," I blurt out. "I didn't mean it to sound like –"

He smirks. "It was a convenience store, not a bank, and you don't have to have to tiptoe around me, Stevie. I'm a big boy."

I don't know why my mind goes somewhere else, but I face punch myself internally. It's either that or bleach my brain.

I take a large sip of my coffee as he stares at me.

"I can fill these out on my lunch break, if you like." He goes on after a moment. "That way, I can get acquainted with the place, and you won't have to babysit me all day."

"Sure." *As soon as I take my foot out of my mouth.*

"Well, we may as well start here. So the register is pretty easy to work. Everything is itemized into categories, so all you have to do is find… let's say, spirits… so you select that and all the options come up. It's a touch screen, see."

I press the 'on' button and the screen comes alive. I hit the spirits, then the whiskey button, and all the different types of whiskey appear on the screen. "You can input a half or full shot, add your mixer in, press add, then use the arrow to go back."

He stares at it like he's seeing earth for the first time. "Neat."

"Did you not use computers, in… there?"

He shakes his head. "Not allowed to use those in the joint. Pen and paper if you want to communicate with the outside world."

"Oh, I thought that was just in the movies?"

"Sadly, no."

"Did you write –"

"To my brother," he says, his voice soft. "And my sister wrote me sometimes, when she could. My parents weren't exactly my number one fans after I got sentenced. Attempted robbery with a loaded gun tends to be seen as a bad influence on my little sister."

"I can only imagine." I have no idea what else to say.

I also don't get how quiet he is, how careful he seems to be with his words. He's so polite… It doesn't fit with his persona, but I guess that old saying about judging a book by its cover couldn't be more accurate.

He doesn't look at me weird, nor does it feel uncomfortable being around him or in his personal space. Like now, which is crazy since I just met the guy three minutes ago.

Calm the fuck down.

"What about you? How long have you been here?" he asks with a slight nod.

"A little over eighteen months," I answer. "Came out to visit a friend and never ended up leaving. My boyfriend –" I stop. *Fuck. What am I doing? Telling him my life story.*

YOU'RE HIS FUCKING BOSS!

He does that one eyebrow raise thing that only select men seem to be able to master, and I move away from the touch screen.

I don't get to finish anyway because I hear the back door unlock, and a few moments later, Roxy, our new chef, walks in. Coffee in hand.

"Hey, Rox," I say, turning to her. Glad the heat is off me for the time being.

She smiles, coming toward us. She's probably one of the best chefs in the state, and it was no secret that Hutch lured her here with a house to live in and a huge salary. She is an excellent cook and makes a busy kitchen look easy. Plus, she yells at the boys from the club for going into her kitchen when she's in the middle of service.

Yeah, I've got a lot of time for any chick who's got balls that big.

"This is Axton, the new bar supervisor." In my periphery, he's still looking at me, and I do my best to keep my eyes on Roxy.

Why is he staring at me, and why is it not weird?

Roxy smiles. "Hey, Axton." They shake hands.

"Pleased to meet you."

"Pleasure's all mine. Hear you've amped up the playin' field in this town in a few short weeks."

"Well, I don't know about that, but the club eats me out of house and home," she says. "I have to keep locks on the cool room because they just come and raid the place whenever they feel like it."

We both laugh.

She's probably a year or two older than me, has long dark hair, and proudly tells anyone and everyone she has Cherokee roots. That, and a whiplash tongue. I think that's a chef thing, though, since most of the chefs I've met over the years are moody. At least Roxy doesn't have the usual mean-streak that goes with it.

"Probably not a bad idea," he agrees.

She tilts her disposable coffee cup and keeps on walking. "Gotta do prep before we open. See y'all later." She heads off toward the kitchen and finger waves with her free hand.

"That was Roxy," I explain foolishly. "One thing I've learned over the years is to keep the chef on good terms, no matter what."

"Got that right. Can't wait to have my first home cooked meal."

I don't meet his gaze as we walk down the length of the bar. I can't even imagine what prison food tastes likes.

"So this is the restaurant side of the Crow," I say as I follow to where Roxy just passed through. "We have sliding doors to keep it partially blocked off from the bar side. It also helps when we have big parties and such to open it up and put more tables in."

He follows behind, and I try not to notice he smells like Brut…

"Then we've got the pool tables, a juke box, and a stage for the band." I turn to him. "Hutch likes country and rock. Since it's a family joint, he mainly has acoustic singers and guitars. The Sunday session is really popular in the summertime."

He nods as our eyes lock. He's still holding his paperwork.

I make my way around the patron side of the bar as we continue past the tables, and I show him the restrooms and the outside kids play area – yep, they thought of everything. And finally, the cellar.

We head downstairs into the dark depths of the refrigerated cool room where all the alcohol is stored. There is a key code to get in since Colt, the clubs security expert, installed high-tech cameras and passwords on literally everything.

"So the kegs are here," I say as I motion to all the barrels and crates. "All the spare alcohol over there. The palettes come in, and there's a lift installed on that side."

"The cellar has a lift?"

I smile. "Saves time, though I wouldn't suggest hopping in there. It often gets stuck."

I turn and because it's dark, I don't see the edge of a crate of wine. As I stumble, Axton reaches out and snags me by the elbow so I don't fall on my ass.

"Shit," I say, laughing off the embarrassment. "Looks like I've had too much coffee this morning."

"Or not enough." He gives me a wink which, for some reason, I'm battling with, because it makes my heart race.

This has got to stop. I can't be crushing on the resident bad boy.

It's because I'm newly single and deprived, that's what it is. And let's face it, there's nothing like the sexy, tattooed, hot ex-con to set any single woman's insides on fire… if only he weren't my new employee…

I swallow hard, adjusting my tank top from the hem as I straighten myself.

"Thanks," I mutter. I head back to the stairs, quick to get out of there with his close proximity. It's making me jittery. I fucking hope that this gets better because I don't want to be jumpy around him twenty-four seven. And it's got nothing to do with him being an ex-con.

"Not a problem," I hear him reply faintly as he follows me.

"So the door does unlock from the inside, and it's handy when you have an armful to carry," I say, showing him the large red plastic button on the wall, and it's at perfect butt height, so I turn and shove it with my ass cheek to open it. "One quick bump, and voila, you're free."

As I turn, he's looking down at my ass, but his eyes quickly meet mine as we look at each other for a few awkward moments.

Rushing to fill the silence, I tell him, "So just be sure to shut it again firmly when you're done." His eyes tip to the floor as he steps through. "The other staff don't have access. Just myself, Roxy, you, and Colt."

"Got it."

"So, uh, I forgot, I've got your shirts on the bar. I'll just go grab them and then if you wanna make yourself a coffee?"

"Sounds like a plan." He's gone all broody again. Long gone is the smirk and the crinkle of his eyes. It's a bit of a shame, since he's so much nicer when he smiles...

We walk back through to the bar, and I pull the bag of shirts out from under the counter.

"Brock said you were about an extra-large, though I see you're quite big in the shoulders…" It's a mindless observation, but I see his lips turn up ever so slightly.

"So, uh, you might need a bigger size."

I hand him the bag and turn to grab myself a glass of water. It feels like an inferno in here.

As I'm doing that, I hear the bag rustle and the plastic wrapping tear.

Wait, he's not going to…

I flick my eyes to the reflective glass where the glasses and bottles of spirits hang, and I get the absolute shock of my life. Axton pulls his shirt up over his head, and I'm met with the full force of his tattooed chest; a bird with large wings spread, skulls, flames, pops of color, but it's not just that, it's how fucking ripped he is.

His body is insane.

His pecs are outlined and flanked by abs that could go for days, his shoulders and biceps show that he lifts heavy weights, and the smattering of hair at his naval… *holy fucking shit.*

He drops his discarded shirt on the bar, then pulls the polo over his head. It's a perfect fit.

I'm not sure why a weird noise leaves my throat as soon as his body is covered up, but suddenly bright, electric blue eyes are staring back at me in the glass. *Fuck.* And now I've just been caught staring. Could this day get any worse?

Maybe now is a good time to start day drinking.

I look away quickly, busying myself with the glass of water I've just overpoured all over the floor, but not before I notice his amusement.

This time, he doesn't hide his smile, but it's really more of a smirk. *I wish he'd stop looking at me like that.* I sure as hell am not going to be crushing on Axton Altman.

Nope, I'm not.

And if he keeps looking at me with that heat in his eyes, I may very well be the girl to knock it all the way back to Stradbroke.

Axton

BRACKEN RIDGE
REBELS
ARIZONA
M.
C.

CHAPTER 3

AXTON

I slink onto the chair next to my brother with a heavy sigh.

"Had a long day?" he muses as I grip the neck on the beer bottle and suck half of it down.

"Almost thirteen hours."

"How'd you like your new boss?"

I can't help but notice the snark in his tone. "Stevie's great."

"Don't be fooled by her pleasant demeanor," he warns. "She's a slave driver."

"Hence why it's eleven o'clock, and I've only just sat down. Monday's are a bitch."

"Welcome to the real world."

I tilt my beer to him as we sit in companionable silence for a few moments. I just locked up, and I've still got to clean the bar. Stevie left an hour or so ago. I try not to look up at the ceiling above us, where her side of the apartment is situated.

"Didn't tell me she looked like *that*." I go on, a smirk

on my lips.

He turns to me. "Well, better keep it in your pants where she's concerned. Hutch won't like it, and you're a prospect."

I hold my hands up. "I get it, don't get my dick wet with my boss. You think I want my ass kicked by Hutch?"

"No, but temptation is a thing, especially when Stevie is easy on the eyes."

I roll my eyes. "Got plenty of pussy at church. Forgot to thank you for the other night. Bambi was waitin' up in my room."

He chuckles. "I don't really wanna hear about it. Long as you're bein' safe and all that shit."

"Thanks, dad, for your concern, but rubbers were a thing before I went to jail."

"Just sayin'. Prospects can't be seen with any chick around church. Got me? Bambi was a one-off. You wanna continue that, do it at her place."

I slap him on the back. "Know it. Don't get all weird on me. I get how it works."

After a few more moments, he says, "Amelia's been asking for you."

I saw my sister the night I got back, when they threw me a party at church. She cried a lot.

I don't like making her cry, or any woman, for that matter. It was a lot for her, and for me.

I wonder if I'll ever be able to make amends with

everyone in my family… I think about my mom and dad and my stomach lurches that they weren't there to see me. Not that I expected a glorious family reunion, but Mom… surely? I always was a momma's boy, but time changes all that.

Both my parents and Brock have made up and they love Angel and the kids. I guess I'm their one disappointment, the black sheep of the family who only brings them shame.

"I know. I'll see her on my day off."

"That's not till Tuesday. Be nice for you to call her from time to time. She's a good kid, Ax, she missed you a lot."

"You gonna start tellin' me what to do, bro? Could've given me twenty-four hours at least to get settled in."

He takes another swig. "Yeah, you're right. So, how's it feel, bein' out?"

I look down at my hands. "It's an adjustment."

I know he worries about me; it's written all over his face. In his eyes, I'm still nineteen years old, spotty faced and unsure of which side of the bed to piss on.

One day, he won't see me that way. I don't know when, but hopefully soon. Everything takes time.

Ten fucking years.

It was the worst mistake of my life. The shadows loom, and I know I may not be able to ever live it down, but that's my cross to bear, not his.

"You know you just gotta ask if you're struggling with

anythin'."

"Know that, appreciate it." I hesitate then add, "Have you heard from Mom and Dad?"

He turns to me as I keep staring ahead, trying to work out what I could ever do to say I'm sorry. Fuck knows I've written letters over the years, but I never wanted a reply. I never wanted to hear the words that they were disappointed in me. I knew it that day in the court room when I plead guilty.

I never want to relive that day.

"Not over the weekend."

"They know I'm out." It's not a question.

"Listen, bro, Dad's gonna take some time. Fuck knows we've had a rough year patchin' things up, so he's probably gonna need a little longer to come around."

"What about Mom?" My heart heaves.

Brock was always Daddy's boy, the favorite, even though Dad never stopped giving him a hard time growing up. Me, however, I was always the apple of Mom's eye, even when Amelia came along. We just always had a connection. Letting her down, out of everyone in my life, is what pains me the most. I'll take it to my grave.

"She wants to see you, but let her do it in her own time."

I snort a laugh. "Right."

"Mom's good, bro, she just needs…"

"Time, yeah, you said it already." I chug down the rest of my beer and go to stand. Bar ain't gonna clean itself. "One thing about time, bro, is I had a lot of it, and I'm not gonna live in the past. I've chosen to make a fresh start, and I get that I let them down, but if they're not with me, then they're against me. Period."

I don't mean to come across as harsh, but I can hardly help it. I start wiping down the bar with spray and a rag.

"Don't gotta get all shitty. Rome wasn't built in a day, that's all I'm sayin'."

I nod. I get it. Big fuckin' disappointment.

And Brock can talk, he has it all. A wife who loves him. A kid who adores him. And a new baby. He's got a business that's thriving and all the nice shit like a home and a nice truck. It's hard not to compare, but I envy him. So fuckin' much.

"Got it. You want another beer?"

"Nah." He sets the empty bottle down on the edge of the bar. "Gotta head home. Why don't you come over for dinner tomorrow, after work."

"I'm not sure I can."

He frowns. "Ax. You're not expected to work thirteen hours a day. You look at your roster. Don't wanna burn out in the first five minutes."

"I know. I'm good. Gotta apply for my contracting license too, then I can get some extra dough on the side with odd jobs. Get some experience."

He eyes me curiously. "Glad to see you're serious about it. Can earn your prospect stripes faster by helpin' out at the club. Just keep your nose clean."

I look up as I start to lift everything off the top of the bar, clearing away the last of the dirty glasses.

"I will," I say. "Got no intention of doin' anythin' else but that."

He tips his head. "See you tomorrow."

I give him a chin lift. "See ya."

He leaves out through the back, and a few moments later, I hear his motorcycle start with a loud roar.

I've got the lend of one of Brock's older bikes but I gotta get some scratch together for my own ride. It's one thing being given the prospect opportunity with the M.C., but it's quite another borrowing someone else's bike. I gotta fix that as soon as possible.

Another forty-five minutes later, and I'm switching the lights off and heading upstairs.

I tread up the two flights until I come to my door. I have a key, but I didn't bother locking it. I turn my head absentmindedly to Stevie's door. I don't hear any movement from inside, which is a weird thing to even be listening for. I shake it off and turn the handle.

The room up here is nice. It needs a little repair; the pipes clang together whenever you run the hot water, and the paint's peeling quite heavily, but that can all be remedied.

To have my own space is like a godsend. I never imagined I'd be this lucky to land on my feet and have this opportunity. Today was rough. I fucked up a lot. I mean, I can pour beer and spirits, but I don't know what some of the drinks are and the register is more complex than Stevie made out. It confuses me a little. I'm better with my hands rather than using computers. I also don't want to look dumb in front of her. That would be embarrassing.

I palm the back of my neck and peel my shirt off. I smirk when I think about catching Stevie watching me get changed.

Let's face it; she's nothing like the girls I would normally go for. For one, she gets to decide my fate where employment is concerned, and reports back to Brock and Hutch. So, I've got to keep on her good side. Looking at my body and doing something about it are two different things. She looks at me like I'm a curiosity, not someone she wants to jump.

My dick twitches at the thought of my hand tugging her long, blonde ponytail as I slide into her from behind. *Fuck.*

It's not my fuckin' fault she's hot as fuck and has lips that could suck the pit out of a cherry.

I head straight to the shower, pulling my boots off and then my jeans.

I start up the water, waiting for the clanging to stop, then climb in once the steam is pouring out of the little space.

Showering in fuckin' peace. Who knew this could be so rewarding?

Something else that's rewarding is rubbing one out without anyone else watching.

My hand slides to my cock as I reach for the soap with the other. The water feels so good on my aching body as I pull my dick nice and slow to start. *Fuck yeah.* I lean back against the wall and let the spray hit my back, resting one hand on the glass in front of me. This shower's so freaking tiny I barely fit.

Without warning, my mind flicks to Stevie in her tight jeans and that tiny white apron. I imagine pulling said apron off and lifting her tank over her head, my hands reaching around to cup her tits.

I wonder if they're big or small or even real, hard to tell with all those clothes on. And I don't mind how tits come, long as I get to suck on them. I groan as I imagine shoving her jeans down, feeling between her legs as I spread her knees wider. *Fuck.*

My hand speeds up as I imagine my cock sliding through her pussy lips, feeling how wet she is as I pluck her nipples and whisper dirty shit in her ear. She shoves her ass back into me, begging me for it as I give her what she wants and shove my cock inside. She groans as I move in and out of her slowly, knowing my size is too big for her tight little cunt. As she cries out, I only pick up speed, then grab her hips as I fuck her harder, squashing her up against the wall as I lose control and bite down on her shoulder. In no time at all, my cum is squirting all over the shower screen as I explode, panting as I expel every drop from my balls. *Fuck, man.*

I turn around, letting the spray wash me clean as I rub a hand over my face, trying to clear my mind.

I can't have a thing for Stevie Hart. No fuckin' way. She's off limits.

The only way I get to touch her is in my shower, in my fantasies.

And it's gonna stay that way.

Amelia hugs me tight as I stand from the table.

"Hi, big brother," she says, all smiles as she hands me a package.

"Hi, little sister." I grin back and give her a chin lift. "What's this?"

"I baked you cookies."

I peer into the brown paper bag and look up at her curiously. "You bake?"

"Yup. Mom's famous sugar cookie recipe."

I still as my eyes meet hers. She slaps a hand over her

mouth. "Axton, I'm sorry."

I wave her off. "It's not a crime to say Mom or mention her name. It's fine." *It's far from fine, but whatever.*

She squeezes my forearm. "She'll come around. I know she will." There's no mention of our father. I know that ship sailed a long time ago. I've accepted it from him, but not from my mom.

I smile and whisper, "You know, you sound just like Brock."

She rolls her eyes. "I do not!"

"Do so." She's so easy to stir. I've missed this most of all.

It's stupid the things you don't realize you need until you don't have them.

"Shut up, the pair of you!" Angel scolds. "And move your asses to the table. I've made your favorite, Axton."

She holds a large, steaming tray of home-made lasagna as I hear the pounding of blood in my ears. *Fuck, it really is the little things.*

"How do you remember that?" I sit down opposite Brock, who's watching the game while holding the little guy in one arm and a bottle in his spare hand.

Rawlings comes barreling through the door. "Can I sit next to Axton?" she yells out excitedly as I pull the chair out for her. She scrambles to sit on it, waving something at me.

"It's Uncle Axton," Angel chastises, putting the dish in

the middle of the table. Then to me, she says, "I remember everything, sunshine. Don't you forget it."

I turn back to Rawlings. "What's that?"

"I painted it for you."

A lump forms in my throat as I look down at it.

"See, that's the house and your motorbike. That's me and you and my horse, George."

She's painted a blue sky with a big yellow sun and green grass below us.

"Where's the rest of the family?" Brock asks, his eyes still on the screen.

Rawlings tuts. "Dad, you have like a billion paintings of us. This one's for Uncle Axton."

"I love it," I say, giving her a big smile. "I'll put it on my fridge when I get home."

She does a little dance in her chair.

"Rawlings, pass the salad down," Angel tells her as she sits at the end of the table and turns the TV off.

"Hey!" says Brock.

"You can watch the replay later."

I smirk. "Some things never change, huh, brother?" He shoots me daggers. Angel always did have him by the shorts.

Amelia passes me the breadbasket, and I take out a slice of crusty bread.

"You did good, Angel," I say as she tells me to dig in.

"Uncle Axton, can you do mine too?" Rawlings asks, passing me her plate.

"Sure thing." I scoop the spatula under a slice and set it on her plate.

"Can I call you Uncle A?" she asks. "Uncle Axton is kind of a mouthful."

"Rawlings," Brock scolds. "Don't be rude."

I laugh. "Sure, kid, I don't mind."

"He doesn't mind!" Rawlings chirps.

"I've got ears, they're not painted on," Brock replies just as the baby gurgles. I watch as Brock turns the baby and places him over his shoulder where a small towel already hangs. *Mr. Dad.* It suits him.

He also seems to know what he's doing.
I give him a nod. "You look like a pro."

His eyes flick to mine. "Man's gotta help out where he can. Plus, I'd rather do this than the diapers."

"Eww, gross," Rawlings says, holding her nose. "Ethan's ass smells yucky."

I snort a laugh before I can stop myself.

"Rawlings, that's quite enough at the table!" Angel says, shaking her head. "Nobody wants to think about that while they're eating, and don't say *ass*, young lady."
Brock chuckles as Amelia dishes up his plate.

"This is real nice," I say, tucking in. "You've got a really neat home out here. Did the place up good."

Brock spent about two years making the old farm a home for them to move into. Plus, there are barns and horses and a huge workshop that Brock added on. There's plenty of room out here. I suspect we'll be spending some time in the shed, working on the bikes. I've got to pay him back somehow for the use of his motorcycle.

"It took long enough," Brock complains. "In the end, I hired contractors. I had a master plan to get Angel to move in with me."

"A master plan?" Angel jokes, pointing her fork at him. "That's the first I'm hearing of it."

"Well, I always knew you'd be mine eventually." He leans toward her, and they kiss across the salad bowl.

Rawlings slaps her forehead. "They do this all the time," she complains. "It's so gross."

Angel smiles as she sits back down on her chair. "So, how's it going over at the Stone Crow?" she asks me as I continue eating. The food is so fucking good, I know I'll be having seconds.

"Pretty good. Pickin' things up all right."

Brock's eyes flick up to mine as he eats with one hand while still patting the baby over his shoulder.

"How's Stevie to work with?" She goes on.

I nod. "She's great. Easy-going. I do what she tells me. We don't have any problems."

"Speaking of which, Kennedy has that paperwork ready

for you to sign for the parole officer," Amelia tells me, chomping on her crusty bread. "She's working from her hospital bed."

"That's great. I'll drop by tomorrow on my break."

"You seem to be fitting in." Amelia continues. "Some of the girls around the club are getting really annoying, though."

I frown. "How do you mean?"

She rolls her eyes. "Asking me about you all the time, like I'm going to let any of those skanks get their hooks into my brother."

"Amelia," Brock says, his eyebrows pinched. *"Rawlings."*

"What's a skank?" Rawlings bursts out, looking up at Brock across the table.

He shakes his head at Amelia. "See what you did?"

"It's a bad word," Angel puts in. "And Amelia needs to watch her mouth at the table with young children around."

"Oops, sorry," she says, wincing slightly as I try not to laugh.

"I'm sure what Axton does in his private life is just that, *private."* Angel goes on, giving me a stern look. *What did I do?*

I scrape my plate as Amelia laughs. "Woah, slow down, nobody's going to steal your food."

Of course they couldn't know how much that sentence

rings true for me. You get really good at eating shit fast, not knowing when your next half decent meal is coming. The shit they serve in prison should be illegal. My gut twists at the thought.

"Can't help that it tastes good," I reply. "Mind if I go in for seconds?"

Angel smiles, perhaps sensing my discomfort, even though I don't show it on my face.

"You don't have to ask. Go for it."

I slap another piece of lasagna on my plate and go for more bread.

Brock hands the baby over to Angel.

Watching them work together in tandem has me fascinated.

My brother was tough growing up, a lot like my old man, though he was never an asshole.

Not for the first time, I realize that this home life shit suits him down to the ground. He never was much of a player; it was always Angel that made him light up like a fuckin' Christmas tree.

God willing, I hope to have something like this myself someday. In fact, when you're incarcerated, the only thing you can think about is the imaginary life you'll one day have.

It embodies all these things; a home, a wife and some kids. *One day.*

I just get the feeling everyone sitting at this table is waiting for me to fuck up, though. I have no reason to doubt they want what's best for me and they do support me, but it's like the elephant in the room. Waiting on tenterhooks to see when I slip up.

I'm a violent criminal, according to my police record, a medium level offender, which means I still have to be monitored, not only by my parole officer, but an independent community officer to make sure I get all the support I need.

I'm so fuckin' lucky to be sitting here with my family. A job lined up. A place to live. Money coming in. I've no reason to feel like the world hasn't just landed at my door.

But there is that thing inside me that still hangs onto the past. That mourns the kid that I was and all that got taken away because of one stupid mistake.

The best piece of advice I got from one of the long-termers for when I finally got out was to not try and pick up where I left off, since the world I once knew has changed. I have to be flexible and open-minded and be willing to change my ways.

Above all else, I have to want to not re-offend. If I was planning on going out and robbing a bank, I would never have gone back to school while in the joint and got my qualification. Soon, I hope to be doing more electrical work and less bar work, but it's good for now. I don't want to pile too much on my plate too soon. Slowly does it.

I've so much to make up for, and I'm not gonna prove any of them right. I want to right the wrongs in my past by paving the way for my future.

It's bad enough when people in this town talk. Yeah, I've already had people cross the street when I walk down it. Even though I didn't commit the crime here, people still talk. That's just how it is.

Not everyone is gonna be so accommodating, and that's something I can live with.

In jail, I developed pretty thick skin. You gotta to be able to survive and take the knocks. If you don't, nobody is gonna remember your name. Nobody's gonna care.

The last thing I wanna do is become a statistic; it'll just give my parents more ammunition to go against me and tell everyone "we told you so."

I miss them.

I'll never go to them, though. I've caused them enough shame.

But I'm done being fuckin' sorry. I'm done.

BRACKEN RIDGE
REBELS
ARIZONA
M · C

CHAPTER 4

STEVIE

"What do you mean, you broke up?" Kennedy looks at me with wide eyes as I sit the chocolates that I bought for her down on the bedside table. She's been in the hospital for these last four days with broken ribs and a concussion, yet I see her laptop open on the side table.

I didn't want to stress her out, but Lukas was due home any day now, and she's going to know something is up when he doesn't show.

I shrug. "He ended things."

Her eyes almost bulge out of their sockets. "*He* ended things?"

I nod. "To be honest, I feel fine about it, K. I wanted more of a commitment from him, and he couldn't do it, even after all these years together. I think we both knew this was coming. We've been apart for so long and in that time, we've established we want different things."

"And you're fine about it? Like, really?"

"Yes, I think deep down, I knew that he's always been

hesitant with the marriage thing. I don't know why, maybe it extends from his own parents' divorce – I honestly don't know. The distance thing has always been an issue for me. He's years away from doing a desk job, and I'd never want to be the one to tell him to come home for good. He loves what he does." *He's married to it, and not me; that's the bottom line.*

"But he was your first," Kennedy says, sitting up in bed as she winces. I help her as she smiles gratefully.

Seeing her banged up like this makes my stomach turn. One asshole is in jail awaiting trial while the other had surgery to remove the bullet Bones put in his shoulder, but that doesn't make me feel any better.

"That's got to make you feel… upset."

"Of course it does. It hurts, but I also know that we've run our course, K. He's all I've ever known, you know? And he has no plans to come back to the U.S. permanently anytime soon. I want to make a life with someone. Settle down. Maybe even have kids. We've never even talked much about any of that stuff. I'm just meant to wait around to *possibly* be a wife or the mother to his children. The truth is, I gave him an ultimatum and he ran."

I try hard not to show my sadness. If I break now, then I'll never resurface. I've always been a strong person, like Kennedy and my mom are, but I've also always worn my heart on my sleeve. I can't lie to save myself.

I've cried a lot over the last few weeks. I even called in a couple of personal days just after we broke up because I couldn't get out of bed. If Lukas walked through the door now and told me he was sorry and he wants to marry me, I'd take him back in a heartbeat. But I know that won't happen. I know him. He's always been very career-driven, not that there's anything wrong with that, but he obviously didn't see me in his future. That hurts more than anything else.

"I'm sorry, I don't know what to say." Kennedy goes on.

I lay a hand on her arm and give it a small squeeze. "It's fine. I've got so much going on to keep me busy. My life's crazy. I'm renovating the apartment, and speaking of which, can you ask Bones if he's got a drill I can borrow?"

"Why do you need to borrow a drill?"

"I need to hang some pictures."

"Why don't you ask your neighbor? How's that going, by the way?"

My heart lurches all of a sudden when I think about Axton. *What's that all about?*

"Good," I say, looking down at my shoes. "He's… nice."

Her brow furrows. "Uh oh."

"Uh oh, what?"

"Why are you looking down?"

My eyes snap back up to hers. "I'm not."

Trust my sister to go all *lawyer mode* on me. I forget she knows body language a little too well.

"Stevie, did something happen?"

I don't even have to pretend to look offended. "No, it didn't. Like I said, he's nice and a fast learner. So far, he's proving to be a good worker."

"Do you feel funny being around him?"

I panic. "In what way?"

"With him being a felon."

Oh, that.

I shake my head. "No, I genuinely think he's here for his second chance."

"Even so, if you feel unsafe…"

"K, I'm a big girl, and I don't feel unsafe, but thanks for your concern. He's not like that, from what I can gather so far. He's quiet, does his job, locks up most nights, and doesn't give me any backchat like some of the others do who should know better."

She still doesn't look convinced. "Well, he's got a lot riding on this job, so it's in his best interests to keep you on your good side and not cause any trouble."

I inwardly cringe. I know that my sister is a lawyer and it's her job to judge people to a degree, but I kinda feel bad for the guy. He made a stupid mistake as a teenager, and now he's got to prove himself to everyone, *forever*, just to make ends meet and keep a roof over his head. Whenever he does anything in life, this will come up.

I know that I don't know anything at all about him, but I just can't even picture him robbing a convenience store with a sawed-off shot gun. It just seems so out of character…

"I know that, and so far, he's been great." *And he's got pretty eyes and a body made for sin…*

"Good, then tell me why you've gone a weird color and you're touching your hair."

I drop the end of my ponytail.

"You've hit your head way too hard," I tell her. "And I haven't gone a weird color. It's stuffy in here… they don't let you open any windows."

She scrutinizes my face. "Is he good looking?"

Shit. Fuck.

"Uh, I haven't really noticed." *Crap. Not the right thing to say at all. She'll see right through it.*

"You haven't really noticed?"

I shrug. "He's not ugly, if that's what you mean."

"This just gets better."

"Well, he's my employee, so it's not really professional for me to comment on how attractive my staff are."

She balks. "I'm your sister. Now I have to know. Give me something… is he anything like Brock?"

I nod. "Pretty much. Blonder, though, and he's got more of a beard and tattoos on his entire…" I trail off. *Fuckety fuck.*

She stares back at me. "He's got tattoos on his entire… *what?"*

"Body, I'm guessing. You can see them all around his neck and up his arms and stuff."

Crisis averted.

She narrows her eyes and looks like she's just about to cross-examine me, when Bones comes through the door and saves my ass.

"Hey, babe," he says, then glances up at me. "Hey, Stevie, how's it goin'?"

I smile back. "Hi, Bones. Pretty good. I was just on my way out, dropped off some decent coffee and chocolate."

"Thank God you didn't bring me any crossword puzzles, or I'd really want to kill myself," Kennedy groans.

I turn to her. "That's not even remotely funny after the ordeal you've been through."

"It was just a joke," she says. "I'm lucky that the boys got there when they did and Sienna was able to get help. Those two assholes were crazy. I can't wait for their day in court."

"I worry about you," I say, squeezing her hand. "This has all been really tough to get my head around and seeing you like this, sis…"

"I know it has, but bad shit happens all the time to good people. I can't change it, Stevie. It happened, and I'm alive and that's all that matters."

I glance to Bones. It's awkward with him standing there.

"So, I'm taking it you two are a thing and that's not changing?"

Bones rests a hand on hers as he sits by her bedside, looking at her with something in his eyes I've not seen before. Devotion is one way to describe it. I know he cares for her, loves her even, and though it's crazy being kidnapped and having guns and police cars, if anyone is going to overcome something like this, it's Kennedy. There is no stopping her.

I wish I had her confidence. I don't think I'd be able to string a sentence together if it were me that had been drugged and kidnapped.

I still don't know if getting involved with Bones is the right thing for her to do, even though I know he's a good guy.

Despite the fact I work for bikers, I still see the danger that being involved with an MC like the Rebels can bring. It unsettles me, yet I know they are the good guys. They don't go around looking for trouble, but if trouble finds them, they deal with it.

"We're a thing," she replies, gazing up at Bones. He leans down and kisses her forehead.

"Good, for a second there, I thought you were gonna go all lawyer on my ass," he says.

Touché. Kennedy has that way about her. She makes

you want to love her and scream at the same time.

I smile. "Well, you should know, Bones, she has a wicked temper, and don't ever leave the toilet seat up whatever you do. Big mistake."

He grins. "Should I be taking notes?"

"I'll send you a list."

"You know, I am still conscious," Kennedy pipes up. "And I just survived a kidnapping."

"Which is why I'm not leavin' your side until you're walkin' again," Bones says.

The chemistry radiating off the two of them is palpable. It makes me wonder if Lukas and I ever had anything remotely close to that. It's like there was something missing. That spark.

"When do they think you'll be able to leave?" I ask, knowing broken ribs take weeks to heal.

"Hopefully in a few days. They want to be sure I have no head trauma, which I've been telling them I don't," Kennedy says, annoyed.

"No offense, sis, but you look like you went ten rounds with Mike Tyson."

She grimaces. "I don't doubt it. I'm too scared to look in the mirror."

"They're gonna pay," Bones mutters, his eyes blazing. "They're gonna pay for what they did."

"You don't need to go all commando on my ass," she

tells him, her eyes softening. "I need you here with me, not back in jail."

Bones leans in to give her a kiss, and I divert my eyes.

"Get a room, you two," I say, grabbing my purse. "And I've gotta run and get back to work."

Bones clears his throat. "Hey, Stevie, been meanin' to talk to you, if you've got a minute."

"Sure," I say. "I'll see you tomorrow, K. Hopefully you'll know more about when you're allowed to go home."

She nods and we hug. "Thanks, Stevie, I'll text you later if I hear anything new."

"Okay." I give her a wave as Bones follows me out into the hallway.

I turn to him. "What's up?"

He palms the back of his neck. "Just wanted to check on you and see how you're doin', with Axton."

Oh no, not you too. "Uh, fine. Like I just said to Kennedy, he's a fast learner and he's keeping his nose clean."

"And you feel fine around him?"

I feel more than fine. "Yes, I appreciate everyone's concern…"

"You'd tell me, wouldn't you? You're not gettin' anyone into trouble if you do."

I put my hand on my heart. On the one hand, I'm touched he, and everyone else, is making sure I'm okay and that Axton is toeing the line, but on the other, I feel bad that everyone is waiting for him to fuck up. "I would tell you, and he's been great. I promise."

He looks relieved. "Well, if that changes, you come see me. Got me?"

I try not to smile. "Uh, okay."

He gives me a chin lift. "So, you're okay with me and your sister?"

Now I do smile. "Would it matter if I wasn't?"

"Some shit went down, gotta be thinkin' about it."

"I am, and it worries me, if I'm being honest. The club does have dangerous elements and Kennedy being kidnapped isn't ranking too high on my comfort level. She's stubborn. She'll say she's okay even if she's not. She's got that whole fight-or-flight mode, always has."

He nods. "Good to know, but I think I can deal with her stubbornness. Her temper, though, that's somethin' else altogether."

He's a good guy. I always liked him, even before he and Kennedy finally got together. Aside from Gunner, he's always been the most light-hearted of the boys and seems to be able to take a joke.

"Tell me about it."

He looks a little awkward before he says, "Guess you know that I know about Dean."

Dean was my sister's husband who died of cancer a

couple of years ago. She's been dealing with the trauma and the guilt ever since he died.

"I figured."

"I know you two are close." He goes on. "What happened to her… I'm never gonna let anythin' bad happen to her again. You got my word on that. You know how all of us treat safety at the club."

A lump forms in my throat at how much I know he means it. "I believe you, but Kennedy won't be a kept woman. She still needs her space."

"I get that. Believe me when I say I've tried to stay away, that I know it'd be better for her to find a man who wears a suit and has a better day job, one that won't get her involved in club shit. It fuckin' kills me that she went through this. You don't know how much."

"I do know," I say, seeing how sincere he is. "And I know she loves you, Bones, so as much as she tells you she's independent and doesn't need to rely on a man, she does need that emotional support. You just gotta be sure that you're all in. If she gets hurt again…"

"I ain't goin' nowhere."

"Glad to hear it."

"So we're good?"

It's kind of sweet he's seeking my permission, in a roundabout way. "There is no stopping Hurricane Kennedy, and if she's happy, then so am I. I just never want to see her banged up like this again."

He nods, relief in his eyes. "Shit's gonna die down now. There's no beef with any club, or anyone else, for that matter, Jack's left town, we're runnin' the car and scrapyard now. Trust me, I want things to go back to normal too. It's why I moved to a small town. I like the peace and quiet, and most of all; no drama."

Jack is the father of one of the fuckfaces that kidnapped Kennedy. They had beef with the club when Steel broke all of Jack's fingers for stealing from them. Little did Jack know, his daughter was out for revenge and wanted compensation for Jack going broke. She was strung out on drugs and out of her mind.

"It scared the shit out of me, when Kennedy got taken," I say. "I thought I may never see her again."

He places a hand on my shoulder and looks me right in the eye. "You know I would never let anything happen to her, and though she's independent, I'll be watchin' over her to make sure. Especially now she has to heal and take some time to get better. Nobody's ever gonna hurt her again."

I wipe a tear from my eyes. "Thanks, Bones, you're a good guy."

He gives me chin lift. "Just let me know, if any shit goes down with Ax, or anyone else."

I smile. "I thought Steel was the club's enforcer?"

"He is, but Steel can be a little intimidating."

"You think?"

He grins. "You've got my number."

I start to walk in the other direction. "See ya later."

By the time I get to work, the lunch rush is about to begin. I pop into the kitchen to see Roxy, and I find Axton leaning against the counter, a dishcloth over his shoulder as he laughs at something Roxy is saying. *Is he getting fresh with the head chef?*

He straightens when he sees me.

"Hey, guys," I say. "Anything change on the bar menu before we start taking orders?"

Roxy smiles, her long dark hair tied up into a hair net as she controls her laughter. *Obviously, something was funny.*

"Nope, but I've got a ton of beef patties today, so we shouldn't run out of burgers."

The hamburger and home-made fries have been a huge seller at lunchtime. A lot of the tradesmen and road workers come in to get takeaway. Roxy and the other two sous-chefs make the patties by hand, and she has special sauce.

"Sounds good. Word is getting around how good the food is," I say.

I glance at Axton. He still has a smile on his face, and I feel a pang of jealousy that I wasn't the one to put it there. Still, Roxy is an attractive woman. And Axton is an attractive man. Plus he just got out of jail, so, I mean, he's probably banged the whole town by now.

It's been ten years since he's been with a woman. Yet, I haven't seen or heard any chicks coming and going next door like how I imagined. Maybe he keeps all of that kind of stuff at the club?

I feel him staring at me as I peer over the large bowl Roxy's mixing something into, stirring around with a whisk.

"What's that?" I ask. It looks like lumpy custard.

"I'm trying out a new beer batter for the fish and chips," she says proudly. "I've just mastered the batter… I think."

"I said I'd be happy to taste test," Axton tells me with a grin. "Haven't had decent fish and chips in… let's see now… yeah, it's been a while."

Though he laughs, I see the pain behind his eyes, but if Roxy does too, she doesn't show it. Instead, she laughs along with him and tells him to come back in ten minutes for the first batch of fish for the taste test.

What is it with me and this guy? I'm like a broken record. Why do I care she's making him smile?

"Well, Roxy does make the best batter this side of the Mississippi," I reply as I turn to leave.

At least he's getting along with the staff, maybe a little too well, but it's better than making enemies and being a pain in the ass. The last thing I need is him upsetting the head chef, and she seems far from put-out.

Plus, he does everything I ask him, and the bar is spotless, so why am I suddenly feeling like three's a crowd?

Another busy lunch rush ensues, and Axton works the bar well, even running some plates out to the tables. I wouldn't say he's the friendliest of people I've ever met, but he's polite enough and never rude. He doesn't really talk to the customers at all and keeps his head down for the most part.

After lunch is over, I go on my break to review some of the invoices. I take refuge in the back office where Colt has all his fancy surveillance equipment set up.

My eyes wander to the monitor showing Axton tidying up the bar and polishing the glasses. After he's done that, he sweeps the floor and keeps serving the few customers that come in. It's quiet again in the afternoon until the evening crowd finish work.

I don't know how long I sit there staring. It's only when I hear someone clear their throat that I'm jolted out of my reverie.

I look to the door and Axton stands in the doorway. One arm leans on the doorjamb, and I notice his bulging biceps as he gives me a chin lift.

"Delivery guy from the distillery is here. Assume it's okay to let him in through the back?"

He always asks when he isn't sure of something. That's something new that I appreciate.

I give him a smile and hope he didn't notice my zombie trance while staring at the surveillance camera.

"That would be great, thanks, Axton," I say.

"I'm happy to help him unload while it's quiet. Rory can cover while we haul." He goes on. "I can see you're busy, and I'm sure paperwork is a bitch to deal with."
He also uses his brain, unlike most of the other staff I have on hand.

"That would be amazing, if you're sure you're okay to do it?"

He gives me a small smile. "Pretty sure I can figure it out."

Funny. I don't see him smiling like that at the customers, only when ladies are present.

I swallow hard.

It's my libido, I realize, as he turns to leave, and I tear my eyes away from staring at his ass.

I don't know why I feel heat every time he's around. I've been attracted to other guys before, even while I was with Lukas. It's only natural, and obviously, I never acted on it, but it was okay to look.

However, I should not be looking at Axton in *that way,* nor should I be picturing what he looks like without that shirt on… or a pair of jeans.

I need to get some freaking work done, yet every time I go to my computer screen, I get distracted. It's because he's off limits, I decide. And all wrong. That's what it is.

I mean, how much more wrong could there be?

The bad boy ex-con with dirty tattoos, a criminal record, and his rough and rugged physical appearance that crosses somewhere between completely understated and sexy as hell.

I press my palm to my forehead.

Just breathe.

It's nothing, I tell myself. *It's just stupid.*

One thing I do like is the presence he has. Nobody's gonna mess with him, and this bar, unless they're really drunk or really stupid. We need that here.

Most of the time when I was bartending at the club, it was just me and Ginger or Summer. I'm not used to having a man behind the bar that can handle himself. Let's see how he does on Saturday night when things in the bar can get a little wild.

A deep, dark, secret part of me likes the thought of it, seeing him in action, seeing what he's capable of and what he'd do when he has to turf someone out. Not that I condone violence, but sometimes people need to be tossed outside with their keys taken off them and put in a cab.

I swallow hard at his bulk and how his eyes dance with humor, even when he tries not to smile. I wonder how that mouth would taste with that prickly beard... *fuck.*

Groaning, I fist the table on either side of my computer. *This has to fucking stop.*

It's the fantasy, a distraction, nothing more.

BRACKEN RIDGE
REBELS
ARIZONA
M · C

CHAPTER 5

AXTON

Friday night tests my patience and my stamina. The Stone Crow used to be the place where dodgy drug deals went down in back corners, where drunks sat at the bar on their usual stools, and brawls broke out.

Now that the Rebels weeded out all the trash, the bar is littered with a different demographic altogether. The families come for the early bird special in the restaurant, happy hour runs six till eight, and then Friday and Saturday nights, there's usually a live band playing light rock and country.

The place is booming tonight.

Hutch put on extra security including the other prospects, Jax and Gears, and a bouncer on each door on weekends. You get caught trying to sneak in here and peddle drugs, then you won't have to deal with the cops, you'll be running from the Bracken Ridge Rebels.

From what I've heard, Hutch runs a pretty tight ship and he's not one of those old, cruddy biker Presidents who are set in their ways and don't like change. He's exactly the opposite.

I never thought I'd see the light of day on a Friday, but Brock and a few of the guys are having a poker night at the club and Brock said I could tag along. Not that prospects are usually allowed to do that, but I guess it pays to have your older brother as the club's V.P.

So when I arrive after 1am, they're only just getting started.

I settle the six-pack on the table and give my brother a chin lift.

There's also Steel, Colt, and Rubble sitting at the table.

The boys all stare at me as I take a seat. "What?" I gruff. "Do I have a sign on my head that I'm not aware of?"

Brock pats me on the back, hard. "Glad to see you made it."

"Wired after tonight, will take me a couple hours to wind down."

"You get to kick anyone out?" asks Steel, knowing how Fridays usually roll.

"Couple got a bit rowdy. I dealt with it."

He gives me a chin lift. "You finish haulin' the blue metal?" He looks dubious.

Little does Steel know, every task he gives me, no

matter how busy I am, I get it done.

Even though I work full time at the Crow, I still have prospect duties to complete. There's no rest for the wicked, or so they say. Today I spread gravel around the front parking lot at the club's entrance. Took me three fucking hours before I started my shift.

But I can't exactly say no to Steel. Not if I want my front teeth to remain in my mouth.

He's solid like me and Brock, but bigger, and even if I wanted to, nobody talks back to the Sergeant at Arms and the Enforcer. I'm lucky they're letting me sit at the same table. This is how club life works.

"Of course. I don't fuck around," I reply.

"Not according to the sweet butts," Rubble says, giving me a look. "Chelsea's been looking for you."

"Christ," I mutter.

Brock gives me a strange look. "You all right?"

I pop the top of my bottle. "I'm fine, why?"

"Thought you'd be up to your eyeballs in pussy, bro."

I run a hand over my face. "Had plenty, but work, along with getting my license, and prospect duties kinda hinder shit a little."

Steel grunts. Colt laughs and Rubble just shakes his head.

"You've been locked up for ten fuckin' years." Steel goes on. "I know I'd be findin' the time."

"My dick's fine, still hangin', thanks for your concern," I add.

I can't tell any of them that before I got locked up, I'd only been with a handful of chicks. I'm really not that experienced when it comes to sex. Though, it's pretty fuckin' basic.

When I fucked Bambi, it was cool and shit; she did all the right things, but I have really no clue if what I did was right. I'm almost thirty years old, and none of my brothers around this table want to hear that shit.

"Could line you up with Bambi again. She's eager." Brock goes on.

"Bambi knows the taste of my dick," I reply, taking a long pull on my beer. "So do most of the girls in this club." That's a lie. I only fucked her, but one thing I learned in prison is you've gotta keep up appearances. If people think you're weak, then they'll just treat you that way.

I never want to appear like that in front of Brock. So, for a while, I gotta talk the talk and most of its trash.

"Must've done somethin' right." Colt laughs. "She hasn't stopped talkin' about you. I think her and Chelsea might be gettin' under each other's skin."

"Plenty of me to go round," I say. "Two can choke on my cock at once if they really want."
Rubble snorts and starts dealing the cards. "You any good at poker?" he asks when our eyes meet across the table.

"I spent ten years in jail. I'm good at all card games." Steel shakes his head. "Nice goin'," he says to Brock. "Fuckin' card shark on our hands here."

"Little bit of competition never hurt anyone," Brock replies, giving me a wink. "Right, Ax?"

I snicker. "Don't worry, I'll make it seem like I'm shit for the first few rounds." I give them a chin lift. "What we playin' for?"

"Anything from five bucks and up," says Colt.

Good. I'm pretty low on cash as it is, and I could do with making a couple of bucks.

A few things I learned in prison were how to fight and how to win at cards. I didn't mind making shit in the workshop, but I tried to stay out of the kitchen.

"You ever get jumped in jail?" Steel asks when the game gets underway.

"All the fuckin' time when I first went in."
Brock swallows hard. I know this is a hard limit for him.

"What about other shit?" he presses, and I know what he's asking.

"You're fuckin' nosy," I retort back with a chuckle. "If you're askin' if my ass is still a virgin, the answer is yes. Not sayin' there weren't times in the early years where a couple fuckturds tried, but I had the advantage of bein' big and strong, and I can't be sure, but there coulda been a couple people lookin' out for me while I was in there."

Brock's gaze meets mine and he looks back down at his cards.

"Maximum is hardcore, but I managed to stay outta trouble, for the most part." I go on. "Then I got transferred to minimum and let out early on good behavior. None of it's a picnic, but you just gotta keep your head up, do your time, and try not to kill anybody."

"I can't imagine ten years without pussy," Rubble says, shaking his head when it's his turn to pick up. "Feelin' a woman's touch…"

"Only had a few years under my belt before I got locked up," I say. "Got plenty of time to make up for it."

"How's Stevie been since you arrived?" Brock chucks a card on the pile in the middle of the table.

"Good," I say. "We get along great. She's a pretty cool chick." *One who I can't stop thinking about and who I've jerked off to more than once in the shower.*

"She says you're a hard worker, not afraid to get your hands dirty," Steel agrees. "Least she's not tellin' us to give you the boot."

"Been checkin' up on me?" I pick up a king of spades and tuck it into my stash.

"Someone's gotta," he retorts.

He's probably right. Trust is earned around here, I get it. I'm still a shit kicker until proven otherwise. Even though I'm Brock's kid brother, that doesn't sway you any favors or guarantee friends until a little bit of time has passed and you've proved your worth.

It's simple, really.

I've just gotta keep my head above water.

"What happened to Nitro?" Steel gives Rubble a chin lift.

From what I can gather, Nitro is about to be patched in, he's the new recruit. Rubble's ol' lady Lucy just found out that Nitro is her long lost brother.

He's helping run the car and scrapyard the Rebels just bought. I wonder why they didn't get me to go help out there. I'm probably more cut out for manual labor in a scrap heap than I am serving drinks in a bar. I don't really like people much, but I gotta be polite.

Except to the assholes who annoy Stevie.

"Had to sort shit out at the yard." Rubble shrugs. "Said he'd be at the next one."

"Weekend after this, we patch Nitro in," Brock says.

"Fucker's been workin' his butt off for weeks without a break. He's got that place turnin' over already. Glad he didn't take off to Phoenix."

"What's in Phoenix?" I ask.

"Another club," Rubble answers. "My old club, but they've reformed and come back swingin'. The Sons of Phoenix Fury. They're one percenters, but good guys. Smokey and I go way back, and Nitro used to be part of the club some years back."

"Heard about the shit that went down with Bones and Lucy," I say. "Long as I get to knock some heads together from time to time."

"You just keep your head on straight," Brock pipes up. "Don't need you gettin' into any trouble till you're well outta probation."

"I fold," Rubble groans.

"Me too," says Colt.

"What you got?" Steel gives me a chin lift.

"Royal flush," I say, laying my cards on the table.

Steel leans over. "Well, I'll be damned." He's got four of a kind and Brock has a flush. "I thought you said you'd pretend to be shit?"

"Fuck," Brock groans. "I forgot how fuckin' good you are at competition."

I laugh, scooping up the cash from the middle of the table. "Nah, I just got a sharp mind, the rest is just luck."

Rubble's about to scoop up the cards and deal again, when there's a commotion at the door.

"Thought the prospects got told to beat it tonight?" Brock frowns.

"They did," Steel replies.

A girl giggles and some keys get dropped, then a male voice says, "Shhhh!"

"Who's going to hear us?" the girl replies with another

giggle.

I haven't been back in town very long, but I'd know that laugh anywhere… what would Amelia be doing here with…

"You're laughin' loud enough to wake the dead," the male voice says.

"Gears. You're not going to chicken out on me, are you?"

"You shouldn't even be here."

Brock and I share a glance.

Oh, fuck. This is about to get ugly.

It would almost be comical seeing their faces when they round the corner and see us — if it weren't my little sister, that is.

Brock and I rise from the table at the same time.

"Shit!" Amelia cries, trying to turn and make a run for it, but I'm across the room quicker and I haul her ass back through the door.

Brock's already got Gears by the scruff of the neck. "What the fuck is this?" he bellows.

If the dead weren't awake before, they certainly were now.

"It's not what it looks like!" Gears tries to protest, holding his hands up in surrender.

"Like fuck it's not!" Brock lands a swift punch to his stomach, and he doubles over as Amelia screams.

"Brock! That's enough!"

He points at her in the face while I hold her by the wrist so she can't wriggle away. "You be quiet, and you…" He looks back at Gears. "You've got about three seconds to tell me why you've got my baby sister here, and this better be fuckin' good, sunshine."

"Brock," Amelia interrupts. "I'm not a baby, and I'm getting sick and tired of you introducing me like that to everyone. I'm not a child!"

"Maybe not." He goes on. "But he's a fuckin' prospect and you're a club sister."

"My car broke down," she cries, frustration lacing her tone that makes my ears ring.

Brock snorts. "Right, so Gears thought he'd just try to fix it up in his bedroom, did he?"

"Calm the fuck down, everyone," Steel says, coming up behind me. "Let's just take a beat."

Amelia, the brave little thing, looks up to him like he's going to be sympathetic. "Steel, do something. These two aren't even going to listen to anything…"

"I'll do something, all right," Steel replies, cracking his knuckles. "I'll go outside, find the shovel, and start diggin' the hole if he doesn't start talkin'."

"Urgh!" she cries out again. "You bunch of buffoons are so annoying. Do you really think we'd come here if we were fooling around?"

I look down at her. "Maybe you've been fooling around

elsewhere and got cavalier."

Brock turns his glare on me. "Axton makes a good point. Maybe you have?"

I'm itching to punch this fucker out. Gears and I get along fine. He's an okay dude, but that doesn't mean I'm okay about him touching my sister…

"Where the fuck's the car?" Steel barks. "I'll get Jax to go check it out."

"That's just charming," she scolds, hands on her hips as we surround her. "You don't even believe me, your own sister."

I haven't been around my sister since she was a kid, obviously. But from what Brock has told me over the years, she gets into a fair amount of trouble all by herself. And I certainly wouldn't put it past her to pull a stunt like this. Even if she is a grown adult, she shouldn't be wandering around late at night on her own. Maybe it's a good thing Gears pulled over, if that is actually the real story.

Brock turns to Gears. "Start talkin'."

"I was drivin' past the turnpike on Oakpark road, when I saw Amelia's car," he says, running both hands through his hair like he's stressed. He should be shitting his pants. "And she had a flat, so I got out to take a look."

All eyes stare at Gears, and while I can tell he's telling the truth, I know there's more to it. I don't believe that Amelia's intentions are strictly honorable. For one, why was she giggling like that?

"So, that still doesn't explain what you're doing here?" Brock barks.

Gears still holds his hands up in surrender, and if he knows what's good for him, he'll keep them there. "I came to get tools."

Steel folds his arms over his chest, never a good sign, his frown matching mine and Brock's.

"Tools?" Steel questions. "That piece of shit truck doesn't have a simple wrench?"

"I took all my tools out so I could pick up the gravel for the yard," he explains. "Didn't get a chance to put everything back in."

By now, Amelia has folded her hands over her chest in annoyance. She's not a kid anymore, but in this club and our family, that doesn't matter. Prospects don't touch club girls.

"You wanna talk to me about what happens to prospects who put their hands on club sisters?" Brock points in Gears's chest. "Just ask Gunner. He got a poundin' for makin' out with Lily years ago when he was prospectin'. Fucker never forgot that night, ain't that right, Steel?"

Steel grunts. No more words needed. When it comes to his little sister, Lily, he's the worst offender.

"Are you done?" Amelia demands. "Or is the Spanish Inquisition over?"

Brock glares at her. "I don't wanna hear your smart

mouth, Amelia. Now's really not the time."

She shakes her head. "I think now is a perfect time. So what if I was fooling around with him? I'm old enough to do what I like without having my two big brothers rattling the poor schmuck's head, scaring us half to death, and Steel over here, ready to bury him alive."

"I'd quit while you're ahead, Amelia," I warn.

"Don't you start," she hisses back.

I hold my hands up. "Be rational, that's all I'm sayin'. You know the rules better than I do."

She can't argue there.

Amelia and I are taking things slow, getting to know one another, so her snapping at me is a little bit of a surprise. Not that I can blame her; it's hard for her to do anything within the MC without us knowing about it.

But even I know it ain't gonna cut it with a prospect.

"I'll do more than bury him," Steel warns.

Brock folds his arms over his chest. He's not done yet. The force of animosity coming off him makes me realize how protective he is. He used to get like this when we were kids and Angel was around. I try not to smile at the memory. Old habits die hard.

"Can we go now?" she huffs.

"That's enough out of you," Brock says, his eyes blazing. "You want to associate with this MC, you know how things work, Amelia Jayne, so don't start throwing tough words around like you're dumb, when you know perfectly well how things roll around here."

She opens her mouth and closes it again. She's not going to argue. She likes coming to church. She likes hanging with the girls and being part of the club, so I know for a fact she's not going to do anything to put that in jeopardy.

"This conversation is becoming really boring." She sniffs, holding her head high. "And I still need a ride home."

"I can take her," I offer, even though I just got there. "I've only had two sips of beer."

Brock gives me a chin lift. "She can wait a few rounds until we're done. Gears, I think the upstairs bathroom needs a clean."

Gears, quite wisely, keeps his trap shut and makes for the stairs across the room without anther word.

"I'm not a child," Amelia huffs at Brock, clearly pissed.

"No? Then why the attitude if he's just fixin' your car? You shouldn't be that pissed off," he fires back.

"Like he wouldn't have had his hands all over her ass given half a chance," Steel pipes up.

"I saw the huge grin on his face."

"We can kick his ass later," Rubble calls from the poker table behind us. "Let's get on with it. I've got a wife and a baby to get home to sometime tonight. I'd like to enjoy the few hours of freedom while I've still got it."

"I'm not sitting here waiting for you all night!" Amelia whines. "I'm tired, and I want to go home."

"Is she always like this?" Steel grunts, storming back to his place at the table.

"Afraid so," Brock retorts. Once Steel's gone, Brock's face softens just a little.

"Amelia, please tell us we don't have to hurt Gears," I say, trying to smooth the situation some.

"You don't have to hurt Gears," she replies.

I pull my arm around her shoulders. "You know how Brock is." I ruffle her hair. "Always was a hothead."

She swats me on the arm but doesn't shove me away. "I'm lookin' out for her," he argues. "That's never gonna change."

She wrinkles her nose. "Just because a prospect gave me a ride after my car tire blew, doesn't mean I'm blowing him."

I wince. "I definitely didn't need that visual."

Brock pinches the bridge of his nose and says, "Amelia, let's not even go there. For everyone's sakes, enough! Got me?"

I can't be sure, but I think she calls him an asshole as she squirms out of my hold and makes for the bar as we walk back to the table.

"You buy their story?" Brock asks me.

"Not a chance," I say. "Though to be fair, I don't think

Gears would purposely try somethin'. He'd be stupid to even think about it."

"Amelia's a pretty girl, and it's not like he's a fuckin' saint."

"I think he got the message."

"He better have," Brock looks up toward the stairs. "I'll put a hole through his head before he touches her."

"I can still hear you," Amelia calls from behind the bar, where she reaches for a soda. "These ears aren't painted on."

"All bets are off when it comes to women of this club. If they're not drivin' you insane, they're tryin' to give you more gray hairs," Brock tells me, frowning. "Just remember that."

"Loud and clear, brother," I say, as we walk back to the table. "Loud and clear."

BRACKEN RIDGE
REBELS
ARIZONA
M·C

CHAPTER 6

STEVIE

There are six of us working the bar Saturday night. When we have a good band playing, the place goes bananas.

I like it when it's busy, when the hours fly by and the adrenaline keeps you on your toes all night. When it's like this, we all work our butts off.

I deliberately try not to take too much notice of Axton, but avoiding him is a little hard. He's everywhere. Working the bar like he's been doing it his whole life. He moves so fast, like a pro, and I'm secretly impressed. He's come a long way in a little over a week.

I've also noticed he's getting a lot of female attention.

Who could blame a girl? He's got the whole bad boy vibe going on in tight, black jeans, a black t-shirt with *The Stone Crow* scrawled across it, and steel caps. *His ass is…* no!

I shouldn't be noticing his ass or anything else. Yet, I lose count of how many phone numbers slip in his hand while he's pouring drinks and collecting empty glasses from around the tables.

There it is again. My jealousy. I've no right to feel this way.

Axton is a grown ass man, with a lot of baggage, and I don't need to be imagining what it would be like to feel his rock-hard body and squeeze his tight ass.

I can safely say that I've never, ever fantasized about someone I work with before, let alone someone I'm in charge of.

His eyes flick to mine suddenly, and I look away.

Way to go, idiot. Now he caught you staring.

I don't know what's gotten into me, but it has to stop. Maybe I just need to find a random guy and get laid. Not that I would know what that's like, since the only guy I've ever been with is Lukas. He's all I've ever known. In fact, imagining myself with another man, when it's all said and done, fills me with dread.

I should be able to let loose, do what I want, have a good time without having to reason with myself that I'm allowed. I'm not betraying Lukas; he broke up with me. We're over and have been for a long time.

Maybe I just need a rebound, that's what people do, right?

The best way to get over someone, so they say, is to get under someone else. Then again, what the hell would I know?

The downfall for me is that I've no idea how to date, or even if I'll ever be at that point ever again. Even though things with Lukas and I were strained these last few years, I still love him. Maybe I always will, and that makes moving on all that much harder, even when I know it's for the best.

As the night goes on, the bar gets busier, the music gets louder, and the patrons are in full Saturday night swing. When I turn to the cooler to grab a handful of beers, Axton and I reach for the same bottle at the same time. Our fingers touch.

One side of his mouth turns up. "Ladies first."

I roll my eyes, but I can't help the smile on my face. "That's awfully chivalrous of you."

"Chivalry is my middle name." He winks.

I grab two more as I avoid his eyes. So fucking blue. I also can't mistake the jolt in my chest and the way my heart rate speeds up when our fingers touch. *This isn't fucking normal.*

I need to get a grip.

If I'm not mistaken, I feel a need that isn't just pressing, it's literally throbbing between my legs. And I know it's all dirty and wrong. It's so fucking wrong, but he's everything a hot-blooded male should be, minus the criminal record. In my fantasy, I choose to overlook that part.

I know he's watching me in my peripheral as I grab the rest of the drinks and pop the tops, placing them on the counter and taking the cash. A few minutes later, I feel a light touch at my hip. Axton's touching me. His fingers brush my skin lightly. I swallow hard as I turn.

He's looking down at me. "You had a break yet, boss?" he asks, concern across his face.

He removes his hand as fast as he placed it there, now that he has my attention.

I can't even form a sentence with that small but searing gesture, and the way he says *boss*...

I don't show it, though. Instead I straighten my back and shake my head. "You worried I don't have enough stamina, Ax?"

The minute the words leave my mouth, I could shoot myself in the foot. His eyes dilate slightly, earning me another heart palpitation. I was meaning: to get through my shift, but now it just sounds dirty.

There's that crooked smile again. He leans down to my ear. "I'm pretty confident you've got that covered." His voice is low and gravely, and it does things to me that shouldn't be legal.

"And, I'm fuckin' hungry, but it seemed rude to go eat before you do. You've been here longer, and you are the boss after all."

I clench my pussy, and I don't fucking mean to, but talk about being hungry and eating and me being his boss just sends me into a tailspin. I'm deprived, that's what it is.

"Again, very chivalrous," I muse, trying to keep myself from blurting anything else out that sounds dirty.

"I'll take one shortly. Feel free to eat first, though." I don't know if I succeeded or failed, but he moves down the other end of the bar, and I avoid eye fucking his ass.

Maybe I need a cold shower instead of a hamburger.

After ten more minutes, I take that well needed break, but instead of going into the restaurant, I take the stairs up to my apartment two at a time to make a sandwich instead.

I had to get out of there. The whole vibe is sending me somewhere I'm not sure I want to be, and it's all my fault. Well, it's his fault too, for being so damn sexy.

I hold a hand to my forehead as I pull out two slices of bread, slam them down on the counter, and slap mayonnaise on both sides vigorously, causing me to poke a hole in the bread as I curse myself. I smack in a couple of slices of turkey and cut the thing in half, slicing half my finger in the process.

"Shoot!" I say, as blood immediately gushes from my skin. The cut isn't bad, but it's enough to warrant a small bloodbath.

Grabbing a piece of paper towel off the roll, I press it against my skin to try to stop the bleeding. Of course, I don't have any medical supplies up here, since the first aid kit is downstairs. I walk back down, leaving my bloodied sandwich on the bench, cursing the day I was born. I don't have time for this shit.

I wander down to the utility room between my office and the back of the bar and pull out the first aid kid while trying to keep pressure on my finger.

I'm rummaging around, trying to find a band aid, when I hear, "Shit, Stevie, what happened?"

My eyes shift upwards, and Axton is in the hallway, a dishrag over his shoulder as he takes out the trash from behind the bar. He drops the bag immediately and comes toward me, frowning when he sees blood seeping down my hand.

"I had a fight with my kitchen knife. Safe to say, I didn't win," I say, pulling at the wrapper with my teeth.

His eyes flick to my mouth for half a second before he takes my hand, removes the sodden tissue, and curses some more. "Looks like you definitely did a good job of it. I'll get some clean tissues."

"I'm fine, really."

"Hold the pressure for a sec, I'll be right back."

"Thanks." I nod and he takes the first aid kit from me and tucks it under his arm.

I walk down to my office and take a seat. It stings like a bitch, but I know I'm being a bit of a baby. I don't need Axton helping clean me up; however, the blood is flowing quite freely now. I hope I don't need to have a stitch.

He returns a few moments later, pulls up a crate, and sits

below me. Taking the paper towel, he drops it on my desk and wraps some clean tissues around my finger.

"You know, I'm probably fine to do it myself," I say, feeling a bit ridiculous.

But it's like he doesn't hear me.

"Was the knife old or new?"

"New," I say, then add, "Why?"

"If it was old or rusty, I'd say you'd need a tetanus shot, but I think you should be all right."

One big hand holds the pressure tight while he takes the band aid from my fingers. "This won't cut it. Hold the pressure tight while I find some gauze and tape."

"Axton, I don't think that's really necessary."

His ice blue eyes flick up at me. He's quiet by nature, but I've never seen him this serious before. It's intense.

"Trust me. I've seen some injuries while I was inside. You don't want to get it infected. Fastest way to do that is to just slap a band aid on it and not treat it properly."

I can't help my small smile. "Are you sure you're not in the wrong trade?"

He smirks. "Thought about being an ambulance officer one time, but I'd end up refusing to help all the drunk assholes or the ones on drugs."

"You never did any drugs?" The words are out of my mouth before I can stop them.

But he continues to rummage in the first aid box and

doesn't even look up. He locates the gauze, disinfectant, and some tape.

"Not after I got locked up. Too hard in prison. Though I smoked enough cigarettes to probably give me lung cancer down the track. Tryin' to give that up."

"It's a dirty habit," I say just as his eyes meet mine.

"Lot of dirty habits, Stevie. Trouble is, most people pick more than one, then they land in trouble. I should know, I wrote the damn book."

I swallow hard as he shakes his head, as if remembering something, and I can't help it when my mind drifts all by itself, imagining all the kinds of trouble Axton could get me in. Mainly in the bedroom.

There goes that throb again...

I clear my throat. "Not me. I was an angel growing up."

He snickers. "I wouldn't doubt that for a second."

I laugh. "You're so quick to believe me. I could have been a devil."

He shakes his head. "Now that, I definitely don't believe."

I watch him as he works, patching me up as he tells me the next part is gonna sting... disinfectant on my wound.

"Why not?" I ask. "Do I have an honest face?" I show him some doe-eyes and a pout as his shoulders shake with laughter.

Fuck me, it's a nice sound. It's the first real laugh I've

heard, aside from the other day with Roxy in the kitchen when he was all smiles. But this is different, and I don't know why.

Wincing a little as he dabs disinfectant on the cut and holds the gauze tight as he wraps my finger up, his smile still traces his lips. "Most people are an open book, if you know what to look for."

"Something tells me you're good at reading people."

His eyebrows raise. "You could say that."

"I'm dying to know what my face says," I cajole, trying not to show him how much my finger hurts. I hate blood, and I hate pain.

I see his eyes crease slightly as he bites his bottom lip. For a guy who's been in prison, he's teeth are remarkably straight. "You really wanna know?"

"Not if it's anything bad."

His eyes meet mine again. "There's not a bad bone in your body, Stevie Hart. I can tell that straight away."

"You can?" I muse. "What else?"

He looks back down and grabs the tape, rolling it out as he rips the end with his teeth. "You don't trust easily."
I try not to let my eyes go wide.

"You're patient and kind, but that's a mere observation, so it doesn't really count. You also worry a lot, about everything."

I swallow hard as I stare down at him, then in small

voice, I say, "You can tell all of that from my face?"

His lips twitch as he wraps the tape around my wound. "And body language."

He's been watching me? Why does that turn me on and not frighten me?

I lick my bottom lip as I imagine how that beard would feel between my…

"You can read people's bodies too?" I try not to whisper it.

He shrugs. "Anyone can. You're forgetting, I had a lot of time to observe. I had to have my wits about me in the joint. You get good at knowin' when you're bein' played real quick, who to trust, who to avoid, and who could potentially whack you."

"Holy shit," I whisper.

His eyes flick up. If I'm not mistaken, they've glazed over just slightly.

It hurt him. Being locked up.

Why do I get the feeling Axton Altman is quite a sensitive man, behind the muscle, beard and brawn? He really is a sweet guy.

"You, for example, are a strong, independent woman. You can hold your own, but sometimes you second guess yourself. I'm no expert, boss, but you should always go with your gut in decision-making. Your gut instinct is never wrong."

I bite my lip as his eyes flick to my mouth.

Something charges between us. It's there. He knows it too. There's a fucking inferno brewing, and it suddenly feels really hot in here.

"That's scarily accurate," I reply when he's done and I have my hand back.

Losing the touch of his warm hands makes me less jittery, but I'm fucked all the same. And I know it's ridiculous, but my panties are fucking soaked.

"You're a beautiful woman, Stevie," he adds. "Though, that's another obvious observation."

We stare at one another, then he shakes his head. "I'm sorry…"

I frown. "I don't know if it's appropriate… to say that…"

"It's true, but yeah, fuck… I'm sorry, I didn't mean to make you uncomfortable."

Little does he know, I'm far from uncomfortable.

"Well, I did ask," I say, because I don't want to make him feel bad. "That'll teach me."

He goes to stand, and I catch him on the wrist with my unwounded hand, stopping him.

"I just…" I sigh, trying to think of the right words. "We work together, Axton."

Have I just inadvertently admitted that I find him attractive?

He nods curtly. "Duly noted."

"And things could get awkward."

He rolls his lips inwards, as if fighting a smile. "Brutal honesty is another trait, and it's not a bad thing. In fact, it's never a bad thing."

I let go of his wrist as he gathers up the mess on my desk. "If it's okay, I'll go take my break now, *boss.*" His tone lingers on that last little word, and something about it hits me right in the middle of my core. The bastard. Maybe he's doing this on purpose.

I wave my good hand at him. "By all means, and thanks… for patching me up."

He gives me a chin lift as he heads for the door. "Anytime."

He leaves the room and my eyes flick to the monitor on my desk, which has all angles of each and every camera in the place. I watch with interest as he appears on the screen, heading up the hall toward the bar, but suddenly, he stops.

I lean in closer to see what he's doing.

He runs a hand through his hair, visibly shaking his head, then he slaps his forehead a few times with the butt of his hand.

My eyes go wide at the gesture. He didn't do anything wrong; even if saying I was beautiful was definitely crossing the line. It doesn't matter how good it felt hearing those words come from his lips, or that I wanted him to keep touching me.

I'm his boss.

This cannot happen.

I need to get laid, and not with him. With some other random dude I don't care about. Surely, that'll fix things.

I need to relieve the want that lurks deep beneath the surface, and I need to do it fast.

If I don't, then I don't know what to do with the burn that ignites inside me every time I'm left alone with Axton Altman.

BRACKEN RIDGE
REBELS
ARIZONA
M · C

CHAPTER 7

AXTON

Every inch of my body gravitates toward the infuriating woman I call my boss.

She's fucking heaven.

Everything about her reels me in. Her touch. Her scent. Her sweet, sweet mouth. Jesus Christ, what I could do to that mouth.

It isn't the first time I've thought about taking her mouth, claiming it with my own as I push her hair back off her face and press her up against the wall.

I knew I was on dangerous territory when she probed me about what I could see in her face. But I can't lie. I've never been able to. And, frankly, she is a beautiful woman, not that she seems to know it.

What I didn't tell her is how I think she also pleases everyone else except herself, she's guarded, and I know from the look in her eyes and from the way she kept biting down on that lip of hers that she has a dark side. Sexually, she wants a man to take her, be rough with her, treat her

body like it's there for his own enjoyment. And I fuckin'
would if I could.

She is going to drive me insane.

I walk back to the bar with a fucking torpedo in my
jeans, and I contemplate, not for the first time, going to see
Bambi or Chelsea. Not that they're Stevie, but they're still
nice girls. Pretty. Completely submissive. They do whatever
you want, and yet, somehow, I just don't know why that
doesn't appeal to me. I don't owe Stevie Hart anything. She
doesn't have the right to my body or my fuckin' soul, yet
here she is, keeping me away from any other woman.

I know I'm gonna rub one out tonight, again. Picturing
her underneath me while I torture her with my tongue. To
taste her sweet pussy… fuck. I don't even know if I'd last
without shooting my load everywhere.

Truth is, I've never gone down on a chick before. And
I've no intention of doing that with Bambi or Chelsea.
When I fucked Bambi when I first got out, it was to feel the
touch of a woman and get off, obviously. With Stevie Hart,
I'd want to take my time.

I imagine all the positions I could get her in, including
fucking her on this bar after closing. Parting her legs,
putting them over my shoulders while I eat her pussy until
she's crying my name all over the bar… *fuck.*

I avoid her for the rest of the night until she clocks off
and disappears upstairs. Then I clean up quickly after Rory

sees out the last of the patrons. I'm beat. I work a half day tomorrow since the Crow is only open for Sunday dinner. Roxy is putting on a smorgasbord. The restaurant is already booked out for the first sitting and half of the second.

But Sunday is the day I don't see Stevie because she has Sundays and Mondays off.

As I trail my ass upstairs, I hesitate on the landing, my eyes flicking over toward her door.

She's so fuckin' close, yet so far.

I don't hear any movement from inside. I wonder if she's a night owl like me, or if she sleeps easily and soundly.

It'll take a few good hours for me to wind down. Usually, I'm too fucked after work to go out. Except for the poker night last weekend, all I've done is work and haul shit for the M.C.

It's actually nice to kick my boots off, flick the TV on, and down a couple of beers.

Taking a shower, I refuse to rub one out with my soap. I already did that once before while imagining her, and I'm hoping if I stop thinking about what happened earlier, my dick will go down and stop reminding me that I need to fuck.

I dry off, pull on some boxer briefs, slug the cap off a bud, and crash down on the bed. Hopefully, there'll be some late-night horror movie on that I can fall asleep to.

I settle back into the pillows and flick the channels.

Having cable is a bonus I never expected.

When I find the horror channel, I leave the movie on that's just started while I make myself comfy.

My phone buzzes, just as I take a swig of my beer.

Bambi: hey big boy, are you still up?

I glance down at my cock. Yeah, it's still up, all right. But I don't need to tell her that.

I don't answer. I know if I do, she'll come on over and we'll end up fucking.

The last thing I want is for Stevie to run into my late-night squeeze in the morning, or worse, hear us.

Then my mind wanders… would Stevie be a screamer? Or would she come quietly?

My dick twitches.

I rub one hand over my cock, my mouth dry as I try my fuckin' hardest not to imagine her like I did earlier; spread wide for me across the bar. I have this fantasy about it, and now I've imagined it more than once, the replay is more vivid than ever before.

Stevie naked. Her legs spread, cupping her own tits while I settle down on my haunches to suck on her sweet pussy.

My hand brushes my cock again, and I squeeze it, snaking my hand inside my boxers to feel myself. I'm not small, and that's not just me being a douche. My cock is decent.

Knowing I'm not going to be able to sleep until I come, I shove my boxers down to my knees, and grasp the beast as I stroke myself once, twice. Then I lean over to the bedside table and pull out the lube, squirt some into my palm, and start to fuck my hand. I work slowly, setting the pace as I spread the oil all over myself.

I close my eyes and go back to my fantasy; Stevie's legs thrown over my shoulders while I fuck her with my tongue. Oh yeah, fuck, that feels good…

"Do you like that, boss?" I growl, licking through her slick heat, blowing on her sensitive skin as she squirms, tightening her knees around my head. Her pussy is so damn pretty…

I lick and suck, paying attention to her clit as I part her and deliberately swirl my tongue around.

"Oh God, Axton…" she cries, her eyes watching me as I smirk up at her.

I lean back and insert a finger, then two, reveling in her pussy taking my fingers and how sweet it looks. She's so fuckin' tight. I resist the urge to slam my cock into her at full force. That's for later.

"What do you want me to do to this pretty pussy, boss?"

"Axton…"

"Yeah?"

I curve my fingers, letting her feel all of me, then I smooth my thumb over her clit. It's enlarged and swollen from my sucking. She's already come once with my mouth, and she tastes like a goddamn dream.

I never knew pussy could be so sweet, but Stevie Hart is like candied apples, and I can't get enough of it.

"I need that big fat cock inside me."

I grin, unzipping my pants as I stand and pull my dick out. "This big fat cock?"

I sheath myself with my hand as her eyes glance down at my movements.

"Fuck, you're so big," she says.

I grin. "Next time that mouth is gonna be wrapped around me while you swallow my cum. Got me?"

Her eyes widen. "Yes, oh God, yes…"

I grip myself harder as she pinches her nipples and moves a hand down to her sweet center. I knock her hand away. "Don't touch yourself. That's my job now. You get to come when I make it happen."

"Urgh!" She throws her head back as I smirk.

"You can't watch me touchin' myself, can you?"

Her eyes pop open. She reaches for me. "I need it, Axton. Give it to me, now!"

I grin, leaning over the bar, my hands on either side of her body. "You're a greedy little boss lady. Tell me what you want this cock to do to you, and I might do it."

Jesus, I love taunting her. She's so needy for it.

"Fuck me, Ax, please, get that big cock inside my pussy."

Fuck. I almost shoot my load everywhere at her filthy mouth.

I lean down and take her mouth instead, my tongue invading hers as my hands clutch either side of her head. I want her to taste herself on my lips. She gasps, wrapping her arms around me as she tries to impale herself on my cock.

"Impatient," I tsk. "Do I get less shitty jobs tomorrow if I make you come more than once? Because I already gave you two."

I hover my cock around her entrance, but don't penetrate. She can fuckin' beg me for it.

"I'll put Rory on garbage duty," she pants.

I wince. "Don't mention his name while I'm about to fuck you. It's just mine I want on your lips. Got me?"

"There's no one else, Ax," she pants. "Just you…"

I cup her face with one hand as I kiss her quickly. "Good girl."

I cup her tits with both hands, tweaking her nipples as she squirms. Leaning down, I suck each one into my mouth, squeezing each breast as I suckle between them both. She groans again, trying to rub against me. I glance down, and her glistening pussy has me all fucked up. I rub a hand through her wet folds as she bucks underneath me. She needs to come again, and I know she's gonna come hard.

I hold my cock and rub it through her slickness, nudging her clit. "Gonna make you come like this first."

"Axton..."

I rub her nub back and forth while my other hand pulls her nipple. She leans back with her hands on the bar, pushing her tits out to me. I could literally pull myself off and cum all over them if I wanted to, but I want to feel her tightness choking my dick, milking me while I forget myself and everything else around me. I need her sweet pussy, and it's all that stops me from blowing right now.

My dick rubs back and forth over her clit, my tip glistening with precum that I can barely contain... I know I'm gonna come hard when I finally blow.

Her neck goes red as color creeps up to her face. "Oh, Axton..."

"Come, baby," I grunt. "Show me how much you like my cock."

She lets go, coming gloriously she moves her hips up and down, throwing her head back as she calls my name.

Just as she recovers, I shove my cock inside her, stilling for a moment while I'm balls deep.

"This pussy's mine," I growl as she cries out. I pull out, then slide back in. "Do you hear me, boss lady?"

"Yes," she stammers. "Fuck, Axton. Oh God, that feels

good..."

I tilt her hips, pulling her ass closer to me, until she's all but lying down on the bar now, leaning up on her elbows as I glance down to where we're joined. I love every second of watching her body move. She's so responsive to me.

"Look at my cock, fuckin' takin' what I want," I grunt. "So fuckin' tight, baby."

I run one hand up her smooth, sexy body and grasp one breast, squeezing it, while the other hand holds her ass as I pummel in and out of her, thrusting hard every time I hit the end of her. Her tits jiggle as I stare at them.

"You do me so good," she cries. "I need it, Ax. I need it just like that, baby..."

I growl as I quicken, fucking her harder, and every time I do, she makes this noise in the back of her throat that has my balls ready to explode.

"Come again, boss. I need you to come so I can too. Your pussy's chokin' my cock, babe. Look at it."

She opens her eyes and looks down the length of her body, her eyes going wide as she tightens her legs around my waist.

"Ax, your body's so hot," she cries, her face heated with lust as I take her.

"Next time I'm gonna fuck you in front of a mirror so you can see everything I'm doin'," I say.

She cries out again as I tilt my hips, grazing her clit

with my pubic bone, and she climaxes, pulling me to her as her nails scratch at my back like a wildcat. I fuckin' love it when she marks me.

I come too, emptying my balls into her as I call her name. I lift her off the bar as she wraps around me, my dick still spurting as I move her up and down while she looks down at me. I milk my cock for all it's worth, while she bobs up and down, her climax taking over her soul. At least, that's how it sounds.

She's so fuckin' beautiful…

My eyes open as I glance down at myself and groan. I just shot my load all over my chest, and it felt like fuckin' magic. My hand's now sticky as I continue to milk myself, wishing she were here right now to clean me up. I wonder if she'd actually do it.

Fuck. I don't need that visual as well as everything else.

I wish more than anything she was in my bed. While I do have a fetish about the bar scenario, I also wanna fuck her in my bed. Spread her wide, take my time, kiss every inch of her body while I explore, learning what she likes and how to make her orgasm last longer. These are all things I don't really know about a woman. Porn teaches you nothing. I want the real thing. I want to learn.

But I know that I can't fuckin' have it, not with her.

I know that I'll likely never know what it feels like to be buried balls deep, to have her riding my cock while I run my hands all over her. And it frustrates me. If she weren't my boss… *maybe I could quit?* I shrug the thought off, imagining what Brock would say.

Quitting my job because I wanted pussy. Yeah, that'd go down real swell. He'd have my balls, not to mention the rest of the MC, and then there's Hutch and his disappointment.

I'm in fuckin' purgatory. That's all I know.

And Stevie Hart is the fuckin' gate keeper.

I pull my boxers off and clean myself up with them. Disgusted with myself because I should know better than to lust after someone I can't have. Fuck knows I've had enough practice at abstaining. But something about the real thing right across the hall, snuggled in her own bed, so close yet so far, has me seeing stars.

There's nothing to substitute for the real thing, but I don't want Bambi or any other chick. That was a mistake. I didn't know Stevie existed then. That might make me a pussy-whipped fucker, but I don't care.

The way I feel whenever we're alone together has me reeling. This thump in my chest and a ringing in my ears. What the fuck is that?

It's like she holds some kind of magical power that makes her a temptress and me a dragon.

Eventually, I'm gonna have to go there, to a woman, if I can't have Stevie, but I don't want to. I want to have her and nobody else. I want to claim her body just like I did in my fantasy.

I want to make her scream my name like she's never screamed before and have her ride my cock up and down while I spurt into her, watching her lose all control.

Wouldn't that be a sight for sore eyes, even if it is a very stupid and dangerous train of thought.

But I can't help wanting what I want. I'm not a perfect person, I've never professed to be, but I eventually get what I want. And that's what disturbs me.

That I can't stay away.

That I've got to have one taste, one bite. One fucking night in her bed.

Instead, I'm resorting to giving myself pleasure with my own palm.

It just won't do.

I have to fight these feelings and pretend she's nothing to me.

It's for the best, for her sake, but mostly for mine.

BRACKEN RIDGE
REBELS
ARIZONA
M · C

CHAPTER 8
STEVIE

I stare at the door. I don't know why every time I glance over, I picture Axton standing there, larger than life. I also picture him in numerous other positions, but I try not to think about that too closely. I've never reacted to a guy like I have to him before, and it's alarming.

I slap an arm over my eyes. I refuse to give in and touch myself, even though I know I need to. I fall asleep, and when I wake, I'm in no better shape than I was the night before.

The way he touched me.
The things he said.
The way his mouth looks when he smiles... and when he laughs? All bets are off.

It's official. I have a crush on my fucking employee.

I run a hand over my face and try to shake him off. It's ridiculous, I know it. Not to mention that he was just being nice helping me when I was injured. I'm reading too much into it.

I know what lures me in the most is the danger that

Axton Altman represents. The fact he's done hard time. He's seen and done a lot. He's a badass.

Still, it's getting obsessive.

Reluctantly getting out of bed, it's after ten o'clock on Sunday morning. It's the one day that I sleep in and don't plan anything.

I do, however, decide to head downstairs to the Keurig and make myself a decent cup. I seriously need to get my own coffee machine, but I only really drink a cup or two in the morning.

Pulling a cardigan around my shoulders, I unlock my door. I stick my head out and listen for any movement. It's doubtful I'll run into Axton, and nobody is at work until after three. Deciding the coast is clear, I head out onto the landing and down the stairs.

It's not quite summer in Arizona, but the weather has been nice lately. Today I plan on going to see Kennedy at the hospital again. With any luck, she'll be out today, and I'll be able to help her pack and get home. I know she's dying to be out of there. I keep getting a million text messages from her, asking to sneak some food and Krispy Krème donuts in.

I switch the machine on and let it warm up as I go in search of something to eat. Since I didn't end up having dinner last night, I'm a little famished, and usually Roxy will have leftovers in the fridge.

I hit the jackpot when I see a slab of carrot cake with thick icing in the fridge. Never wanting to go near a knife again, I use a fork to cut myself a slice and place it on a plate. Wandering back to the machine, I stick in a pod and the milk. I nibble away at the cake as I lick my fingers, knowing that this will definitely not fill me up. Maybe I'll pick up some brunch from the Coffee Bean and take some of that French toast Kennedy likes with me. Someone has to keep her alive, and the food she's getting over there sounds disgusting.

When my cup fills up, I blow into it and take a long sip. I sigh, knowing that I'm going to have to make the investment soon. I deserve it. Even if I do only drink two cups a day.

I take the steps carefully, holding my cup in one hand and the cake in the other. Just as I get to the top of the landing, Axton comes rushing out of his room and smacks right into me, almost sending me flying back down the stairs.

I make a strangled cry in the back of my throat.

"Fuck!" he says, grabbing onto my forearms as I wobble on the top step. My coffee splashes and spills down my top as I gasp. "Stevie… I didn't see you…"

"Axton, Jesus, you gave me a heart attack!" He lets go of me when I'm safely on the landing.

"Sorry, I didn't realize you were up yet."

It's then his eyes decide to travel down my body, and I

realize at about the same time he does that I've got skimpy sleep shorts on, a tank top that barely contains my breasts, and now a big wet patch down my front. And I don't even have enough hands to yank my cardigan closed.

I internally facepalm myself.

His eyebrows shoot up as I feel the heat rise in my cheeks, but his eyes don't linger long.

"Uh, that's okay. I'm obviously just accident prone at the moment," I say, trying not to sound like a loser. "I needed coffee in a hurry."

"I just fuckin' burnt you!" He looks pissed off with himself as he runs a hand through his hair.

"No." I shake my head. "You didn't. It didn't make contact with my skin. I'm fine." *Please, ground, swallow me whole now.*

"Are you sure?" His eyes flick to the large coffee stain on my tank and then he looks down at his boots almost immediately.

What the fuck? So, I'm not imagining it... he is checking me out?

"Yes, I'm sure. I didn't expect to see you running out of there like a bat out of hell, that's all."

One corner of his mouth turns up, but he doesn't say anything. It's then I realize he's going over to the club.

He's wearing a leather cut with the word 'Prospect' on the front, along with his usual ripped jeans, black t-shirt, and heavy boots.

He looks like the ultimate bad boy. I can see his tattoos peeking out of the shirt around his neck.

It's also then that I realize how fucking good he smells. He's just showered, his hair's still wet and slicked back off his face, and he's trimmed his beard... not that I should notice that small, trivial detail. But it seems I notice a lot about Axton Altman that I shouldn't.

"My bad. I'm in a hurry, kinda slept in. I've got some shit to do over at the clubhouse."

"They have you working over there on a Sunday?" *Why did I ask that? I need to go put some clothes on...*

He nods. "There's no such thing as a day off when you're a prospect."

I smile tentatively and move around him toward my door. "Well, don't work too hard," I say as he follows my movements, even as he begins to descend the stairs. Jesus Christ, my ass is hanging out of my shorts.

"I'll try not to." He gives me a chin lift. "Have a nice day off."

I don't give him a reply, scurrying back into the safety of my apartment, mortified.

After dumping the cake and my coffee on the kitchen island, I throw my cardigan on the bed.

What a total loser.

I go change my top. Tossing it in the hamper, I pull on

another one, catching sight of my appearance in the mirror as I groan.

My ponytail is lopsided, I have socks on, and one is pulled up high, the other down low. And my sleep shorts *literally* show half my ass. I slap my forehead. I should've known better than to try and sneak around half dressed when I know full well I share this place with another person. I'm used to living alone.

I also didn't expect he'd be mowing me over at the top of the stairs.

I eat the rest of the cake over the kitchen sink, washing it down with my coffee as I decide to go back to bed for a while and pretend none of that ever happened.

He smelled like he just walked off the set of a goddamn Gucci fragrance commercial.

I can still smell him long after he's gone, and that *just had a shower* scent that never gets old. The way his eyes dipped to my chest… and he swallowed hard when he stared at his boots.

I shake it off.

I'm acting irrational. The man just got out of prison. Anything in a paper bag is going to turn his head. I mean, the man went without sex for ten years. He's got girls crawling all over him.

I wince as I recall the chicks at the bar all weekend, mewling over him like lost little kittens.

They don't seem to mind, or care, about what he did while they're eye fucking him.

Yet, I heard him come upstairs last night, and I didn't hear another set of footsteps. It's not like he can't bring chicks up here. Even though I know for a fact Hutch probably told him not to, it doesn't mean that he won't. It also doesn't mean a girl, or two, didn't come up later and leave really early. *Stop already!*

What is wrong with me?

He's a flesh and blood man. All men stare at breasts, it doesn't mean that he's interested.

Maybe it would be better if Axton worked somewhere else… but then I'd have to explain to Hutch why and, quite frankly, I'd rather have a hot poker shoved into my eye.

That also wouldn't be fair to Axton. It's not exactly his fault I can't stop obsessing over him.

I need to start acting like an adult and not a juvenile.

My rabbit is calling, yet I can't bring myself to do it. If I get off while picturing his face, we're never going to be able to work together again.

This is my purgatory, and I'd better get used to it, because I like this job. And I'm not giving it up because my hormones are on a merry-go-round.

Since I can't see Kennedy until after two o'clock, I

stop by to see my friend, Cassidy, who works for Colt, her old man, at Bracken Ridge Security. She usually doesn't work Sundays, but she text me to say she's catching up on paperwork and Colt won't be there, meaning we can gossip. Colt has been part of the club for quite a few years and has just been appointed as the Regional Officer; he'll be helping Steel with the prospects and keeping tabs on any new movements in town with other clubs. Or so Deanna tells us. She knows a lot more about club news than anyone since she's Hutch's daughter.

Cassidy also works part-time at Lily's salon. Lily is Steel's sister and Gunner's ol' lady.

I'm lucky to join a club where most of the girls get along. Even the sweet butts.

I definitely turned a blind eye at the clubhouse on some of the parties — not that the boys do anything illegal, since Hutch doesn't stand for drugs in the club. But there are always parties, and now and again, things get a little crazy.

I guess you can't expect anything less from a biker clubhouse.

I bring a bag of donuts from the Coffee Bean and two caramel lattes. Cassidy looks relieved when I knock on the door for her to let me in.

Ever since all the shit that just went down with Kennedy, everyone is on still on high-alert and taking extra precautions, so it does not surprise me when I see a motorcycle in the lot.

"Is Colt here too?" I ask when Cassidy opens the door and spies the donuts.

She takes the bag from my hand with a grin. "Nope. I got stuck with Jax," she says. "But he went out to get us some lunch."

"I got your favorite coffee."

Her eyes go wide, and she locks the door behind us. "I knew we were friends for a reason."

I laugh, looking around the small space. It's situated in between Steel's auto and Rubble's towing business. Then I see Cassidy's desk in the back, littered with paper.

"Looks like you're going to be here a while," I say, as she slumps back into her chair, and I sit opposite, handing her coffee over. "Hope Colt's paying you overtime."

She smirks. "As much as I love him, I like to have a few hours to myself."

I snicker. "Like that, is it?"

She takes out a donut and chomps half of it down, making little moans as I take one out for myself. "You've no idea. We're thinking of moving in together, now that Bones and Kennedy are inseparable and probably want their alone time."

"So, Amelia will be looking for a new roomie?"

"I know, she'll be devastated. I'll have to break the news to her soon, but there's really no point in staying. I'm rarely ever home."

"What a problem to have," I muse, licking my sugar-coated fingers.

"What about you? How's your roomie going?"

It's an innocent question, but my mind immediately jolts back to him dressing my wound last night, then this morning's debacle on the stairs.

I look down at my hands. "It's going fine."

"Uh oh," she says, taking a giant sip of her latte. "Tell me everything."

"There's nothing to tell," I protest.

Cassidy is also one of the few people who knows about my breakup with Lukas. I put off telling Kennedy because she has been in hospital, and I didn't want her to stress. It was nice having Cass to offload to. She's a really good listener, and we've become close.

She eyes me speculatively, and when our eyes meet again, I throw my hands up in frustration.

"You can't say anything to Colt."

Her eyes go wide, then she pretends to zip her mouth shut. "Tell!"

I sigh and slump back in my chair. "I've been having weird thoughts about Axton."
She dives back into the donut bag without taking her eyes off me. "Weird, like how?"

I put my face in my hands. "Promise not to say

anything?"

"Jesus, Stevie, I promise. Now hurry up, I'm getting old over here."

I take my hands away and curl my knees up on the chair, hugging them. "Weird as in… *illicit.*"

Her eyes go wide again as her lips curl into a devious smile. "I can't say I'm surprised. He's hot."

I slap my forehead. "Not you too."

"What?" She shrugs. "Just saying it like it is. I've got eyes. So do most of the women of Bracken Ridge. It's okay to look."

"Not for me, it isn't! I'm his boss."

She almost chokes on her donut. "That's so hot, but so taboo all at the same time."

I glare at her. "You think? Which is exactly why this is bad."

She eyes me carefully. "Has anything happened?"

"No!"

"Woah, keep your hair on," she says, amusement on her face. "But do you want it to?"

"Of course not."

"Why not?" She shrugs.

My eyes bug at her. "Are you serious right now?"

"What? You're consenting adults."

"Yes, consenting adults who work together. This is so not helpful, Cass."

"It is kinda saucy, though, don't you think? I mean, he's got a great body, a nice face, sexy eyes, and that whole bad boy vibe going on."

"That's exactly it. It calls to me on some other level, one that has no rational explanation."

"You can't help who you're attracted to." Cass goes on. "It's as simple as that. But you're not acting on it, so stop beating yourself up."

I sigh, knowing she's right. I look down at my feet.

"You're not planning on acting on it, right?" she presses.

"Don't be stupid, Cass. Forget I even said anything."

She wipes her fingers on a napkin and then gives me a sympathetic look. "Has he said or done anything?"

I shake my head. "No. It's completely unrequited, although, he did look at my boobs this morning when he spilled coffee on me."

She raises an eyebrow.

"Long story." I go on, sighing. "He just got out of jail; he'd find a mailbox attractive."

"I don't know? From what Amelia says about Axton, it sounds like he's looking to settle down. It's not like he's banging every chick at church."

This piques my interest. "He's not?"

She leans forward on the desk. "Nope, not even close."

I frown. "What's wrong with him?"

She shakes her head. "Poor guy can't get a break."

"He's been in jail for ten years, Cass. Most guys would be out banging all the way to the moon and back."

Cassidy doesn't share my sentiments. "Not necessarily. Sometimes they go the other way. Just think, everything's changed since he's been inside. Ten years is a lot of time. Everything's different for him. For some, it's probably overwhelming."

If I'm honest, I like the idea of Axton not screwing anything in a skirt. Not that I have some weird boss/ employee hold over him, but the thought pleases me, nonetheless.

In my fantasy, which has only just made itself apparent, Axton only has eyes for me.

"More like the MC are keeping him up all hours of the day and night, when he's not at work, that is."

"Well, he's a prospect, and he has to prove himself to the club. It's what he signed up for."

"He's a hard worker." I go on. "Never has a bad word to say about anybody, and he keeps to himself. Maybe that's why I'm attracted to him; he's not like the other guys around here."

"He's new in town. It'll wear off."

"You think?"

"I'm certain. But you know what?"

Finally, I think she's going to give me some words of wisdom. I glance up at her.

"You could always bone him and get it out of your system." She laughs as I reach for a pencil from the desk and lob it at her head.

"Very funny. It's the last time I'll ever tell you anything."

"Don't be such a spoilsport. I think it's a good idea."

"Yeah, about as good as a hole in the head."

There is absolutely no way that anything is going to happen between us. Period.

It's a phase, that's all.

And, if worse comes to worse, I can always try to roster him on opposing shifts.

That's got to be better than the alternative. *Anything* has to be better than this.

BRACKEN RIDGE
REBELS
ARIZONA
M · C

CHAPTER 9

AXTON

The club run on Sunday after lunch clears my head. Thank fuck Brock let me borrow his old bike until I can get enough scratch to get my own. Can't exactly be part of an MC and not have wheels.

It's on days like this, when my mind is clear, that I begin to remember.

My mind flicks to my parents.

Disappointment floods me when I think about them, especially Mom, and how much I regret everything that went down. I can't help thinking that maybe it's better this way.

I know Brock has made peace with it, and he and Dad even get along now, which is something I never thought would happen. Not after their tremulous relationship when we were kids. Brock's always been pretty level-headed. The only time he's not and sees red is when it's got to do with Angel, and now his kids.

Brock invites me over for dinner, but I remind him I

have to get to work. I've got the evening shift, and it's the first time that I'll be working without Stevie, so I don't want to fuck it up.

I'm never gonna get past prospect stage if I don't show everyone what I'm capable, and that's what Hutch and Brock want to see. And if I have to bust my ass for a little bit until I can get my electrical license and go out on my own, then that's what I have to do. I'm no stranger to hard work.

Sundays are a different crowd; usually it's the early bird oldies and families for the smorgasbord.

I grab something to eat on the fly and try not to groan when two staff call in sick, so it's just me, Rory, and another girl, Emmaline, running the bar.

Tonight, though, Steel, Gunner, and Nitro decide to drop by for some grub and beer.

Steel gives me a chin lift as they take a seat at the bar.

While the club doesn't advertise they own the place, nor is it a biker bar, the boys drop in from time to time to keep an eye on things.

"You doin' okay?" Steel gives me a chin lift.

We didn't exactly get time to chat on the run today. In fact, I'm just stoked that I was able to get a ride in without having to stay back and haul gravel again. I'm hoping that they think I'm doing a good job. The last thing I want is to be given an easy ride.

"I'm good," I say, popping the lids of three beers and settling them down.

Gunner gives me a fist punch and Nitro a chin lift. I don't know much about him, being he's new to the club like me, but he seems like an all right kinda guy. He didn't give me any shit when I picked up the gravel from the scrapyard. He was actually quite accommodating.

When you're a prospect in other clubs, it's notorious that you're a shit kicker. While Steel likes to give me a lot of stick, as does Brock, for the most part, everyone's pretty cool. I don't know if it's because I'm Brock's brother, or they're waiting for me to fuck up and say *I told you so*. I'm not gonna give them any reason to think that, not in this lifetime.

"You boys headin' in for some grub?" I ask, taking a few moments to have a break.

"Bet your ass." Gunner grins. "Could smell that roast from across town. I love my ol' lady, but she prefers to keep sweaters in our oven."

Nitro grunts a laugh and Steel shakes his head. "The apple doesn't fall far from the tree," he says. "When God was handin' out culinary skills, Lily was at the back gettin' her nails done."

"What about you?" Nitro gives me a side-eye. "You any good at putting shit together in a kitchen?"

I shrug, not wanting to seem like a douche by

telling them I'm not a bad cook. "I do okay. Got a bit of experience, from bein' in the joint, though I tried to stay outta the kitchen as much as possible."

"They let you cook?" Gunner asks. "What, with like knives and shit?"

"When I got released into minimum security, the inmates have the option to take cookery class. Thought it was better than fuckin' woodwork — made enough wooden spoons and bookshelves to see me a lifetime — and it's better than laundry duty."

They snicker.

"You findin' it hard bein' out?" Nitro asks, taking a pull on his beer.

"Nope," I say honestly. "All I gotta do is think about my first few years in maximum, and that pretty much sets me on the straight and narrow before I even have a bad thought."

"I spent a few weeks in the joint for a petty misdemeanor." Nitro goes on. "Worst fuckin' few days of my life. Don't know how you did ten years, bro."

"Neither do I sometimes. Swear to God, if they took teenagers around a maximum-security prison as a field trip, I guarantee you'd think twice about doin' bad shit."

They nod in agreement. "Just keep doin' what you're doin'," Steel tells me, his face serious. "And you got nothin' else to worry about."

I nod, pushing off the bar to go serve a customer. My

heart jolts in my chest when I see Little Mick standing at the bar. I swallow hard. He's a former inmate who ran a lot of different operations inside, one of them being smuggling drugs and cigarettes. He was the go-to guy and he's shady as fuck.

Instantly, my hackles rise.

"Axton?" he says, a grin on his face. He's missing teeth, has messy black hair, and is wide-set and tall. He's a big motherfucker. More to the point, I don't know what he's doing here. "Well, I'll be damned." Something in his tone tells me that he's not at all surprised to see me here, and it makes me all the more suspicious.

"Mick. Long time, no see." *It'd be fuckin' great if I never saw you again.* "What can I get you?"

"I'll grab a Bud, bro."

I don't know why he's calling me that. I never was his bro and I'm never gonna be.

I turn, grab his beer, and pop the lid off. He hands me the cash and I avoid his gaze. I know he's assessing me, sizing me up.

"Those your crew?" He nods over to the three bikers all watching him.

It's like the slippery fucker just can't help but draw attention to himself.

"Damn straight."

He smiles, but it ain't kind. "Got yourself set up all nice

over here. Should give you a standing ovation."

"That won't be necessary. When'd you get out?" I know exactly when it was, but it's best he thinks he wasn't missed.

His eyebrows raise in surprise. "Six months back. You got any jobs goin' here?"

One of my hands turns into a fist. "Nah, man, we're fully staffed." I try not to let the tension show on my face, so I laugh. "Can't exactly see you as a barman."

He takes a long neck of his beer. "Wasn't talking about pouring beers, my man."

My eyebrows knot together instantly. "I'm clean, bro, you know that. We don't push drugs here, and the MC doesn't exactly like outsiders spittin' on their turf." *Fuck you.*

Of course, the MC doesn't peddle drugs or guns or any illegal shit, but he doesn't need to know that.

He smirks. "Come on now, surely, you're up for a little cash on the side? I know how hard it can be to make ends meet, and if I recall, you do kinda owe me."

I stop in my tracks. I don't want to raise my voice or cause alarm because I don't want Steel and the boys heading over here. I can handle this asshole myself.

"I don't owe you shit."

He rubs his chin, and I've never wanted to knock someone's head off so fuckin' much.

Coming here into *my* workplace. *My* town. *My* life. He needs to fuck off before I change my mind and bury him.

"Come on, man." He laughs. "I'm just kidding. You should see your face."

"I think it's time you finished your beer and got out of here."

"Next thing you're gonna say is, 'I don't want no trouble,'"

"Well, that's a moot point. I don't."

"We got a problem here?" For a big guy, Steel moves fast. He towers behind Little Mick like a monster. His jaw set tight as he keeps his eyes on him.

Mick turns in his chair. "No trouble, man," he says, waving his hands in the air. "Axton and I served time together in Stradbroke. I was in the area and wanted to pay him a visit. For old times' sake."

"Yeah, well, I think you've outstayed your welcome," Steel says, not mincing words.

I think he's about two seconds away from hauling Mick out the door.

He snickers. "Sounds like you're kicking a man out, not very hospitable for a small town."

"Trust me when I say, you don't want me repeatin' myself," Steel says.

He chucks back his beer. "Here I was thinking it was safe to visit an old friend." He stands, brushing imaginary lint off his pants. "I'll be seeing you, Axton."

I fold my arms over my chest. "No, Mick, you won't."

He drops his bottle down with a thud as Steel moves aside to let him past.

It's not like anyone on the planet with half a brain would pick a fight with Steel willingly.

I nod to Steel as Mick walks away. "I had it under control."

He turns back to me. "Didn't seem that way. As the Sergeant at Arms, it's my job to keep prospects away from shit, especially with you on probation."

"You gonna babysit me now?"

He points at me. "The cops are lookin' for any fuckin' excuse to lock your ass back up. He looks like a no-good piece of shit. Let's hope he fucks off."

"You got that right."

"What'd he want?"

I don't know if I should lie. I mean, technically I've nothing to hide, and I know Steel wasn't born yesterday, but I think the less he knows about Mick, the better.

"I've no idea, assholes gonna try shit, especially ones I spent time with. He's just passin' through. Lookin' for a hit." He stares at me. "I'm clean. I don't do drugs. Never have since I got locked up."

Steel rubs his chin, not happy with that answer. "Yeah, well, you need all the help you can get, prospect. But, you still don't have to do everything alone now, you hear me?"

I'm not sure if he understands I'm a grown man with a set of balls hanging, but I unfold my arms and keep busy, clearing the couple of empty glasses surrounding us.

I'm not happy he thinks I can't stand up for myself. "I got it, I was handling it just fine."

"That's debatable."

"Scumbags like him are always gonna be hangin' around, lookin' for trouble. I'm ready for it."

He eyes me suspiciously, and it makes me wonder if I really was doing a bad job of trying to get rid of him. I know Steel's protective stance over the club, the women and his brothers, is legendary, and now I've seen it for myself.

"You better be ready, because you know what they say about ex-cons?"

I give him a chin-lift. "What's that?"

"Once a con, always a con."

"Not me. I'm not goin' back inside. Got too much goin' for me."

He means well, but I still wanna punch him in the throat.

"He shows his face in here again, let me know."

"I can handle myself."

"Next time, he may not be alone."

The man's bullshit radar is exceptional, I'll give him that. Little Mick knows every loser and deadbeat from here to Timbuktu, of that I'll guarantee.

He thumps me on that back and I think that's the end of our conversation.

I don't show it, but it unnerved me with Mick showing up here. What's his endgame, exactly?
I don't owe him shit. If he thinks I do, he's sadly mistaken.

I can only hope he takes the warning and fucks off, but that stab in my chest tells me that it was no coincidence he was here. I only hope he doesn't ever come back.

I'm cleaning up the tables, when I hear the front door open. I thought Gash had locked it, so I holler over my shoulder, "We're closed."

I look in the reflective glass behind the bar and see a small, blonde, woman in a pantsuit and a smart trench coat. I'd know those eyes anywhere, and the curled, blonde hair, even though it's been a decade.

My mother.

I stop what I'm doing and stare at her.

"Axton," she says as my throat goes dry. The glass I'm polishing cracks in the dish towel.

I turn and toss it in the sink, then, looking up at her, I say, "Mother."

She's beautiful, she always has been, but even in her mid-fifties, she's stunning. She's always been well-kept, and the years have proved to be kind. She hasn't changed a bit.

"I hope it's all right that I'm here." She goes on, clutching her purse. It's the only sign she gives me that this could be slightly awkward. Like Brock, Mom's always worn her heart on her sleeve. As much as Brock likes to think he's like Dad, he gets most of his traits from Mom — the good ones anyway.

"Of course." *What else can I say?*

She steps closer. "I'm sorry that I didn't come sooner."

I nod, resting my hands on either side of the sink as she looks at me. "Would you like a drink?"

She nods. "A strong martini would be lovely."

I turn and fetch a glass and as I turn back, she's moving behind the bar. I still as she comes closer.

"Axton." She begins to cry, folding her arms around me as I face away from her. "I'm so sorry, my baby… please forgive me, please forgive me…"

I close my eyes. So much pain, so much time. I don't know how to be her son anymore. I don't know how to be like this; close to someone.

I turn, and she folds into my arms. I kiss the top of her head but don't say anything.

I'm choked up, my chest feels heavy, and I wipe one of my eyes that has traitorously started to leak.

"It's been a long time, Mom," I say when she cries into my chest and doesn't stop.

"Too long," she agrees. "I wanted to come when you got out, but your father said to give it some time, let you adjust…"

"I had ten years to adjust, Mom." I try not to let the bitterness swallow me whole.

While Brock and Dad patched things up a year ago, things with me are still on the outs. I guess you just can't put some things in the past. I always was a momma's boy anyway. Dad only had time for Brock in between serving in the military and the stints when he was home. It was hard on everyone, then Amelia came along.

As if reading my mind, she pulls back and says, "Amelia's been giving me updates. I hear you're doing very well since… since you got out." *She can't even say it.*

Reaching over, I pull a tissue from the box and hand it to her. She blots her eyes, her mascara smudging slightly.

I make her drink and pour a shot of whiskey for myself, tossing it back while the burn eases the pain.

"I'm doin' okay."

I pass her the martini and look down at my boots.

"Will you look at me?" She cups my face, her small hands warm and comforting.

I look up.

"You're so much the same," she says, her voice small. "But so different at the same time."

"I grew up." I shrug.

I hold her gaze. "I wanted to come to Stradbroke," she begins. "But your father wouldn't allow it. Neither would Brock."

"It's no place for a lady," I concede. "I wouldn't have wanted you to see me like that, not ever. It was bad enough bringin' shame on the family."

"You weren't yourself," she says, like that makes everything all right. "I blame myself for not seeing the signs. We should've seen it coming… things were bad for you back then."

"Mom," I say, holding her by the shoulders as she raises her glass to her mouth for a sip. "It's water under the bridge now. I want to move on."

She nods, her eyes tearing up again. "I don't expect you to forgive me…"

"Mom, I should be the one saying that to you. I'm the one who committed armed robbery, remember?"

She swallows hard, a faint smile on her lips. "My baby," she whispers. "I prayed for you every night, that you'd be safe. When you went away, it cut your father deep, Axton. You've no idea what it did to him. He was a wreck for months. I tried so hard to convince him to go see you, but he just couldn't. He just couldn't do it."
I nod.

I've had years of time to feel bitter, to feel like the world owed me a living. Having my parents disown me was just the icing on the cake. I was angry, upset, but mostly, I was disappointed in myself.

I've learned a lot in ten years, and one of those things is patience.

Everyone's waiting for me to fuck up, but I'm not gonna give them the satisfaction.

My mom, though? I think she's always been in my corner; she just didn't know how to show it.

"It's okay, Mom."

"It's not okay!" she cries. "I don't expect that we'll get back to a good place immediately, but I want to try. I've missed you… you don't even know how much. When they took you away…" Her shoulders begin to shake.

"Why don't I make you a coffee while I finish up and we can talk."

She gives me a watery smile. "I'd like that."
I take her drink from her hand and place it down as she takes a seat at the bar. As I go lock the doors, Gears comes back from the kitchen, and I give him the heads up that he can go.

I clear the rest of the glasses and place them in the dishwasher as Mom's coffee pours from the coffee machine. I've learned how to make cappuccinos, though I don't advertise it.

"You're going to do so well for yourself," she says, watching me. "Brock told us that you got your qualifications to be an electrician while… inside." She can't bear to say *prison*.

"I did a lot of study. Now I have to get some hours on the job and obtain my license and certification. The club has given me a chance to prove myself, so until then, I'll be here."

She smiles as I hand her the coffee. "I'm proud of you, Axton," she says. "I know we've got a long way to go, but I know you're a good boy."

"I'm a man now, Mom. I grew up fast."

Her eyes drop to her cup. "I can't bear to think about what you had to go through."

I look at her levelly. "Mom. I did the crime, I had to do the time. It's how it works."

"I know that, but you had no priors…"

"Mom, you don't have to make excuses for me. I held up a convenience store, under the influence, with a firearm. Granted, the gun in my hands wasn't loaded, but I still could've killed someone. That's on me. I've made peace with it, and in time, I hope you will too." After I got arrested the cops found another small firearm tucked into the back of my jeans, this one was loaded.

"You're my child," she says. "And I'll tell you the same thing I said to Brock; that I want a relationship with my son. Your father needs a little more time, but he'll come around Axton. I know he misses you as much as I do."

My lips twitch. Disappointing my father isn't high on my list of things to be proud of. I'm an epic failure in his eyes, and I get that, but if he'd look a little closer, he'd be able to see I've changed. I'm not the same person I was when I went inside. If he can't see that, then it's his loss. I'm done having to repent all of my sins forevermore.

I'm good with myself and who I am now. If he isn't, then it's time we both moved on.

She sips on her coffee and looks at me thoughtfully.

"You don't have to defend him. I get he's angry, but I'd be lying if I said I wasn't disappointed. I thought he'd want to see me after all this time." I shrug off the bar to keep myself busy at the sink. "I thought about comin' over, but I didn't think I'd be welcome, so I stayed away."

Mom dabs her nose with the tissue, and I really don't want to set her off again. "We're the parents. We should have met you when you got released."

I run a hand through my hair. "In all fairness, that would've been weird. You did the right thing. I've needed this time to get settled and get into a new routine, get used to things again."

She nods, taking small sips of her coffee.

There's so much to say, but I need to get my ducks in a row.

If Brock wears his heart on his sleeve, then I'm the opposite. What you see isn't what you get. I'm a closed book. I've been burned too many times, on the inside and out, and I keep my cards close to my chest. It's how I'm wired now. I don't know if I can be anything else.

I look back down at the couple of glasses I'm rinsing and say, "He doesn't know you're here, does he?"

I feel her eyes dart to me quickly, and I have my answer. "No, but I am going to tell him, and while I know he needs some time to process things and get his head around it, I've made it clear I am having a relationship with my son." She clears her throat. "I don't know if Brock filled you in, but… I left him last year."

My eyes go wide. No, Brock did not mention this.

"Mom? What happened?"

She nods sagely. "I'd had enough of him ignoring Brock. I saw him and Angel, and I knew they'd gotten back together. I wanted to be a part of his life again, and the same goes for you. If your father doesn't like it, then he's known me long enough by now to know who I'll choose."

"That's kinda selfless of you, Mom, but I don't want to be the cause of arguments between the two of you," I say. "It'll just give him more ammunition to keep me away."

She waves a hand at me. "He'll do no such thing. In fact, I want us all to have dinner next week, when you have a day off."

"Mom…"

"Amelia will come, Brock and Angel and the kids too.

You're a part of this family, Axton. I want to show you how much."

I know mom means well, but Dad's made it pretty clear that I'm nothing but scum. I'm dead to him. I have no intention of going to a family get-together, but I don't want to upset her again tonight. I'll let her down gently later.

I give her a chin lift. "That'd be nice." *Fuck, I'm such a liar.*

"I hope you mean it. I want this to be a fresh start for all of us," she says, hope in her eyes for the first time tonight. "I love you, Axton, please always remember that. I never once stopped loving you. You were always in my heart."

There's that lump again. I look up at her and know she's sincere. She's a good mom. I know she means it. We all have regrets; we all make mistakes.

"Right back at ya, Mom. It's good to be back."
I only hope I can live up to her expectations.

I can't turn back time, but I can move forward, and that's exactly what I intend on doing.

BRACKEN RIDGE
REBELS
ARIZONA
M · C

CHAPTER 10
STEVIE

"**S**hhh!" Deanna whisper-shouts as I try to get my key in the door.

"Why are you shushing me?" I bellow back at her.

"Shhh! The both of you!" Cassidy says, taking over when I can't get it in the keyhole.

"This door's fucked," I say. "Well and truly."

"You're just saying that because you want to be fucked, well and truly." Deanna snorts, belly-laughing like she's hilarious.

"I'll have you know, all I really want right now is coffee and Aspirin," I groan.

The cool night air is quickly sobering me up.

We had a few drinks at Zee bar and the girls walked me home.

"You're welcome to come up, sleep on the couch?" I say, when the latch finally unlocks.

"Can't. I've got to be up early for a quote in Phoenix,"

Deanna says with another snort. "I blame you two for feeding me too many cocktails!"

Deanna is in her final year of school, she's doing her associates in decorating and design, and she's starting to branch out and get some jobs. In fact, it was the reason we were celebrating tonight. Too bad some of the other girls couldn't make it.

I wasn't even going to go because I was with Kennedy all day, but she was tired and turned in early. Plus, Bones was there, and having him around protecting her made me feel a lot better.

"Don't blame us," Cassidy retorts. "You did it to us. You know, you don't have to flash the barman your tits to get free drinks."

Deanna slaps her on the butt. "Very funny, I didn't flash him. I'll have you know, my money maker does just fine without having to get naked in a public arena." She circles her face to indicate what money maker she's speaking of.

"Anyway," I go on. "Why are we being quiet? There's only me and Axton here."

"It must be good, living next door to the hottest guy in town." Deanna goes on. "I might make a play for him, that's if you don't object?"

The thought irritates me. Like when Roxy was flirting with him in the kitchen. I should've told them both to get back to work.

I shrug. "Why would I?"

"He'd fuck like a maniac," Cassidy agrees. "Being in jail for that long. He's got that strong, muscular body that screams, 'I go for hours.'"

I scrunch my nose up. "Do you guys mind? I have to work with him. I'll never look at him in the same light again."

"Bet you would like him working under you." Deanna smirks, nudging me in the ribs while Cassidy snorts with laughter. She's an idiot when she's drunk.

"Is he good with his hands?" Cassidy pipes up. "Or are his skills more of the oral nature?"

"Good one!" Deanna laughs as they cackle.

"The cab's waiting," I tell them, not wanting to encourage them any longer. "And you two are disgusting."

"Disgustingly cool," Deanna says, linking her arm with Cassidy's. "You just won't admit it."

"Get upstairs. I'm freezing my ass off out here." Cassidy stomps from side to side, trying to stay warm.

"I will if you two ever shut up," I complain, pulling my key from the lock.

They giggle again as I shut the door on their retreating figures.

It's quiet once I'm inside. The landing light is on, which is helpful, as I try a couple of times to make it up the stairs without falling over. I didn't think I was *that* drunk, but it seems Deanna, despite what she says, is a bad influence.

I snort a laugh as I remember Cassidy and I pulling her down from attempting to dance on top of the table. Zee bar isn't the type of place you go to party. It's sophisticated.

I stumble, swear loudly, and then drop my phone, which clatters back down the stairs.

A few moments later, I hear Axton's door open.

"Shit!" I whisper, trying to go back down the stairs without falling over.

"Stevie?" Axton says. His hair's all disheveled and his jeans are unbuttoned and… holy smokes, he has no shirt on.

"Who else would it be?" I ask, then realize I just said that out loud. I slap a hand over my mouth and laugh. "I dropped my phone."

He takes the stairs down to me, right before I almost topple backwards, retrieving my phone and then steadying me at the same time. "I heard."

"Whoops, sorry, I hope I didn't wake you." I try not to stare at his body, but it's a little hard to miss.

The eagle tattoo across his chest, its wings spread far across from one side to the other. It's a thing of beauty. He's muscly, his biceps bulge and his abs rock hard. There's a small smattering of hair that leads down his torso, past his belly button, and disappears into the top of his jeans. I swallow hard, imagining his cock.

"I think maybe it's time for bed," he suggests, his one

hand on the small of my back while he holds my phone in the other.

What a great idea. Your bed, or mine? I snort out loud at the thought.

He looks down at me with one eyebrow arched, amusement on his lips. "Something funny?"

I shake my head. "Nope."

"You sure?"

We get to the landing, and as I turn to his door, he places his hands on my shoulders and turns me toward my own door. "How about a nightcap?" I suggest.

His hands momentarily freeze on my shoulders before he lets go.

"I think you may have had enough."

He's right, but when I drink, I get an awful lot of gumption.

"Coffee, then?"

"It's late," he says, even though I can hear the TV on from his open door.

"What are you watching?"

"Fright Night."

I snort with laughter. "You like horror movies?"

He nods, his eyes staying firmly on mine, and oh how I wish they'd run down my body like he did the day he spilled my coffee. I want him to notice me.

"Me too, always have, ever since I was a kid. Kennedy hated them. She made me turn them off and then she'd have to sleep with a light on."

He gives me a chin lift but doesn't say anything.

"I don't suppose you have Aspirin?"

He smirks. "You pre-empting a headache, boss?"

I fucking love how he calls me that. I'd like to hear it while I'm riding his...

"Uh, I'm kinda thinking I shouldn't have knocked back that last cocktail."

He hands me my phone. "I'll go grab you a couple."

He doesn't invite me in, which is the right thing to do, but it doesn't stop me from wandering over to his door and walking inside after him.

It's neater than I thought. He doesn't have many possessions, which is normal since he's only just got out of the clink.

His bed is in the middle of the open plan living area. That too is neat and tidy, aside from the duvet that's peeled back where he was just lying.

When he comes back with the Aspirin and sees me standing there, he stops in his tracks.

"I like what you've done with the place," I say, pointing to the curtains like that's meant to mean something. "And that's one hell of a TV."

It takes up one side of the wall. As I glance at it, someone is in the middle of a killing spree.

"Here you go." He holds out his hand and drops the

tablets into my palm.

"Thanks."

Our eyes meet, and he looks a little bit uncomfortable.

So I decide to ask him. "Do I make you nervous?"

He blinks a couple of times before he says, "Uh no, it's just… like I said, it's late and I'm half naked."

My eyes drop again to his chest as I take in another assessment.

I shrug. "I kinda like it."

His mouth snaps closed, and I've no idea what he's thinking or what he was about to say.

"Sorry," I mutter. "It's been a while."

His lips do that twitchy thing I'm so fond of. "What's been a while?"

I wave a hand in the air as I blurt out, "*It*. You know… sex."

He makes a sound in the back of his throat that goes straight to my core.

Instead of acting surprised or telling me I'm highly inappropriate and ill-mannered, he doesn't. In fact, he seems interested in this topic.

"How long?"

I look up at him. He's so fucking beautiful. And I'm not just saying that because I'm drunk, his boss, and completely fucking horny. "Well, let's see now…" I count on all my fingers, then give up. "A year or more."

His eyes brows rise up in surprise. "That's a while."

"Yes, it is."

"But it's not ten years."

I wince. "God, how did you cope?"

He rubs his chin. His beard is another thing of glory about him I can't seem to get enough of either. "With difficulty."

Without thinking, I reach out and cup his face. He's warm, really warm, and his beard is surprisingly soft, not scratchy like I thought it would be.

"I've never kissed a man with a beard before."

"Stevie…"

"You don't want to?"

"I didn't say that."

"Then what?"

He's gone completely rigid, and I can't tell if my touch is pleasing him or repulsing him. He's so hard to read.

"You're my boss."

I shrug. "So?"

He shakes his head. "And you're drunk."

"I know what I'm doing."

He smirks. "Oh, you do, do you?"

I nod, albeit a little too much. "Yep."

My hand trails down to his chest where I feel his pecs, my pussy clenching, as I want so much for him to touch me back. I'm on fire, and it isn't because of the alcohol.

"We shouldn't do this," I'm sure I hear him mutter, but it's faint.

"Does that mean you don't want to?" I whisper.

"Didn't say that either."

"Then what?"

He steps closer. "I don't want to take advantage of you."

Fuck, he's so warm. My hand splays down his abs, feeling the faint trail of hair beneath my fingers. I glance down and see the bulge in the front of his jeans.

I'm turning him on.

"I've thought about it," I whisper. "I know it's wrong, and I'm drunk, and I shouldn't, but I… I can't stop thinking about you, Axton. What do you think that means?"

He groans when my fingers graze the top of his open jeans. "Fuck," he whispers.

I've never wanted a man so badly. Not just any man. *Him.* I want him.

"My sentiments exactly." I don't wait. I reach up and brush my lips against his as he stills.

He smells good, like soap and men's deodorant. Like sex.

It's soft at first, and his beard feels amazing. I'm surprised how much I like it. My other hand glides up his arm as I feel his body, wanting him to reciprocate so badly. He doesn't, not until my hand brushes south over his cock…

"Stevie," he groans, as I feel his hardness through his

jeans. Fuck me, he feels big, and so delicious. I want to take his dick out and play with it all night long.

His tongue meets mine and then his hands rest at my hips as he deepens the kiss.

And it's so fucking good.

My hand rubs him up and down, and on every stroke, I get more and more excited. My panties are dripping and my nipples pebble, begging to be touched.

"It'll be our secret," I say, when we break free. "Touch me."

One hand snakes up my body to clutch my breast and I gasp out loud. The other hand cups my face as he kisses me again, this time with wild abandon.

I've never been kissed like this, even with Lukas, ever. Even in the early days when we first fell in love.

This is… something else. Primal. Urgent. So damn hot.

He completely takes over, walking me back over to the bed as I continue to fondle him, and he rubs my nipple with his thumb.

"You're so fucking beautiful," he tells me as I cling to him. I'm so fucking needy.

"So are you," I whisper back, frightened he'll back off when he realizes what we're about to do. And make no mistake, I want it. I want it so damn bad.

He moves his lips down to my neck, kissing, nipping, sucking as I wrap my arms around his neck and pull him into me. His cock grinds against me as I moan.

His hand squeezes my butt, and he groans in appreciation, then he moves the other hand down to my skirt and he stops. I move my hand down to cover his and slide it under the elastic.

When he finds me slick and wet, he curses. I'm too far gone to even care how embarrassing that is. I hold his wrist, guiding him as he runs his fingers through my pussy, rubbing my clit as I close my eyes and hang on for dear life.

"Fuck, boss," he whispers in my ear as I make incoherent sounds I've never heard leave my mouth before.

"You get me so hot," I tell him. "So fucking hot." I need his hands all over me, but I can feel the tension building, and I think he feels it too. He doesn't penetrate, but he keeps rubbing and circling as his tongue caresses my neck, and I lose all self-control.

"Oh God," I moan. "Oh yes, right there, Axton… oh… oh…"

He watches me intensely as I begin to unravel, my climax building as he continues his slow but sweet torture. My orgasm erupts and I cry out, my body shaking from the impact as he holds me around the waist, and I come all over his hand for what feels like a glorious lifetime.

When I come down, his eyes are fierce as he stops what he's doing.

"Axton?" I question as my eyes pop open. His hand

pulls out of my panties.

"I, uh, I'm sorry, this is a mistake. I shouldn't have done that…"

My eyes water from the intensity of what he just did to me. "Doesn't feel like it. In fact, it feels very right." I want his cock inside me. I need it, *now.* I want to be wrapped around his body. I want him to claim me and fuck me stupid in his massive bed. Why does he have to take the moral high ground?

"It'd be taking advantage of you when you're intoxicated."

"I want it," I plead, knowing he does too. There's fire in his eyes that can't be mistaken. "I know you do too."

"Not like this."

"Your cock disagrees with you." I look down at the bulge in his jeans. "I want to play with you, Axton, we can have fun together. That's all it is."

He shakes his head. "Not when you're… like this."

I put my hands on my hips. "Like what?"

"Like I said, drunk. I shouldn't have made you…"

"Come?" I finish for him. I shake my head, shame creeping up my neck and burning my cheeks. "I get it, you don't want me. It's fine, I'll leave."

"Stevie." He tries to reach out, but I dodge his grasp.

"I'll see myself out."

"Please don't be mad…"

I ignore him, and I can't get out of there fast enough. I slam his door behind me and go to my own door, unlocking it after three tries.

When I'm inside, I sink against it and slide down to the floor.

Oh my fucking God.

What the hell just happened?

The man is as frustrating as all hell, and I know I sounded like a needy bitch, but he was into it. If that missile in his jeans was any indication.

I slap a hand on my forehead. *What have I done?*

It should be me taking the moral high ground, not him…

Dropping my phone, I kick my shoes off and strip down to nothing, then crawl into bed.

I don't even turn the television on. Instead, I reach into the drawer and pull out my vibrator.

I don't even need to lube the thing up as I switch it on and swirl the tip around my clit. It's still swollen and in need of more. I come quickly, circling the tip around and around, all the while imagining it's the real thing; Axton's cock teasing me before he shoves into me hard.

I do just that.

The vibrator isn't huge, nothing like what he'd be, and it turns me on even more knowing how big and hot and thick he is. I push it into my pussy, hissing at the vibrations as I turn the bunny ears on, so I get two vibrations at once.

I come again, hard this time, and I call out because it's so intense. Not as intense as what his magic fingers just did to me, but good enough.

Each time I come, I picture his face. His body on top of mine. His cock ramming into me over and over as he thrusts in and out, taking me to heaven and back.

He's an asshat for rejecting me, even if it was the right thing to do.

I keep at it until I'm spent. Until I'm so sated and orgasmed out that I lie completely still.

I fall asleep wondering if I'll ever get to touch him again.

BRACKEN RIDGE
REBELS
ARIZONA
M · C

CHAPTER 17

AXTON

I stare at the door for what feels like an eternity. My feet feel cemented to the floor.

My heart thumps in my chest wildly like a racehorse.

Fuck.

What did I just do?

Oh, I know exactly what, the question is why?

I run a hand through my hair. I should go after her, apologize. She's clearly intoxicated and I'm 100% sober.

I go to my door, swing it open, and march out onto the landing. Then I stare, like a fool, at her closed door, shaking my head. *What the fuck am I doing?*

I'm just gonna make things worse.

As I turn to leave, I hear a cry. I listen harder, *shit!* She did leave pretty mad, so now I've upset her and made her cry… I don't mean to, but I press my ear to the door, but I hear her call out again… then I realize… she's not crying. She's crying out.

I step back, startled, when I hear my name, and then a moan. It's the most fucking perfect sound I've ever heard. It makes me want to smash the door down, go in there, and finish the job myself.

I cross the landing back to the safety of my apartment in a couple of strides.

Why did I have to meddle with it? Why can't I just stay away from the one woman I can't have?

I rest my head against the door as I close my eyes.

She's so perfect.

Everything about her, it reels me in like a moth to a flame. She's natural. What you see is what you get, and I dig that. I like it when a chick doesn't need to try too hard.

And she's so fuckin' cute drunk.

And now I've had my hands in her pants. I've also had a brief taste of her pussy, and now I know I want more.

Two seconds ago, I was all about going over there to say I'm sorry, but now I'm picturing all the ways I could take her and make her say my name like that in real life. With me doing it, not her hand or some sex toy.

A small smile splits my face. I palm the back of my neck.

I can't honestly say I'm truly sorry.

Intoxicated or not, she shoved my hand down into her panties. Yes, I should've taken the high road and stepped back and tried to get her to leave. Not continue until she's coming hard with my name on her lips.

But the truth is, I liked it. I more than liked it, and I wanna do it again.

I pinch the bridge of my nose, then run my other hand down to my cock. Yeah, it's straining to get out to the point of being painful. I'm gonna have to do something about that… again.

Pushing off the door, I go over to the fridge and down a bottle of cold water. I feel like I need a stiff drink, but that's not gonna solve the issue of what I've now got flooding through my veins.

I've got a big fucking crush on my boss, yet *crush* seems so juvenile.

I know I haven't had a whole lot of experience with chicks, and I really thought that would all change when I got out, but the truth is, ever since I laid eyes on Stevie, my mind's been occupied with her.

Then it occurs to me; doesn't she have a boyfriend? I'm sure she mentioned it…

Something rears in my chest, and I'm unsure of the feeling. It feels a little like a slow boiling rage. Imagining another man's hands on her, where mine have been, makes me want to punch a hole in the wall.

I don't care that she isn't my girlfriend. The fact that she's my boss obviously makes it complicated, and the fact she has a boyfriend. I feel protective toward her, as if I have a right to be a green-eyed monster when I barely know the girl. It doesn't stop me, though.

I want her beneath me, squirming, her eyes scrunched closed as I pound in and out of her.

Stevie calls to me on another level, one I can't explain, and it's probably because I can't have her. That must be what it is. Infatuation.

Now I know in the morning it's sure to be awkward, which is why it's probably a good idea to make myself scarce. I've no idea if she's going to even fuckin' remember, but that's probably wishful thinking.

I make my way to bed, pulling my jeans off and sheathing my dick. It's gonna be another long, lonely night with just me, myself, and my palm, but that's nothing new.

I don't see her the next day. She has Mondays off, not that I'm keeping tabs, but I cover her days off and she covers mine.

I admit, I hid like a coward down in the cellar, rearranging the barrels, boxes, and cartons, and then I moved onto the cool room.

I don't even want to think about last night.

First, my mom shows up unexpectedly and we have a heart to heart, then Stevie comes stumbling into my door and… well, I know the rest. I'm almost dreading running into her. Maybe if I lay low on my day off and stay at church, it might be for the best.

If she ends up firing me for taking advantage of her, then I'm fucked. I mean, it takes two to tango and all that, but let's face it, she was shitfaced.

"You look like you sucked on a bag of lemons," Brock says from the doorway as I jolt with surprise and bang my head on the cool room door.

"Thanks, fucker," I complain. "You scared the livin' shit out of me."

His shoulders shake.

"What's goin' on?"

"Same shit, different day."

"Heard Mom came to see you."

I roll my eyes. "Good news travels fast."

"Welcome to the gossip capital of Arizona, brother, and no, before you ask, I had nothing to do with it."

"Didn't imagine for a second she'd show up here."

"How'd it go?"

"Pretty good," I say. "She hasn't changed a bit."

"Is that a good thing?" he asks.

I turn to him as I haul a carton over my shoulder to move it to the back. "We all know I was always a momma's boy."

Brock grins, remembering, but then sobers quickly. "I'm

sorry, man," he says.

I frown. "For what?"

"For it bein' so shit for you when you just got out, for neither of them comin' to see you."

I shrug. "It works both ways. I could've shown up there, said I'm sorry. I am the one who did what I did."

"You're too hard on yourself."

I turn to him. "No, Brock, I'm not. You think the sun shines out of my ass no matter what I do, but we have to accept the fact that I'm an ex-con. I brought shame upon the family and sometimes the fallout can't be rectified."

He shakes his head. "I don't think that, but you're my brother. You can't keep blamin' yourself. At some point, you have to forgive yourself and move on."

"Isn't that what I'm doin'?" I put my hands on my hips.

He gives me a chin lift. "You used to do that, too, when you were a kid. You'd put your hands on your hips, as if you weren't sure if you wanted to try and fight me or back down."

"Things change, Brock. I don't back down."

"Glad to hear it."

"I also forgave myself a long time ago, but we can't deny the fact that Dad hates me, and I have to live with it."

"He doesn't hate you. Remember, he hated me for the better part of ten years. I'm not stickin' up for him, but he's changed. We get along now better than we ever have. With

Dad, you just gotta tell it like it is, and he'll respect you more for that."

"What if I don't want his respect?" I challenge. "What if I just say, *go to hell*? Who is he to me anyway now? We're strangers."

He pushes off the banister and steps down onto the concrete floor. "I'm not pushin' you to do anythin', bro, you know that. It was good of Mom to come, but I know it's early days. Dad is a difficult man to deal with at the best of times. He's proud, and he's set in his ways."

I narrow my eyes. "You don't have to sell me on him. I know exactly who he is and how we were raised. I was there for the most part."

He squeezes my shoulder protectively. "I'm supposed to kick your ass, bein' a prospect and my little brother, but I've yet to find anything you haven't done that you've been asked."

I can't help the twist of my lips as I fight a smile. "Told you in Stradbroke. I'm not gonna let you down."

It makes me wonder if he's not sniffing around because he's heard about Little Mick, though I'm pretty sure Steel's got better things to do. It is a small town, after all; people talk and the old saying about bad news traveling fast is certainly true in Bracken Ridge.

"I know you're not. When is your parole officer comin' next?"

I shrug like it's no big deal, yet I have the date etched into my brain. My parole officer has the power to rule my life at the click of a button. Fuck knows, they never stop reminding me.

"Next week. Now that Kennedy's out of action for a week, Amelia gave me the paperwork, and I'll go over to Bones' place to sign it."

"This club is lucky to have Kennedy."

I nod. "Can say that again. She's a good woman." I begin to mount the stairs.

"What about you? Any new pussy around the place?" Brock follows on behind me.

I don't get to answer. At the top of the stairs, Stevie comes careering down from the top floor, headed to the back door.

And I just landed right in her path.

I open my mouth, then close it again. She stops in her tracks and looks up at me. I can't lie; I'm delighted when a lovely pink color shades her neck and rises into her cheeks. Why that is so agreeable to me is anyone's guess. Maybe it's because I'm picturing her ass turning bright pink after I spank it. Jesus fuckin' Christ.

When Brock's standing next to me, he gives her a chin lift. "Stevie."

"Brock."

"How much of that did you hear?" He frowns.

"Axton was about to tell you about the new pussy in the neighborhood."

I almost choke on my own saliva. Hearing her say pussy jolts electricity straight down to my balls. But now she thinks we're talkin' trash. And I don't know why that bothers me so much.

This is all I need, a fuckin' wood right in front of my brother.

Brock snorts, not at all sorry for being so crude in front of her.

"Sorry, Stevie, just guy talk. Didn't know you'd be standin' there," I blurt out, shoving Brock in the shoulder before he can do any more damage.

"I'm used to it," she says, eager to get out of there. "I've heard worse in this place, and the clubhouse, for that matter."

She avoids looking at me again and fumbles at the door.

"Are you goin' anywhere in your truck?" I ask, forcing her to look at me.

She does, swallowing hard, then plays with the end of her ponytail. I imagine it wrapped tightly around my fist…

"Uh, yeah," she says, her brow furrowing.

"I noticed one of your tires was kinda flat this morning when I went to grab a breakfast burrito."

"Oh, it is?" she asks, looking surprised.

Brock turns to look at me. "Breakfast burrito?"

I roll my eyes. "Bacon, eggs, spinach, and cheese, or whatever you want, all wrapped up in a burrito."

Brock winces. "Holy fuck, that sounds disgusting. You actually eat that shit?"

"Better than shit on a stick," I say, staring at her while she avoids my gaze. "Anyway, I pumped the tire up this morning, but you have a slow leak. It'll have to go into Steel's to get repaired, so don't leave it longer than a few days."

She bites her bottom lip and then casts her eyes upwards. "That was awfully nice of you, Axton. Thanks for noticing. I should be more observant of these things."

"Anytime."

I don't know if it's just me, but the air around us feels like an inferno.

I can tell by her mannerisms that she's embarrassed about last night. Me? I can't stop thinkin' about it. It's why I've been hiding out in the cellar for most of the morning.

When her eyes finally meet mine, she says, "Well, I've got to go see Kennedy, so I'll see you boys later."

Brock gives her a chin lift.

"Later," I say as she reaches for the door and disappears through it.

It's like she couldn't get out of here fast enough.

I run a hand through my hair, then I notice Brock frowning.

"What was that all about?" he grunts.

I give him a look that tells him he's a little slow. "Uh, her tires."

"Not that part."

"Her hangover."

"Try again, sucker."

"Don't know what you mean, bro."

"Don't give me that look."

I frown right on back at him. "What look?"

"You got somethin' goin' on?"

I swallow hard. "Nope. Look, she got a bit drunk last night and came in late. She's probably just embarrassed that I saw her."

I'm not a very good liar, never have been, but Brock smells bullshit like most people breathe air.

"Good of you to notice her tire."

"I'm observant." I shrug.

He points in my face. "You can't fuck the boss, Ax." I smirk. "Wasn't plannin' on it."

"Plenty of pussy at church to be had. You got all the chicks askin' for you, and not just the sweet butts," Brock says.

"Yeah?" I at least have to make it seem like I'm interested.

"Don't seem so surprised, it runs in the family. Before Angel, I had chicks swingin' off my dick left, right, and center. Had pussy up to my eyeballs."

"Please don't give me that visual again."

"Just sayin'."

"Comin' from the mouth of a man who's married with two kids."

"That's just the point." He goes on. "It won't be like that forever. You'll settle down too, one day, if it's what you want."

I rest a hand on his shoulder and give him a shake. "I've been out a week, bro. Let's not get carried away. Now, are we done with the Spanish Inquisition?"

"Fuckin' breakfast burrito," he mutters, shoving me backwards in the chest. "Swear to fuckin' God."

"Don't knock it till you try it."

"They said that about settlin' down in a small town, and look at me now."

I walk toward the bar. "Spoken like a true Altman."

I just hope I haven't scared Stevie off for good.

BRACKEN RIDGE
REBELS
ARIZONA
M · C

CHAPTER 12

STEVIE

He fixed my tire? Okay, temporarily. But still, that was kinda sweet.

I couldn't look at him in the eye for more than a few seconds, though.

I admit I was embarrassed. I acted like an ass last night, ogling his bare body, barging my way into his apartment, and then he made me… *I can't even say it.*

I slap my forehead.

And now he's fixing things for me.

I should never have made the first move. Never.

I cringe. He must think I'm insane.

Like Brock, he's stoic and very serious, and I can't get any type of lead on what's going on in his brain.

My mind thinks back as I start my truck. He definitely kissed me back, and oh my… he's definitely a chef's kiss on the smooching rector scale. The way his jeans hang low on those hips, his muscled, sexy body, and tattoos covering the entirety of his chest and his arms, he hits me in the core like nobody else ever has. The sexual attraction I have to him isn't something I've experienced before, and a part of me knows it isn't *just* sexual. He has a very sweet nature, he's smart, and I don't honestly think there's a bad bone in his body.

Not that I even know him well enough to be making that kind of judgment call.

I could literally slap myself.

I have to confront him, apologize and assure him it won't be happening again. As much as I want to, I know that the reality is so much more sobering.

The reality is what keeps me from ruining everything.

I rest my head against the steering wheel and thump it a few times.

This is why I should never drink. Having said that, I've drank plenty of times and never came onto a guy like I did with him.

It's like Axton Altman just brings out the animal in me without even having to do anything.

I'm his fucking boss!

That was so awkward back there. I could barely look at him or put a sentence together, and I'm pretty sure my beet red face was a sure giveaway to my humiliation.

I'm all for being confident and owning it, but I'm not like my sister. Kennedy could march into hell and order the devil around at her whim, but I take a little warming up.

I go visit Kennedy at home and stop off to get some groceries and a few of her favorite things.

She's been texting me about how sweet Bones is being and how they're practically living together and he won't leave her side. The pair of them are like lovestruck teenagers. Talk about gag.

Nothing makes me more satisfied than seeing my sister settled and happy. She's been through so much after her husband's death.

I know it wrecked her, even though they were almost separated at the time. Kennedy hung in there and did everything possible to make his life a comfortable one until the very end.

We both moved here for a fresh start. I didn't plan on working for the Rebels MC but the opportunity arose when we took a day trip down from Phoenix and fell in love with the town.

The rest is history.

It didn't matter where I was located at the time, being that Lukas was away anyway, I could make a home anywhere. I knew he preferred the cities more than I did, but there's just something about a small town and a tight-knit community.

I lift my head from the wheel. I don't need Axton coming out back and seeing me in a state of *whatever this is*, so I put my foot on the brake, pull the car into gear, and high-tail it across town.

I definitely can't confess to Kennedy about Axton. She'll have a fit, plus, she'd tell Bones, then Axton would get his ass kicked by the club. Even though I'm not technically a 'club girl,' I still work for the Rebels; and considered property of the club. One thing the Rebels have above all else are their rules. And in this club, rules are not meant to be broken.

I spend a couple of hours helping Kennedy get organized, putting the stuff I bought her away, and set her up with her laptop so she can look over some case files. She's going to be off work for at least four to six weeks.

Seeing her holed up in bed, battered and bruised, makes me angry. We both know being involved with this club involves risk, but judging by how close she and Bones are, it's clear she's picked a side. And, after all Hutch as done for me, I guess I have too.

I decide to go to the art supplies store and get some new canvases. I paint and sketch for fun; it's one of the many *not so great* things about me that nobody knows aside from Kennedy and Lukas. Not that my ex was around enough to know that it's one of the only things that relaxes me in times of stress. I picked it back up again when he got deployed.

Bracken Ridge doesn't often have the most amazing art supplies, so I have to buy a lot of what I need online.

I've been sketching a lot lately. Old buildings. The

desert. The Bracken Ridge skyline from the Canyon is one of my favorite places. I swear the sunsets are the most amazing natural phenomenon I've ever seen. I take photos on my phone and recreate the scenes later. I don't have much room in the apartment, but I make do.

At the moment, because I'm waiting on more paint, I've been sketching more and more. Sometimes I can get lost for hours, not even realizing where all the time went.

It also helps me take my mind off things.

Like the way Axton felt when I kissed him. I wish I could stop focusing on that, but I can't help it.

I loved Lukas, a part of me always will. But what happened last night with Axton wasn't like anything I've ever had with Lukas. There was no fire there like there is when Axton merely touches my skin, or even looks at me a certain way. He doesn't even have to do anything else, and I feel like I'm going to combust.

What does that mean?
I'm a shitty person for comparing two completely different men. They are nothing alike.

What I can't get over in all of this, is the intensity of Axton's eyes. How they are like staring into an endless, turbulent ocean. One where the waves crash one minute and still the next.

Clearly, my brain is ignoring my demands because it wants to keep rehashing everything I know so far about

Axton and why the hell I'm not put-off that he's an ex-con who has a history of violence and is starting at the bottom of the food chain being a prospect.

None of these facts seem to stray my decision in wanting more, even if that is a ridiculous fantasy.

It's about ten o'clock when I finally stretch my limbs and switch off my sketching lamp.

I drew the front of the Stone Crow. I thought I might give it to Hutch in a frame, to say thank you. One side of the building is the old ruin that it was in an old photo from the nineteen forties, the other half transitions into the new structure that it is today.

I have to say, I'm mildly impressed. I know Hutch likes old things, so this is kind of a mixture of the old and the new. I'll finish the shading and some more of the finer details tomorrow, then I'll get a frame.

Going to the fridge, I realize I'm too lazy to bother cooking, so I take a can of Dr. Pepper and guzzle half of it down. I begin putting my pencils back in the box, when there's a tap at my door.

Curious, I look through the peep hole.

Shit!

Standing at my door, his larger-than-life body towering there like freaking God's gift to women, is Axton.

It's like he can hear my goddamn thoughts.

I wonder for a fleeting moment if I could go and hide

and not answer, but that would just be weird. I shouldn't have to hide in my own apartment.

With my heart hammering in my chest, I tentatively open the door.

He looks up from his boots and our eyes lock.

I wish the ground would swallow me whole right about now, but I hold my head high. Pretending I'm fine around him has suddenly become something I really have perfected, when in reality, I'm far from fine.

"Axton," I say with surprise. "Is everything okay?"

He's holding a paper bag with something in it. "Sorry, I wasn't going to knock, but I saw your light was on, and I wasn't sure if you'd eaten yet."

I open my mouth and close it again. *Why is he worried if I've eaten?*

"I, uh, actually, I haven't," I reply sheepishly. "I've been..." *Don't tell him what you've doing all day. He doesn't need to know about your life.* "Busy."

He hands the bag over. "Roxy had some tacos left over. Seemed a shame for them to go to waste."

There's a slightly awkward silence between him handing me the bag and me trying to work out what the fuck I'm going to say.

"That's, uh, so thoughtful of you."

He palms the back of his neck. "Listen, about last night..."

My eyes flick to his suddenly as I rub my forehead. "Yeah, about that…" I trail off.

We may as well address the elephant in the room.

"It was wrong of me… and I just wanted to apologize." He goes on. "You were clearly intoxicated, and I don't want you to think that I took advantage of the situation. I should've… I should've kept my mouth and my hands to myself."

Oh, those fucking hands… I remember him pinching my nipple, and I clench my pussy just thinking about it.

"I wasn't *that* drunk," I blurt out before I slap a hand over my mouth. "I mean, um, I knew what I was…" *Shit. What do I fucking mean?*

His lips twitch like he's fighting a smile. He does that a lot.

Why am I a blithering mess? I'm not a pushover, I never have been, but he does something to me that just isn't normal.

"Careful, boss, you sound like you're digging a hole for yourself."

My eyes go wide, and I feel the humiliation creep up my cheeks all over again. Why do I keep blushing like a freaking imbecile?

"Well, I think we can both agree that it was… wrong, on more than one level, and unprofessional of me to come onto my employee… intoxicated or not."

He shifts his stance, resting one hand above his head on the door frame as I try not to melt into a puddle on the floor. *He's sex on a stick.*

"Oh?" he says, rubbing his other hand through his beard as I watch his movements. "Do you mean me, in general, or the fact that I work for you?"

I clear my throat. "Why does that matter?"

"Just making conversation." He shrugs like it's no big deal.

Right, because discussing the pending sexual frustration I'm having is just like discussing the weather.

I don't think I've ever been so embarrassed.

I take a deep breath. "Workplace… *situations* rarely ever work. In fact, if we continued, then it would only cause conflicts at work… and, in turn, that causes more issues… and problems, and I don't do workplace drama, or office romance, so to speak..." Office romance? *Kill me now.*

He bites his lip as if stifling a laugh. "Gotcha."

I plough on, since I'm in up to neck anyway. "And it was an error in judgment, on my part. I don't blame you when I practically threw myself at you. Trust me, I'm embarrassed enough."

His eyebrows knit together. "There's nothing to be embarrassed about, I was there too."

"I just think it's best if this is where it ends, if we can just… forget it ever happened." Even as I say it, the thought of never having him touch me feels like absolute torture.

He nods like he understands, but his face shows confusion. "I guess."

I frown, and even though I should end this conversation, I don't, instead, I say, "Are you saying… you don't regret it?"

He chuckles slightly. "Is that what you want me to say?"

"No," I begin. "I want you to tell me the truth." *Shit, do I?*

"Are you really ready for that?"

"Of course."

He looks up for a second, like he's trying to gather himself. "Fine. I'm not sorry for doing what I did, I'm only sorry for the simple fact that you were… dru… uh, slightly inebriated and that, yes, you're my boss and that does complicate things."

He doesn't regret it, then?

It hits me like a hurricane that I'm in a lot deeper than I first thought. I'm stuttering and blithering like a fool. In truth, I don't like how vulnerable I am around him and the fact he has the power to unravel me like this without even doing anything.

"But we can both agree it's crazy to continue." *Right?* His eyes meet mine again. The clear blue reminds me of an ice storm, but the way he's looking at me is far from icy, it's more like a volcanic eruption.

"Sure. The last thing I want is for things to be awkward between us," he says, his voice low and gravely.
That's a little hard, considering he's had his hand down my pants. "I agree. So it's settled."

"So we'll agree to… what exactly?"

"Working together," I say quickly. "And that's it. We'll be colleagues."

He nods, and I try desperately not to notice his bulging bicep as he folds both arms across his chest.

"You're right. It's probably for the best."

"Good." I nod. *Glad we've got that sorted out.*

"So, we're fine?" he questions, his hand once again rubbing through his beard.

I nod. "Yep."

"Cool."

I wave the bag at him. "Thanks for the tacos."

He tips his head. "Anytime."

"Goodnight then, Axton."

"Goodnight, Stevie."

He steps back, his eyes still on me. I could be wrong, but it's like he's reluctantly pulling himself away. "Oh, I should mention," he says as I begin to shut the door, giving him a friendly wave.

I halt for a fraction of a second.

"The walls are very thin around here, so if I hear my name on your lips in the throes of passion again, *boss,* I'm not sure I can promise that I won't break this door down and have my way with you so I can hear it with my own ears, face to face."

My eyes go wide as he turns his back on me and disappears into his room without a backward glance, the door closing abruptly behind him.

I stare after him for a few solid seconds before I shut my door quickly, holding the paper bag to my chest as I lean back against the door.

So now he's just playing with me?
And what the actual living fuck? Did he hear me using my toys… Oh My God.

This is fucking madness.

I palm my forehead, feeling a fever coming on. He couldn't have… I mean, I was a little bit inebriated, as he said, but I don't think I shouted his name out loud, certainly not loud enough for him to hear… unless… unless he was listening?

I should be horrified, and I am, sort of. Another part of my dark, depraved mind likes the fact he heard me pleasuring myself, imagining it was him. The only thing that sobers me is remembering I have to work with this man and stop having illicit thoughts about him and that delicious tongue of his…

I've no idea how I'm going to ever live this down… I'm screwed, no matter how I look at it.

And he fucking knows it, the sly son-of-a-bitch.

BRACKEN RIDGE
REBELS
ARIZONA
M · C

CHAPTER 13

AXTON

The next week is awkward, to say the least, but it doesn't escape my attention that Stevie is doing her best to try and keep her distance.

I shouldn't have said what I said, but I couldn't help it.

I spent too long locked up regretting what I did to come into my new life on the outside to not be honest. She asked me, and I answered. She might be able to lie to herself and pretend that we don't have a spark between us, but I'm not going to.

Fuck being professional. When have I ever been that? Let's face it, as soon as this gigs over in a years' time, I'm free to do what I want. Including her.

The thought sobers me. A whole fucking year? Could I wait that long, to have her? I know I can't. I want her now. I want her to shut her pretty little mouth while I grab her by the throat and tell her what to do.

She might be the boss of me in the bar, but she ain't the boss of me in the bedroom. And if I'm being frank, I'd love to get her on her knees where she can take me balls deep into her mouth as I ram down her throat. That'll teach her to try to tell me what we are and what we aren't.

Fuck.

Remembering the way her mouth tasted… and how responsive she was when I made her come in less than a minute… yeah, I'd be lying if I said I didn't want more of that.

I toss the garbage out back into the skip bin, and movement out of my periphery catches my eye.

"Thought I'd find you here," Little Mick says as I turn toward him.

"I work here, fuckface," I say, my jaw tightening. "What the fuck are you doin' here?"

He points at me. "We're not over, Axton. Everyone knows when you get out, debts need to be paid. If I'm to ensure your safety, then that comes at a price. There are a few people who wouldn't mind using your head as a battering ram."

I don't waste a second. I have him by the throat, hauling him up against the brick wall. He's bigger than me, but you know the old saying about the bigger they are, the harder they fall? Yeah, I'm not sure if that really applies in this situation, but I act on instinct. "What the fuck did you say to me?"

He tries to swing, but he's a fat fucker, and I've got

more muscle than him as I pin him down.

"You don't wanna do this," he gasps.

"I'm gonna say this nice and clear for you, so you better listen and listen up good," I growl. "I. Owe. You. Nothing. You got that? Don't come around here again. If I see you one more time, I'm gonna put a fuckin' bullet in your brain."

I shove him backwards as he tries to stand. I can smell the alcohol on him from a mile away, and it's probably to my advantage that he's slightly wobbly on his feet.

"Those are tough words, Axton, but like I say, once you've been in the joint, you gain enemies. Some who haven't forgotten you turned your back on them. That comes at a price."

"You shut your fuckin' mouth!" I sock him in the face as he puts both hands in front to try to block me. "You fuckin' hear me?" I belt him a second time, then another, then I punch him in the gut.

Motherfucker doesn't even get a swing in.

Yeah, I didn't spend all that time in jail working out and developing my fighting skills to be overpowered by a fat, overbearing asshole like Mick.

He guffaws, holding his stomach as I shove him until he's out on the pavement. "Stay the fuck away from me. If I see you around here again, you won't just be dealing with me."

I pull the gate closed, locking it, and make a mental note that this needs to stay closed at all times until he's slithered back under the rock he crawled out from under. What the fuck is his problem?

I run a hand through my hair as I calm down. Turning around, I see Stevie at the back door, frozen as she stares at me wide-eyed.

I move toward her, grabbing her by the elbow as I yank her inside and bolt the door behind us.

"You saw nothin'. Got me?"

"Axton," she warns.

I let go of her. "I'm sorry. That guy, he's bad news."

"Why were you punching him?" She reaches for my hands. They're a little swollen, but not bleeding. I know Mick's jaws gonna be sore for a little while, and that's the only thing that makes me smile. "And why are you smiling about it?"

I sigh, not wanting her to let go of my hands, so I let her assess me.

"He's someone I did time with. He's been hangin' around the bar."

"And out back?"

I shake my head. "That's the first and only time. Until he's out of town, keep it closed. When deliveries come, I'll go unlock it."

"Axton, this is serious. We should call the police."

I stare at her. "No cops. It's not that serious, he's just tryin' to get a rise out of me, make me retaliate."

"It seems like it's working."

I sigh. "He caught me by surprise, that's all."

Her eyes narrow, her green, emerald-colored eyes meet mine, concern all over her face. "It looked a little more than being caught by surprise. Was he threatening you?"

I don't want her to panic or call the cops.

"I told you, it's under control. He's a piece of shit. Some ex-cons don't like the fact some of us want to move on in life and not do any more dumb shit. He's sniffin' around because he's scum, that's it."

"Axton, it's not wrong to go to the cops if you need…"

"I don't need anything. Let's drop it."

She lets go of me. I know my tone's harsh, but I don't need him wedging his way into my life and making Stevie worry. I'm sure getting punched in the face is enough to give him a clear and final warning that I'm not gonna take more of his shit.

"If you say so. I just don't want him being a problem in the bar."

"He won't be."

She nods as if she's trying to believe me, but if I were her, I probably wouldn't believe me either.

"So, we're good?" I press.

She nods. "Yes, of course, but your hands must hurt a

bit? You punched the guy square in the face."

I shrug it off. "Nothin' I haven't done before."

Her eyes go wide. "As long as you're okay?"

I give her a chin lift. "I survived being stabbed in prison, boss. I'm pretty sure I'm gonna be okay. He didn't even touch me."

She swallows hard, and I know I've probably said the wrong thing. But this is who I am.

I was in the joint, and that's that. I'm not proud of it, but it took ten years of my life. If I didn't learn anything from being in there, then there'd be no fucking point to anything.

"Listen," I go on, my voice lowering. "Don't mention any of this to Brock, or anyone from the club, okay? I don't need to worry them."

She still looks a little concerned. "Maybe giving them the heads up might be good, then they've got your back if you need it."

I'm more than capable, but I nod to placate her. "I will, in my own time." Then I do the unthinkable; I brush a piece of her hair back off her shoulder. I can't fuckin' help myself and the second I do it, I realize my mistake.

She freezes. "He won't be a problem."

"Ax…"

Fuck. I can't even handle this.

I need to get my electrician's license ASAP and get the fuck on out of here and away from her. She's got the power to render me to my knees. She's got the power to break me.

"I said, it's all right."

"You're not the boss here, remember," she says, moving her hands to her hips. "If he's hanging around the back of the building, it's unsafe…"

I walk her back into the wall and she lets me. I don't touch her, but I cage her in.

"I took care of it. If you think I'll let that piece of shit do anything to you, then you clearly don't know me very well."

Her eyes dip to my lips. "Axton, we're at work."

I smirk. "You're thinkin' about it, aren't you?"

"About what?" Her lip trembles. I want to pull on it with my teeth…

"About us."

"No," she lies. "I… *we* agreed."

"You like rules, Stevie? Is that it?"

"What kind of question is that?"

"A simple one."

"I guess… I follow them. That doesn't necessarily mean I like them."

I smirk, I could fucking suck the face off her right now. "Well, I don't. Not where you're concerned."

She lets out a slow breath. "I don't know what that means, but we should get back to work."

"I don't think anyone's gonna miss us, since it's just you

and me."

"Still…"

"Tell me to back off, then I will."

She frowns.

"What?" I prompt when she doesn't speak.

Her voice is quiet when she says, "What if I don't want you to?"

"You should."

I push off the wall to leave, but she grabs onto my shirt, scrunching it into two fists as her eyes grow fierce.

"I'm not afraid of you," she says, her face serious. She fuckin' means it.

One side of my mouth turns up. "You sure about that?"

"You won't hurt me."

"That's true enough, but I will hurt anyone that comes near you."

"Like dangerous men?" she prods.

"There's no one more dangerous than me, *boss*. Just remember that."

"I've seen the way you look at men who talk to me."

I snort. "Talk? Not much talkin' goin' on. All they're doin' is ogling your tits and your ass, wishin' they could do more."

She stares at me, still holding my shirt. "Are you going to wrestle every guy who ogles me, Axton?"

"Trust me, I won't be wrestling them," I mutter.

"I know exactly what you're doing."

"Really?" I question, our eyes locking. "And what is that, exactly?"

"You know fine well."

"Tell me," I taunt.

"You're the bad boy ex-con with a boatload of baggage and a sexy swagger. You act as if you don't know the effect you have on women, that you're oblivious to it, but you know exactly what you're doing. You're doing this because you're not supposed to."

I laugh. "Not supposed to?"

"You know the rules Hutch has in place, and a part of you wants to rebel."

My jaw clenches, and she half smiles, knowing she's right. I'm a low-life prospect and Stevie is far higher on the Richter scale than I am.

"Is that so?"

She nods. "Tell me I'm wrong, then."

"So what if I did want to rebel?"

"You're really going to go against the Prez?"

"Maybe fuckin' you would be worth the punishment, if that's what you're gettin' at?"

She stares at me. "I can't believe you just said that."

I shrug. "Why? It's the truth. I told you once before, you'll always get honesty from me, whether you want it or not. The question is, do you want me to?"

"Do I want you to be honest, or to fuck me?"

I can't help it. I reach up to cup her chin, my thumb dancing over her bottom lip as I stare at her mouth. I want to take her so fuckin' bad.

My heart jolts at her honesty. I lean close to her ear and say, "The question is, *boss*, do I affect you enough to disobey him?"

She lets go of my shirt and looks down at the floor.

I tilt her chin up with my hand. "Thought so."

"You don't know shit," she whispers.

"I bet if you dug a little deeper, Stevie, you'd find out a lot of things about me that you didn't know."

"Like what?"

"Like I spent enough time followin' rules, and I don't like feelin' like I'm a caged bird. When I got out, I promised myself I'd only do things that made me happy, fulfilled and fuckin' joyful."

I feel her tremble beneath me, and it makes me all the more excited.

"And, what makes you joyful?"

"You."

I crash my lips to hers as she mewls. My tongue forces entry, and she groans when our tongues collide. She grips me at the hips and pulls me closer, and I can't help but smirk, cupping her face as I deepen the kiss.

"Can't fuckin' stay away from me, can you?" I growl.

"It's a bit hard," she pants back. "When you're right under my nose twenty-four-seven."

I push my body into hers so she can feel my erection, and I don't even care if I fuck her right here on the stairs. *She's mine.*

"Axton!" Brock yells, my eyes immediately flicking open. I step back from Stevie like she's burned me.

"Fuck," I mutter, running a hand through my hair. I adjust my dick as her eyes flick south and she smirks. "You think this is funny?"

She grins even wider. "Better answer him before he thinks we're up to no good out here."

She ducks under my arm and takes off toward her office, strutting her little ass as she goes. If Brock wasn't here, I'd be going after her, hauling her over my shoulder while I carry her upstairs to my bed.

I watch her, my eyes glued to her ass as she stalks off until I can't see her anymore.

I mutter several curse words before calling out to Brock, "I'm back here!"

A few moments later, I meet him in the hallway, carrying a case of beers I just picked up from the back. I have to make it look like I'm doing something, instead of what I want to do, and that's to bang my boss.

"What's up?" I say as he moves to the side to let me pass.

"Came to see Stevie, actually."

My back to him I frown. "Oh yeah, what for?"

"Need to run somethin' by her from Prez."

"Everything okay?"

I drop the case on the side of the bar. We haven't opened the doors yet, so I've still got half an hour to stock the fridges and get all the chairs off the tables ready for service.

"Yeah, Hutch wants to hold the annual art auction here. The high-fliers in the Bracken Ridge council finally recognize that the Stone Crow isn't a strip club, and they want catering for two to three hundred people."

I whistle through my teeth. "Didn't know there were that many art buffs in Bracken Ridge?"

"You'd be surprised," he says, then a moment passes before he adds, "Steel said some guy was givin' you some stick the other night."

"It was nothin' to worry about."

"Who was it?"

I don't want to have to fuckin' lie to my own brother, but I also don't want him to worry. "An inmate that was passin' through. Nothin' to it, He had a beer, then left."

"A little coincidental, don't you think?"

I shrug. "Didn't think much of it, to be honest. You know what some guys are like when they run into you once you're out. They've all got little dick syndrome."

He gives me a chin lift. "Well, you got any trouble, you

call me."

I shove him in the shoulder. "I'm not a kid anymore. Not sure if you noticed."

"Never too old to have backup."

"I don't need it, but thanks all the same."

He slaps me upside the head, and I'm too slow to duck, then he walks off laughing to go find Stevie.

Unlucky for me, I've got a bar to open and the window of opportunity to do bad things to my boss just closed.

Some guys just can't get a fuckin' break.

BRACKEN RIDGE
REBELS
ARIZONA
M · C

CHAPTER 14

STEVIE

I'm glad for the safety of my office so I can decompress. What in the actual fuck just happened?

I try to calm myself because being around Axton is like swallowing liquid plutonium, and now I'm just waiting to go off like a firecracker.

I grip my hair with both hands and tug. I can't exactly scream the place down in frustration, but that's how he makes me feel. To make matters worse, he and Brock continue to talk to one another until Axton opens the front doors.

Now why do I feel so cheated? Was I actually going to let him have his way with me, just like he suggested? I have no defense.

My phone rings suddenly, making me jump out of my skin.

I look down and see it's Lukas calling me. My eyes go wide, and for the first time since we broke up, I wonder if I should answer it.

I don't know when I became a coward all of a sudden.

I take a deep breath and hit the green button. "Lukas," I say as I stand and go over to my office door, closing it.

"Hello, Stevie," he says.

I run a hand through my hair. "Hi, how are you?"

"I'm good," he says. "I'm sorry to call you while you're at work."

"That's okay, I'm in my office." *I wonder what he wants…*

I had all his stuff shipped back to his mom's, so it can't be that.

He laughs a little nervously. "I don't really know why I'm calling."

"You don't?" I ask, taking a big gulp of my cold coffee. I wince.

"I… I miss you, Stevie."

I spurt coffee all over my desk, then begin to splutter and cough as I hunt around in my desk for napkins.

"Stevie? Are you okay?"

"Sorry, my coffee went down the wrong pipe," I say, ungraciously wiping my chin as I cough.

He laughs. "How have you been?"

My heart hammers in my chest at his admission.

"I've been fine, Lukas, thanks for asking."

He is the one who dumped me, but I still don't have a right to be snappy at him. Especially when I got over missing him some time ago. He isn't an awful person, in fact, he's a good person. We were best friends once, when things were less complicated.

"What have you been up to?"

I don't want to do this right now. "The same thing. Running the new bar. I've been really busy setting everything up."

"Sounds like you need a vacation."

"I wish." I laugh.

"Well, that's why I'm calling, actually."

"Oh?" I say. "You're on vacation?"

He pauses. "No, not exactly… I… I wanted to know if you could get some time off."

I frown. "What for?" I don't like where this is headed.

"Stevie, I want to give things another try… with us." I pinch the bridge of my nose. "Have you changed your mind on marriage and kids and all the things you decided you don't want anymore?"

He sighs. "You don't have to say it like that. I know you deserve better, Stevie; someone who could give you all those things you deserve, and be home once in a while. I thought that wasn't me. I thought that by setting you free, it would mean we could move on."

A sadness falls over me. I've never protested about him being in the military. I was supportive of his career. But whenever the subject of marriage and the possibility of kids came up, it was like my words fell on deaf ears.

Somewhere in the six years of doing this, we've grown apart. What we want are two completely different things and it made sense when he ended things, as hard as it was, but I've accepted it. I was a coward. I never wanted to hurt him yet, somehow, I could never summon the courage to leave him first…

"What do you mean by *thought,* as in, past tense?" I ask, watching Axton and Brock on the monitor.

"Stevie. I've been going over things, and I think I may have made a terrible mistake," he says. "I don't know what I was even thinking…"

My hear hammers in my chest. "Lukas…"

"I need to see you."

I swallow hard, ready to throw something against the wall. "Lukas, you broke up with me over the phone. You can't just spring something like this on me, and then what? I jump on a plane, and everything is magically fixed?"

This man that I loved more than life threw me away after six years together without so much as a bon voyage card. He decided, not *us.*

He sounds distressed next when he says, "Please don't be like that. I know things have been a little off lately, and I take full responsibility for that. We've been in a bad place for so long."

"Lukas, let's just take some time out, all right? I think that's what's best. I really can't do this right now."

"Say you'll think about it, about seeing me."

I shake my head, knowing that's the last thing I want.

"That isn't going to happen. I can't get time off and, frankly, it's rude asking me to. I'm trying to move on, Lukas. It's what you said you wanted. I'm adjusting to life by myself in a different way now. Things are moving forward for me, and you have to understand that you can't just pop in and out of my life when it suits you."

"I'll come to you," he blurts out.

Panic rises in me.

I should want to face him, to be able to say the things I needed to say that day on the phone when he ended things. But now it just feels all wrong. I don't need closure like some people do. I just need to be left alone.

"Please do not do that, Lukas."

"Why not?" he stammers.

"Because, you could have done that months ago and you chose not to. I deserved a lot better than that, but coming here now, it won't solve anything. It'll only open up old wounds, for both of us."

I don't know why he's saying all of this, but it isn't what I need right now. He doesn't get to do this all over again.

"I'm sorry…"

"Listen, I have to go, okay? We'll talk later."

He sounds hopeful when he asks, "So you'll call me soon?"

No. "Yes, but I need to get my head around things."

"Take all the time you need," he says.

"I really have to go. Goodbye, Lukas."

"Bye, Stevie. Take care of yourself. Think about it."

I hang up and toss my phone on the desk.

Tears leak out of my eyes like traitors. That's the voice I loved for so long, the one that always knew how to calm me, to cheer me up when I was sad. But the simple fact is, he played a part in the demise of our relationship, so he can't just toss me to the curb, then show up again. I don't understand how things are going to change. By going on vacation?

I shake my head and realize I need to get out of here. I don't want to run into Axton like this, and the cold water has definitely been poured all over me.

I pass Rory in the hallway and ask him to tell Axton I'm going out to the cash and carry. Now seems like a better time than any to stock up on the bar snacks and clear my head.

Especially after what Axton just did to me in the hallway. I'm confused as fuck and need to decompress.

The only thing I feel toward Lukas is sadness.

When he came home the last few times, he was so distant and distracted, he didn't want to do anything or go anywhere. He didn't want to engage in our life together. I became the ghost in the relationship.

I get that his job is highly stressful and dangerous, but it was obvious to the both of us that the love in our relationship had died. There's nothing there. I knew it a long time ago. I fought for us, but it wasn't enough.

I don't break down until I get back in my truck, loaded with boxes of potato chips and bar nuts.

I cry in my car, my hands shaking as I let it all out.

Love fucking hurts. This much I know.

How can I still hurt for someone I don't even want? Yet, pine for another man I've only just met?

All I know is that Axton Altman liquifies my insides at the slightest look or touch. He does things to me that I shouldn't feel down in my very core, but I do.

I fucking do, and I've no idea what I'm going to do or how to stop this. I feel that we've already gone too far as it is.

I remember his growly words as he backed me up against the wall: *Can't fuckin' stay away from me, can you?*

He's got a filthy mouth and somewhere deep down inside me knows; I can't get enough of it.

The afternoon flies by, and I keep myself busy. We're still short-staffed, but that's nothing new.

After work, Roxy decides to serve fondue for all the

staff so we can take a load off and catch up, not that I feel like socializing. But as the manager, I guess I have to make it seem like I'm making an effort.

There's me, Rory, Emmaline, Roxy, Ginger – because we roped her into helping – Gears, who was on security, and Lily's friend, Katie, who is also helping out in the restaurant, and Axton.

I help Roxy bring out the two fondue pots as everyone chats and mingles in the restaurant.

I notice Axton is still at the bar, tidying up. I need to stop acting like a baby, take control of this situation, and start acting like a manager and not a sap.

"Hey, Axton, leave that till later, the fondue is getting cold," I say as he glances up from stacking up all the chairs. He's a workaholic, I'm starting to realize.

He gives me a chin lift. "Won't be long."

I watch as he continues to place all the chairs up on all the tables, ready for the cleaners in the morning. He's been quiet for the rest of the afternoon, almost like he's avoiding me as much as I am him. I know this nonsense has to stop.

"I don't know where Roxy comes up with these ideas," I go on, haphazardly trying to make conversation. "Fondue hasn't been in fashion since the seventies."

I hear him grunt a laugh. "I'm sure it's not the greatest thing for the waistline either, but you've got to live a little."

"Did you want a beer?" I ask, walking behind the bar to

grab myself one.

"Sure."

I grab two and knock the tops off, taking a long draw of mine as I hand him his over the counter.

His eyes meet mine as he's about to take a sip, and he frowns, halting just before the bottle hits his lips.

"What's wrong?" he asks.

I look at him, surprised. "Nothing."

"You've been crying."

My heart hammers in my chest. Mr. Fucking Observant.

"No, I just have allergies."

His forehead creases even more at my lie. "Did I upset you earlier?"

"No!" I whisper-shout. "This isn't about you, though we do need to talk about that."

"So you have been crying?"

"Drop it, Axton, please. I'm your boss."

"So what? Does that mean I can't ask you if you're okay, and if there's anything I can do?"

"No, it doesn't. But it's personal, and I'm fine, thank you. Let's drop it."

"Listen, I didn't mean to get rough with you back there." He goes on as my heart races, realizing that he does think it's about him. That I didn't like what he did.

Little does he know he's the only fucking thing in this place that makes me forget every shit thing that's going on in my life.

"You weren't, Ax, but we should talk about it..." I look over toward the partition that separates the bar from the restaurant. "Later."

"Your place or mine?" He smirks.

"Axton."

He holds up his palms. "I'm kidding. And you don't have to keep reminding me that you're my boss, I'm well aware of it."

"Really? So did you accost and growl at all of your former bosses?"

"My prison warden was a sixty-year-old man who resembled a sumo wrestler, so that's a no."

I want to be angry with him and lead us back to the fact that what we keep doing is wrong, but instead, I burst out laughing. He does too.

It's lovely when he smiles. It's all heart. My heart skips a beat as he watches me.

"Can you be serious for five minutes?"

He wipes his eyes. "You know, ever since I was a kid, I never liked people gettin' upset. Mom and Dad fought a lot when we were younger. Dad always made her cry, and when he was away on duty, she got sad all the time, so I'd try to do something, *anything,* to make her smile."

I imagine Axton as a little boy, blonde and blue-eyed, the apple of his Mom's eye, and I can't help but smile.

"What did you do?"

He shrugs. "Whatever I could. I once made her mac and cheese, which was a total disaster, so she didn't have to cook. Of course, Brock complained till the cows came home about how bad it was and refused to eat it, but Amelia was too little to care. Another time, I brought home some flowers I'd picked from a house down the street, only I got chased all the way down the block by the angry resident for stealing her prized roses."

I laugh harder, imagining him running away as fast as his legs would carry him with stolen flowers while being chased.

"Did you make it home with any flowers left?"

"Barely." He grins. "Mom loved them, of course. She always had that way of making you feel special. You knew you were loved when she looked at you."

I try not to wince. "How's it going now, with your parents?"

His eyes flick back to mine. "Mom came to see me the other night. It was good seeing her again. It was hard, but I'm glad she did. I miss her."

"And your dad?" I press.

He folds his arms over his chest, and I can tell it's obviously a sore spot. "I don't have a relationship with him at present. I'm hoping that will change."

I love how positive he is, even when things seem bleak

or can't be fixed. I wish I could be more like that.

"Does your dad still hold a grudge because of what happened?"

He nods. "I'm not deluding myself in thinking I was ever on Dad's radar, since that was always Brock. The first son. Good at everything, and he even won a football scholarship. He was the golden boy, and I looked up to him. He was a good brother growing up; we got along. But Dad and I have always been on the outs. When I got locked up, it was just another way for Dad to say 'see, I told you so, he's a bad kid.'"

I feel a lump in my throat. "That's awful, Ax."

"I don't need sympathy," he says. "But you asked, so that's how it is for me. I don't know if we will ever make amends, but Mom wants us to have dinner sometime soon. That's gonna be fuckin' hard."

"Just take it at your own pace," I say, giving him a smile. "You're a grown man now. If your dad can't see what an amazing, kind, and caring person you are, then it's his loss."

"That's nice of you to say, but I'm not always all of those things."

I shrug. "Who is? But you're a good person, that's plainly obvious. Your dad needs to take the stick out of his ass."

His lips twitch in that sexy way of his as I try not to

glance down at his mouth.

He purses his lips, but doesn't say anything, then takes a long draw of his beer as I watch him.

"What?" I say.

He shakes his head. "Nothin'."

"Axton."

He grins, taking another pull. "You're kinda cute when you're mad."

My eyes go wide, and before I get the chance to say anything, he adds, "*Boss.*"

"Axton! Stevie!" Roxy bellows as she sticks her head through the partition window. "Will you hurry the hell up? It's getting cold already!"

"Sorry!" I reply, giving Axton an eye roll that she doesn't see.

"Be right there," Axton drawls.

"She's so bossy," I grumble as soon as she disappears.

I turn to leave, and I feel Axton's hand on my shoulder as I step into the patron side of the bar.

I turn toward him.

"If anyone put those tears in your eyes, Stevie, I'll find out."

I feel my chest lurch. "What do you mean?"

"I'm protective, of the people I care about, that's what it means."

I swallow hard. "You don't need to do anything, it's

under control. It's nothing."

He stares at me with a ferocity that almost makes my blood curdle. He's so fucking hot.

"I'm not a man to be crossed, so whoever the schmuck is, he better stay away from you."

I literally have no words. I open my mouth and close it again as he removes his hand.

I should tell him that it isn't about a schmuck, even though it is. That he can't just say things like that or touch me. I'm not his girlfriend or anything close to it. But I soon realize, this is who Axton is. I like he's being more open with me, even if it is kinda personal.

I try not to notice how much he affects me. How much I like his towering, possessive presence, and how much I fucking need it. Not that I knew it until just now.

I can barely breathe when he's around.

Maybe I like his alpha side.

Maybe I like his possessiveness.

And I definitely like him touching me.

However, I pity anyone who does actually cross him. I know he meant the things he said. Axton doesn't seem to do anything half-assed.

"Let's go eat some fondue," I say when I can't think of anything else to divert the conversation. His intensity is too much.

One eyebrow raises, and I turn my back on him and

head to the restaurant. *Fleeing* would be a better term.

I know without even looking back that his eyes are on my ass, and I don't know if it's the primal reaction he projects, or the fact that I like him looking, but I sway my hips just that little bit more.

I'm dancing on the edge of the furnace, and where there's fire, someone is bound to get burned.

BRACKEN RIDGE
REBELS
ARIZONA
M · C

CHAPTER 15

AXTON

It's late as I toss my plate into the sink and yawn. I didn't eat much, after all. I've never been a big chocolate kind of person, but everyone had a good time and had a few laughs.

Stevie left before any of the others to get an early night, and I know it's because of what I said.

I don't give a shit.

I know some dickface made her cry and I'm gonna find out who it is and knock their fuckin' head off their shoulders. I run a hand through my hair and adjust my dick.

Just thinking about her… fuck, man, if I had a woman like Stevie, I'd never want for anything more for the rest of my life.

And I distinctly remember something in the back of my brain about her having a boyfriend… where the fuck is he?

I saunter back to bed, flicking channels, when I hear a faint knock at the door.

My heart lurches at the sound as I jump up and toss the remote behind me.

Sure enough. Out on the landing, dressed in an oversized hoodie with her hair tied back in a long ponytail is the woman of my fantasies.

I crack the door open.

"Did anyone ever tell you not to open the door late at night?" she asks as I rest one arm on the door frame and give her a chin lift.

"Did anyone ever tell you that it's dangerous to go knocking on the doors of strange men?"

She bites her bottom lip. "You're not strange." Then with a quirk of her brow, she adds, "Are you?"

I shake it off. "What's up?"

"I... I couldn't sleep..."

Fuck, she looks cute in pajama bottoms and a hoodie. This is also the first time I've seen her without makeup on, not that she wears very much to begin with, but her skin is slightly pink and so damn pretty. She has the clearest complexion and a very small smattering of freckles on her cheeks that I haven't noticed before.

"Were you after a nightcap?" I cock an eyebrow, and she fiddles with her fingers nervously.

I've never seen her like this. "Can I come in?"

"Of course."

I pull back the door wider, noticing her eyes flick down my body as she takes in my bare chest and my boxer briefs. She's lucky I didn't answer the door naked...

"Are you a night owl?" she asks as I close the door.

I'm so fucking aware of her presence in this small space that it almost overwhelms me.

"Yup, always have been."

We stand toe to toe as I palm the back of my head. She keeps her eyes firmly on mine, though I know she just checked me out again.

"I'm sorry to come barging in here like this…"

"You can barge in on me anytime," I say, then add, "What's up?"

She looks down at her feet. "I don't even know what I'm doing here."

I cock a brow. "Really?"

Her eyes shoot to mine. "What do you mean?"

"I think I know."

Her eyes dilate a little. "You do?"

I'm not going to touch her. She has to want this as much as I do, and I think she does… what else would she be doing here in the middle of the night?

I nod, folding my arms over my chest. "It's not wrong, to give your body what it needs, Stevie, but I need to know."

"What?" she whispers.

"Don't you have a boyfriend?"

She shakes her head. "Not anymore."

"Was he the one who upset you?"

She breathes in and out slowly, reluctant to answer,

then, "Yes."

I feel a strange amount of possessiveness over this woman I barely know. But hearing she hasn't got an old man is music to my ears.

She bites her lip, and this time, I can't resist. I reach over and pull her lip free.

"The next time you do that, I'm gonna sink my teeth into you instead."

She visibly swallows as I try hard not to grin.

"You hear me?" I add when she says nothing.

She nods. "I… I can't stop thinking about the hallway."

"What part?" I've got all night and she's not going anywhere.

"The part where you said it'd be worth the punishment to fuck me."

I glance at her mouth. "Your dirty little mouth does things to me, boss. I don't know if I can take much more."

She watches me intensely, then says, "I mean, nobody has to know… right?"

This time, I don't hold back my grin. "I'm not gonna tell if you don't."

She watches me as I reach to her and free her ponytail with one hand, letting her long, golden hair flow down past her shoulders. "You're so fuckin' beautiful," I say.

She swallows again. "I need your touch, Ax," she whispers, her eyes closing. "I need it like I need air."

She reaches out and I catch her hand, planting it on my chest. "You feel that, Stevie?"

She nods.

"You feel that heart beating hard in my chest? That's for you, because of what you do to me. Because I can't stop thinkin' about you too, because I've been jerking off imagining it's you doin' it to me. What do you think about that?"

Her eyes leave mine and wander down my body, as does her hand. She feels my chest, my abs and then she goes lower. My dick twitches in anticipation. I want her to touch it.

I want her to squeeze my cock and rub the fuck out of it.

She hesitates, then she cups me, and I groan, my eyes still on hers.

She breathes hard and fast as she fondles me, her hand stroking and squeezing, my cock getting harder and thicker at every touch and every second that passes that I'm not inside her.

I hiss when she cups my balls. "Fuck."

"Axton," she whispers.

"Yeah, babe?"

She slides her hand under the elastic of my briefs and grips my cock in her hand. "Shit," she whispers again. "So big."

A smile creeps on my face as I yank my boxers down,

my erection springing free.

She stares down at it, her mouth open as I revel in the shock on her face.

Yeah, I know, but seeing her face like that just adds to my satisfaction.

"Love you touchin' me, Stevie."

She grips harder, and I pull her closer. Sheathing me, I watch her fascination as she tugs on my cock and precum leaks out of my tip. I don't think I've been this fuckin' hard for a woman. In fact, I know I haven't. Even in prison, when all I had were my fantasies and the dream that one day I'd get to do it again.

"Pull your top off," I tell her. "Wanna see your tits." She closes her eyes for a second and then does as I ask.

My eyes lower as I see her naked breasts for the first time. And they're fuckin' glorious.

While not big, they're perky and round, her nipples dark and peaking, perfect for suckling. I reach out and cup them, tweaking her nipples with my thumbs as she swears in a low whisper, a flush of red creeping up her neck.

Her hand jerking on my cock quickens. I don't wanna come this fast, but seeing her tits and her enjoying my touch, I almost lose it. I can't actually believe she came to me.

I lean down and squeeze one breast and suck on her nipple. She cries out, her free hand snaking into my hair as she grips it tight. The movement goes straight to my balls.

Sucking harder, I pluck at the other nipple with my fingers as she slithers around, groaning when I step one knee between her legs so she can have some friction. While I want to touch her pussy again, I know I want to enjoy this first and take my time. I ain't goin' nowhere.

I move to her other nipple as she continues to pull on my dick, then trail one hand down to hers to help her slow it down.

"Don't wanna come yet," I breathe as I move my mouth up to hers and we kiss, long and passionate, our tongues colliding as she mewls at my touch.

She's so sweet. I'm in awe of her, and I can't wait to taste the rest of her.

I bite down on her bottom lip and pull it. "Fuckin' love this dirty mouth."

"Axton," she cries out, rubbing herself harder against my knee as I smile and move my mouth to her neck. I bite down softly. I don't care if I leave a mark. In fact, I hope I do.

"Such pretty skin. I wanna mark you all over, Stevie. Fuck, that feels so good."

She murmurs something, and I watch as she sinks down to her knees and pulls my boxers all the way down so I can kick them off. She sheaths my cock a couple of times, then takes the tip into her mouth.

I just about blow my load as she begins to suck me like

a lollipop. I can't even believe my eyes; I feel like rubbing them just to make sure I'm not dreaming.

"Oh, fuck," I groan as her other hand cups my balls and she squeezes my dick, sinking her mouth down on me farther.

I've had a couple of blowjobs before, but her mouth on me is like wildfire in my blood.

Seeing her pretty lips wrapped around me, takin' me deep, it makes me wanna blow right down her throat. And I just might…

"This cock is so fucking big and hard. You taste so good," I hear her say as my eyes snap open.

"I need it, Axton. I need you."

I lift her up as she wraps around my body, and I plunge my tongue into her mouth as she squeals.

"Fuckin' turning me on so bad, Stevie," I growl, striding toward the bed as she clings onto me.

"Tell me what you want."

"Your mouth on me," she says. "Do dirty things to me with that mouth."

"I better put you on your back, then."

Jesus I'm really gonna fuckin' do this.

I plop her down on the bed as I drag her PJ pants off and stare down at her bare pussy. I run a hand through her folds as she moans, cupping her tits as she watches me.

I've never gone down on a chick before, but I'm so

fuckin' down for her being my first.

I drop to my knees and pull her ass to the edge of the bed. "Spread your legs," I tell her. "Sit up on your hands so you can watch me."

She does as I say as I circle her clit with my thumb, and she moans for me.

"I need it," she whispers. "Please Axton… please…"

"I knew you'd be beggin' me," I mutter, fascinated with her pussy.

I spread her apart with one hand and run my fingers through her crease. She's so slippery that I contemplate just sliding right in her and fucking her senseless, but she's told me what she wants, and I want to give it to her.

I lean down and run my tongue through her pussy as she bucks into my face. She tries to close her legs, but I push them back apart.

"You taste so fuckin' good," I tell her as I do it again, tonguing her clit as she tries to rub against me. "Be a good girl, and I might let you come."

My brain spins as I insert a finger, and she cries out again, begging me for more. I spread her again and suck her clit, my eyes moving up to watch her as she squeezes her eyes closed and jerks at the same time.

I wonder if my beard feels good or bad, but just as I wonder, she grips one hand in my hair and says, "You've no idea how good that feels, Ax."

I know she's close. I insert two fingers and begin to fuck her slowly with them, all the while I tug on her clit, sucking and licking until she begins humping my face as I give it to her. I curl my fingers deep inside as I stroke, and she climaxes so fucking loud she could wake the dead. It goes on and on as she clutches my head, and I continue to let her come undone until she releases me.

I let go of her clit and remove my fingers. "Eyes open," I tell her as her gaze snaps to mine.

I stick my fingers in my mouth and suck. "So fuckin' good," I tell her as my other hand rubs her back and forth, spreading all of her juices so I can prepare her for my cock. It's leaking so much that I know this won't be as slow as I'd have liked.

"Inside me," she gasps. "Now."

I chuckle, stepping back to find my wallet as I roll on a rubber. She watches me as I make light work of it, stroking myself as she scoots back up the bed. I tower over her, crawling on top as I take her legs in each hand and wrap them around my waist.

I hold my cock and rub the tip through her pussy, her nails digging into my back as her green eyes stare back at me.

"Tell me you want it."

"I fucking want it. Give it to me," she whispers.

I chuckle again as I lower my cock to her entrance and

push the tip in slightly. She gasps at the intrusion, and I groan at how tight she is. It's fucking glorious. I run my hands up the sides of her body, skimming over her tits, and reaching up to hold her hands above her head, then I thrust inside.

As I sink in, I almost lose it over how tight she is. How her body responds to me is so fuckin' gratifying.

The sound she makes as I settle deep inside her is like a siren's call, and it speaks to me on another level.

When I've been with other women, it was nothing like this. Of that, I'm sure.

It was just sex, a means to an end.

This feels like I may actually explode if I don't come soon, yet I want to make it last.

I pull out and slam back in again as she jolts forward. I like fucking hard, but I could do her hard, soft, slow, upside down, as long as I get to feel her body and be the one making her lose control.

I like Stevie like this, enjoying it, no worry or upset on her face, just pure bliss. It's a far-cry from earlier in the day when I knew she'd been crying. I still want to get to the bottom of that, but for the moment… I roll my hips back and forth as I slowly slide in and out of her.

I make sure she feels every fucking inch of me, and if I'm too much, she doesn't say it.

Instead, she goes between closing her eyes tightly and

opening them to stare at me in awe.

Her mouth opens to a perfect *oh,* as I fuck her good and slow.

"You like my cock inside you, boss?" I grunt, holding my body weight off her so I can see all of her and gain traction at the same time.

She grips my ass, encouraging me as I pick up the pace just a little bit. "Oh God, yes," she cries. "Just like that, just there, oh, Ax…"

I grind down harder, riding her through another orgasm as I watch her face. She calls my name over and over as I drive it home. Knowing I'm not gonna last, I slow the pace after she's done and roll onto my back, flipping us over. *Oh yeah, now we're talking.*

There's nothing sweeter than a hot woman riding you. I sit up and kiss her, my hands clutching her face as our tongues meet, and she clutches my biceps, giving them a squeeze.

It's safe to say I think she likes my body. Or maybe it's just my cock, but it doesn't matter. I'll take what she's giving.

"Ride me," I tell her in between kisses. I give her ass a squeeze as she rests her hands on my shoulders, and I sit back to watch the show.

My eyes dip to her tits and I reach for them, cupping them, lifting and pushing them together while my thumb brushes over her taut nipples.

She moves back and forth, sliding her wetness all over my dick. I'm buried so deep, I'm right on the brink… I want to last longer, but my fuckin' boss is ridin' me hard right now, and I've never been so fascinated.

I slide one hand to her neck and hold it there. Her hand runs up my arm affectionately, and I can't be certain, but I think she likes the kink.

"There's so many things I want to do with your body, babe," I mutter, watching how her body moves, how well she takes me.

"It's yours," she whispers as I grin, gliding my hands to her hips as I move her up and down.

I curse every bad word I know as I thrust up into her. We fuck furiously, harder, faster as I sit up and whisper in her ear, "Come for me. Let me hear you tell me how much you love it."

She loses control again, and I bite down on her shoulder as she convulses, squeezing my dick with her tight, beautiful cunt, and then I lose it too. I shoot my load, groaning as my release blurs my vision, and I keep pumping until I'm spent.

We're both covered in sweat as I flop back down onto the pillows, taking her with me.

"Jesus, that was…" She trails off.

She lays on my chest as I wrap my arms around her.

"That was what?"

We're both panting, and I can still feel my dick throbbing for more of her.

"Fucking great," she says as I chuckle.

"Had me worried there for a minute."

"There's nothing to be worried about where that monster is concerned."

I lick my bottom lip. "Is that so?"

"Yes."

"Monster, huh?"

She yawns sleepily. "Uh huh."

"I think I like the sound of that."

"I've missed it," she whispers, so faint I barely hear it. "Sex."

I frown, remembering her mentioning this before. "How long did you say it's been?"

"Ten months."

"No shit."

She buries her face into my shoulder. "My ex... he was the last guy..."

She's not been with any other man in ten months?

I kiss her hair. "I'm sorry you were upset."

"He called me," she whispers.

I run a hand down her back, I don't ask her anything, I figure if she wants to tell me something, she will.

Then a few moments later, she says, "He wants to get

back together."

My body stiffens. I know I've only known her for a short time, but I'm damn fuckin' sure that I don't want that to happen.

"How do you feel about that?"

She sighs deeply. "It's over, Axton. It was over a long time ago. He wanted out, I let him go, and it was traumatic and painful, but in the end, the passion was gone between us. We were more like long-distance roommates. Relationships are hard. I gotta tell you, you're not missing out on much." She yawns again.

"You want to fall asleep with my cock still in you?" I ask, loving how warm she is. I've also never slept a night with a woman in my bed.

She giggles. "Maybe?"

I grunt a laugh.

I don't think I've felt happiness like this in a long time, and fuck knows how I've dreamed of falling asleep with a beautiful woman wrapped around me.

We're far from done.

Little does Stevie Hart know, I'm only just beginning.

BRACKEN RIDGE
REBELS
ARIZONA
M · C

CHAPTER 16

STEVIE

Axton rolls his hips back and forth, in and out as I run my hands over his big, solid shoulders. This is how it's been all night. I fell asleep for a while, then woke up to him playing with my body all over again.

"Mmmm," I murmur as he spreads his legs wider, hitching my ass up slightly so he can go deeper. "That feels so good."

Just when I thought I was all closed up for business, Axton provides me with more orgasms than I've had in a year.

He looks down at me as I stare back up at him, both of us spent, both of us wanting more at the same time.

A smile creeps on my face as he rolls those hips just so, brushing my clit with his pubic bone as I come again for what might be the hundredth time…

"That's it, babe, takin' me so good," he whispers in my ear.

I groan, throwing one arm over my eyes, the other

gripping the sheets as my pussy clenches. I feel every single inch of him as I melt farther into the mattress.

He doesn't let up. He just keeps rolling those hips as the bed squeaks slightly at every thrust.

"Axton?" I say, from behind my arm.

He pants. "Yeah, boss."

God, I love it when he calls me that…

"How are we ever gonna keep our hands off one another?"

He grunts a laugh. "Tryin' to fuck you here, babe, and you should be watchin' me."

I remove my arm. "I can't."

He chuckles. "You can't?"

"It's too much."

He reaches down and kisses me. His beard feels so fucking right against my skin.

Remembering him between my legs is a highlight I'll keep in my brain forever. The way he tickled my skin… shit, I could let him eat me out forever, and this… this is just sweet torture.

"Why you smilin'?" he grunts a few moments later.

I run my hands up his body, past his pecs, tracing the tattoos scattered all over his chest.

He's a fine specimen of a man, solid, hard and warm.

"I was just remembering your amazing oral skills."

He grunts, reaching a hand down to squeeze my

breast. "Yeah?"

"Oh, yeah."

"Would you be surprised to know that it was my first time?"

My eyes snap open. "W... what?" I stammer.

He smirks, then quickens his thrusting, making me forget my own name as he reaches up to the headboard and grips it. "Wrap your legs around me," he says.

I do so and he moves up to his knees. It's so deep, hitting my core with every thrust. My tits sway as he pumps in and out of me.

"Damn," I mumble. "So good..."

He chuckles. "You should see from this angle." His eyes dip down to where we're joined, and he groans. "That sweet little pussy takes everything I've got."

"This sweet little pussy is gonna be sore tomorrow," I pant as I throw my head back and come like there's no tomorrow.

Axton quickens, grinding his hips hard against me. "I'm gonna come," he grits out.

And he does, in all his glory, as I watch him unfold, his cock jerking inside me as he empties himself.

It's such an incredible sight, watching Axton come undone.

He collapses on top of me, panting hard like he's run a marathon. "I don't know about work, boss, but I could keep this up full time."

I slap his ass. "I wouldn't complain."

He chuckles again, lifting off me as he pulls out and rolls onto his back. We both sigh at the same time as we stare at the ceiling. He disposes of the condom quickly in the trash before coming back to bed.

"Let's get back to that first time thing… when you went down on me," I say.

He puts one arm over his eye. "I shouldn't have said anythin'"

"Why not?"

"It's kinda embarrassing."

"I don't think so. In fact, I kinda dig it."

He turns to peek at me through his arm. "You might not believe this, but I didn't have that much experience with girls before I got locked up. I was too busy partying and taking drugs to care too much."

I run a hand through his messy hair. "I'm sure you made up for it once you got out."

He shakes his head. "Not really. Only got with one chick, and I didn't go down on her."

I frown, not because of the chick. I get it; he's been in jail for ten years, so I can't expect him to be a saint. Even if I don't like the idea, and I definitely don't want to know who it is.

I want to ask why he didn't, what makes me so special,

then his clear blue eyes flick to mine, and he says, "With you, it feels different."

My heart lurches. "Axton."

He chuckles. "Don't worry, I know my place."

I cup his cheek. "You're a sweet man, Ax, but you know this is just sex, right? We can't be anything more."

Something crosses his eyes as he nods. "Yes, of course. I'm not stupid."

"How will we hide it?"

"I don't know, but I've gotta make a point to stop staring at your ass."

"That'd be a good start."

He laughs, but something's changed in his eyes. I hope I didn't offend him by saying we can't be more, but we can't. I mean, it's not like we want people to know… right?

The other staff, for one. It's definitely not a good look.

He brushes a hand over my hair as he caresses my face. "I like how you're makin' out this isn't over yet."

I blink a couple of times. "I'm not gonna state the obvious."

"What? That we shouldn't?"

"These things rarely end well."

"Why? If the sex is good, and I'm a good boy at work and do whatever you say." He smirks.

"Then maybe you'll reward me again."

I like the sounds of that more than I should. "You're a

bad influence."

"Hey, I'm the employee. I've still got my training wheels on."

I laugh out loud. "Shit, Ax, if that was training wheels, then I'm pretty sure I'm screwed."

He leans over and kisses my forehead. "Spoken like a true queen."

I shake my head and I'm about to get up and get dressed, when he presses an arm across my chest. "Where do you think you're going?"

"Uh, back to my apartment."

He shakes his head. "Nah, I don't think so."

"Are you holding me here against my will?" I muse.

"No, but I'd like to."

He kisses me again, then ever so softly, I hear him say, "Stay."

My heart lurches at how sweet he is.

In all honesty, he's a conundrum. On the one hand, he's this big, larger than life tattooed man, with a dirty mouth and very rough hands, who fucks all night long. Then on the other, he's sweet, thoughtful, and endearing, touching me softly and making sure I'm okay.

I know he's obviously had sex before, but knowing I was his first oral partner, still thrills me. But, I don't want to think about those that came before me, and I'm terrified to ask if there'll be any more.

I can't do that because he'll read more into it, and if that happens, I'm in a whole world of fucked up.

It's better if this stays casual.

I snuggle back under the covers as he spoons me against his naked body.

"Okay," I whisper.

He kisses my hair again, and it's the last thing I remember before falling back asleep.

"The figures are excellent, Stevie. I'm really impressed with your hard work, keepin' the team together, and the doors open with all the staff shortages and people bein' sick," Hutch says as I sit across from him in his office.

I don't come to church as much as I used to, and I've never been in his office before.

It's exactly what you'd expect from a MC President.

He sits behind a large, solid mahogany desk with a closed laptop. Bottles of bourbon line the wall behind him. He has a small fridge to one side, along with a printer and photocopier and some cabinets. And memorabilia all across the walls, from Harley Davidson banners to signed Metallica concert posters. It suits him.

Hutch himself is a dominant figure, and if you didn't know he was the leader of the Rebels MC you'd certainly get out of his way, regardless.

He wears a bandanna around his forehead, with his long hair tied back. He has a handsome face. His beard is graying, but he has a charisma about him that screams silver fox. And those deep blue, penetrating eyes. It's like a school principal when they ask you a question and you can't lie to them. He'd see right through it.

"Thanks, Richie, that's awfully nice of you to say."

I can't call him Hutch because it seems very informal, yet he's asked me repeatedly not to call him Mr. Hutchinson, so I just call him by his first name and that seems to go down okay.

"You've done all the hard work."

"Not just me. You and the boys got the place revamped in a short space of time. It's amazing what new paint and flooring can do."

He watches me, rubbing his chin. "How's the new chef?"

"She's brilliant. I'm sure I've put on at least five pounds since she arrived. One of the perks of the job is testing the new creations."

He gives me a chin lift. "And Axton?"

I swallow hard and keep his gaze. "He's fantastic. I haven't got a bad word to say about him."

"He's been pullin' his weight?"

I nod. "He's very efficient, learns fast, and doesn't cause any trouble." *And he fucks like a maniac.* "I am a little worried, though."

"Oh?"

"He's always at work. We only give him one day off, so I was wondering if you'd extend that to two days. Sometimes he's working twelve hours and rarely takes a break."

"I suppose," he says. "If you're worried about it."

"I just don't want him to burn out. The job is demanding, and you are on your feet all day."

He nods slowly, giving it some thought. "I suppose we could ease up on the hours. It'd give him more time to get his prospect duties done."

It's not like I want to get involved in club business, but I can't help myself when I say, "And I know he's keen to start taking some practical training for his electrician's license. It could be a good opportunity for him to use one of those days for that, instead of being behind the bar."

I wonder if the man can read minds because he assesses me with watchful eyes.

He's not, I tell myself. *This is how Hutch is, stop reading into it...*

If he could read minds, he'd see that I reluctantly dragged myself out of Axton's bed this morning, to which he then promptly dragged me into his tiny shower, and we ended up having sex again with me pushed up against the tiles. I'm thoroughly exhausted. The man's insatiable.

I wonder if Hutch thinks I'm telling him what to do, but instead, he says, "I'll have to think about it, see if we can put him to better use. But I'm glad to hear he's toeing the line. There'll be some paperwork from Kennedy to sign off on for his parole officer."

I nod. "No problem."

"Everything else okay?"

"Yes, I have a couple of interviews lined up this week. Hopefully, we can get some more staff on board. The Sunday smorgasbord is a huge success, and we're thinking of doing an all-you-can-eat mid-week to try and get some more customers in when it's quieter."

"You know you have my full support, Stevie."

I smile. "Thanks, I'm really happy here."

"You get stuck this week, let me know, and I can send Jax along with Gears to help clear shit up, wait tables, whatever."

"That'd be great. Gears has been doing security detail on the weekends, and he's not half bad."

"Long as he's actually doing something and not leering at the ladies all night."

I stifle a laugh. "No, I think with Steel and Brock hanging around from time to time keeps him on his toes."

"Glad to hear it."

"I also heard back from the art society and they're happy with the quote I gave them for the three course meal, which means in two weeks, we'll be hosting the annual Art Society dinner at the Stone Crow."

Hutch doesn't grin a lot, but when he does, the whole world lights up.

"Maybe I should've knocked down a few more walls and built a bigger restaurant." He smirks.

"Well, having the folding doors certainly helps." We can open the bar area right up to fit more tables in, just like we did for the charity auction a few weeks ago.

I'm thinking about entering a piece of art anonymously for the private auction. The art society does some good work for the community through helping young people get back on their feet, offering their building for women's refuge meetings, and a few times a year, they do a drop-in donation day.

"I'll look forward to seeing what Roxy has planned for it," he says.

"Don't worry, she's already working on the menu, as we speak."

His eyes crinkle. "I don't doubt it. The rate this is going, we could definitely expand to takeaways, but we'd need to find another venue and a decent cook."

"Well, Gears helped Roxy out a few times in the kitchen without any fuss," I say. Not that I should probably be telling him that, since Gears is a prospect and not really supposed to be in the kitchen. "He could certainly do more, if given the opportunity."

"It seems a shame to waste him," Hutch agrees. "But until he's patched in, he can't run anything by himself. I'll keep it in mind, though."

One thing Bracken Ridge needs is a decent takeaway. The burgers and fish and chips around town are disgusting and there's no large franchise to compete with.

We may have to be a littler pricier on some things, but people would pay to get a decent burger.

"I'll let you know once Roxy has the menu and run any new staff by you before I employ them," I say.

He gives me another chin lift. "Thanks, Stevie. I struck gold when I found you. You need anything, just let me know."

"Thanks, Richie. I'll see myself out."

I stand and leave the room, closing the door behind me.

I'm always a little nervous whenever I have to meet with Hutch because while he's nice to me and always gives me praise, he's also slightly intimidating.

But I'm feeling like I've got a spring in my step as I head out to my truck. As I'm passing by, one of the car doors opens in the lot, and one of the girls who hangs around the club— a sweet butt, as the boys call them — turns to look at me.

"Hey, Stevie, right?" she says.

"Yeah?" I reply, warily.

"Hi, I'm Bambi." She sticks her hand out, and I awkwardly shake it.

She seems nice enough, but I've no idea what she's doing here, since the club's quiet during the day. Then she clears it up. "I'm here to clean the clubhouse. Those boys are messy fuckers, and I get all the shitty jobs because I'm new around here."

"Oh," I reply. "Nice to meet you."

"Hey you work with Axton, right?"

My heart rate kicks up several notches. "Yeah, he works for me at the Stone Crow."

She does this little pout thing that immediately gets under my skin. "Well, can you give him a message?"

"Sure." *Because I'm his personal beck-and-call girl.*

"He hasn't called me back."

What a tragedy.

I feel like saying, "Maybe there's a reason for that?" but that would be needlessly catty.

"Is that the message?" I ask, fishing my car keys out of my purse.

"No, I need some dick, specifically his."

My eyes go wide, and as they meet hers, she has a smug smile on her face.

So, this is the chick?

My stomach lurches imagining them together. I wish I could bleach my brain.

I find myself asking, "Did you guys hook up?"

She shrugs. "Couple of times. When he first got out, fucked me good, but now there's crickets chirping."

My stomach literally rolls. "How nice for you, but since he's my employee, I think it would be highly inappropriate to deliver that message."

That's like the pot calling the kettle black.

She turns to look at me sharply. "Well, I have to get to him before Chelsea does."

"Chelsea?"

"Ugh, I know, right?"

I blink a couple of times in confusion, but she's already stalking off toward the clubhouse doors, her ass hanging out of her short shorts.

Bambi. Chelsea. How nice for him that he has a legion of followers. My jealousy swirls.

I've no claim over him just because we spent one night together, obviously, but I'd be lying if I said I didn't feel a little jealous, and stupid.

Stupid to think that he isn't just playing with me to get another notch on his belt, to brag that he'd bagged the boss lady.

Stupid to believe that I thought he felt something more from me, that it wasn't just about sex.

What a fool.

All for the cheap thrill of having him in my bed, or in

this case, *his bed.*

My skin prickles as I rub the sides of my arms. Maybe I've made a mistake.

She's rattled me, without even knowing it.

BRACKEN RIDGE
REBELS
ARIZONA
M · C

CHAPTER 17

AXTON

I try not to notice every single little thing Stevie does, but that's nearly impossible.

The woman's in my line of sight every goddamn second as we work the bar together.

It's busy tonight because the local darts team has moved over from their derelict clubhouse to hold their meetings here, and it just so happens that it's burger night. The entire bar and restaurant are hopping.

Stevie's been unusually quiet, as if she's purposely ignoring me, or maybe I'm just imagining it?

She managed to conduct a couple of interviews this afternoon, so hopefully soon, we'll have some more staff on board to lighten the load. One thing's for sure, I've never worked this fuckin' much in my entire life.

Later on, while I shove a burger down my throat out back, I manage to catch Stevie on her own. I snag her by the elbow as she walks past.

"Shit, Axton!" she squeals, pushing against my chest.

I grin, pulling her to me. "Alone, at last."

She wriggles away from me as I watch in amusement. I know it's because she doesn't want anyone to see us, and I should be grateful for that; however, another part of me wonders if it's because she's ashamed and not because I'm her employee.

"Axton, what are you doing out here, in the dark?"

I hold up my burger. "Eating."

She shakes her head. "You can take a proper break, you know. You don't have to lurk out here, scaring me half to death."

"I know what I'd rather be eating and where I'd rather be lurking."

Her eyes narrow, and it's then I realize she might actually be serious.

I step back. "Are we okay?"

"Of course," she says, smiling. *Uh oh.* "Why wouldn't we be?"

"Because you've been avoiding me all night."

"No, I haven't. I've been busy doing my job."

I rub my chin. "Uh huh."

"Well, I've got to get back." She goes to leave, then over her shoulder, she says, "Oh, Bambi says hi, by the way, and Chelsea wants you to call her ASAP."

My eyes go wide as I toss my burger on the hallway table and snag her backwards.

My hands on her shoulders, and reaching down, I whisper in her ear, "Are you jealous?"

She tries to wriggle free, but I grip her harder. "Don't be absurd."

A sick smile crosses my lips. "You are, aren't you?"

"Apparently you fucked her good, and she needs your cock," she blurts out.

I bite my bottom lip. *Shit.*

"You've no reason to be jealous, she was just a chick I banged when I first got out. I told you that," I say in her ear.

"I'm not jealous," she repeats.

"Really? Kinda seems like it."

"I need to get back out front."

"So you're pissed at me because I got my dick wet after gettin' out of the joint? Before I even knew you? Seems a little harsh."

"I'm not pissed."

"Really?" I reach a hand down to her ass and give it a squeeze. "So you don't mind if I do this?"

"Axton…" She tries to swat my hand away.

I run a hand over her breast and give one a squeeze. "Or this?"

She groans, and I reach down and cup her pussy through her jeans. "What about this?"

"Ax, we're at work."

"Let's go into your office."

"We can't," she pants, her chest heaving.

"We can. I'm on break, and you're the boss."

"You don't get to fuck me when I'm pissed at you."

"Ah, so you are pissed?" I begin to creep my hand down the front of her jeans as she, once again, begins to push me back with her ass. "Why?"

"Because I'm stupid, all right?"

I stop my ministrations. "Why would you say that?"

"Because I don't exactly relish in being another notch on your belt, but that's on me. I'm the one who came to you and practically begged you for it."

"You're actually serious with this shit?" I say, spinning her around. "For one, I never thought for a second you were just another notch on my belt. I also didn't realize I wasn't allowed to have a past."

"A past?" She snorts. "This was last week. And it's fine, whatever. I just don't like being anyone's sloppy seconds, that's all."

Our eyes lock, and I stare at her, confused. I've never treated her like that, and I don't know what to say or do. I don't have the capacity to understand women and their moods, though this one seems fairly obvious. She's jealous, but it's for no good reason.

She stalks off, and I let her, staring after her in disbelief. *What the fuck just happened?*

I don't know what this pain is in my chest, but it feels

like a truck slammed into me.

Sloppy seconds?

I haven't even been with another woman since I started to have feelings for Stevie. That's how things used to work when I was a kid, or so I thought. I guess I really have been away too long.

Running a hand through my hair, I ditch my burger in the bin and get back to work. I bypass behind the bar and tell Rory I'm going to clear glasses and make myself useful anywhere else but here.

I see her in my periphery, watching me, but I don't turn. I just keep my mask in place as I continue to keep my head down.

I don't actually know what to fuckin' say, and I feel like she's way off base.

When I'm done with the glasses, I go make a nuisance of myself in the restaurant. I hate waiting tables, so I help clear instead. After that, I take the trash out.

I haul a couple of bags and slam it into the dumpster.

When I turn, something hits me square in the face, and I stumble backwards. A blow comes from the other side as I hold my hands up to protect my face.

I'm being fuckin' jumped.

Out of all the places I thought I'd ever be in fuckin' trouble, I didn't plan on it being in Bracken Ridge, at the back of the local pub while putting out the trash.

I immediately get my bearings, and as another blow comes at me, I block it.

I don't think, I just punch. There're at least two, and the one in front goes down, then another blow comes at my back, and I just about pass out. I get hit again to the back of the legs, falling to one knee; some fucker is beating me with a crowbar.

Bent over, I run at him and knock him over, pummeling him as hard as I can while hoping there isn't anyone else about to hit me over the fuckin' head.

I overturn him, but it doesn't last long, the fucker behind me recovers, and I dodge another blow, the crowbar hitting me in the arm as I cry out.

"Should've taken the deal with Little Mick," one of the guys says as he wipes his bloody nose. "This all could've been avoided."

I look behind him and see another guy, spinning a chain around as he comes toward me.

They have backup. *Fuck.*

Where's my brother when I need him? I could take two, but I doubt three, with weapons.

The dude swings again, and I punch him hard. He drops like a sack of potatoes, and I grab the crowbar, though I've only got one arm now and I can feel the side of my face swelling.

I'll go down swinging, of that, they can be sure.

"You can tell Little Mick to go fuck himself," I spit. "Is that fuckin' clear?"

The guy snorts.

"Axton?" I hear Stevie cry from the doorway. Then she sees what's going on. "Axton!"

"Get back inside! Now!" I yell at her.

Luckily, she's smart and does as I say. I hope like fuck she's gone to get backup because I'm a dead man if she doesn't.

"Once a con, always a con," the guy with the chains says. "Should've stayed where you were inside, would've been a whole lot safer. I think I'm gonna enjoy fuckin' you up. Why Mick said to keep you breathin', I'll never know."

"Fuck you!"

"Hurry the fuck up." The other guy grimaces as he circles me. "That bitch has gone to get help. We don't have long."

"We need him conscious," chain guy replies, his eyes never leaving mine. "Unfortunately."

The guy to my right lunges again, and I swing with all my might, clocking him in the ribs as he cries out, doubling over. I land a swift kick to his head, and he falls backwards.

A blow comes from behind, and I clock him at the same time he does me.

A moment later, I hear the back door swing open.

"What the fuck?" Brock roars.

Thank fuck.

"Hurry!" chain guy spits, taking off for the gate. "We're outta fuckin' time!"

They drag the fucker I kicked with them and make it to the gate as Brock and Nitro get to me.

"They're getting' away!" I bellow.

The gate slams, and by the time Brock and Nitro get over to it, they've secured it shut.

"Fuck!" Brock shouts. "I'll find you fuckers! You're dead, you hear me? Fuckin' dead!"

Nitro grabs Brock's arm to save him from probably mounting the wall and taking off after them.

I'm back on my feet by the time they reach me. Nitro picks up the crowbar from the ground as Brock hauls me to my feet, holding me up.

"Should've brought my gun," Nitro mutters.

"What the fuck happened?" Brock barks.

"Got jumped."

"Can see that. The question is why. Who were they?" Brock asks, anger in his eyes.

I have a split second to decide whether to come clean or to lie. But I know I can't do that.

I hang onto my arm, knowing that something's broken. "They were sent by an inmate I did time with," I say. "To fuck me up after I didn't wanna get involved with Little Mick."

Nitro and Brock's eyes meet, and I grimace through the pain.

"The dude from the bar the other night?" Nitro asks as they help me to my feet.

"He hit me up a few days ago," I begin as Brock helps me to the back door. "Said I owed him, wanted me to do a job for him. When I refused, he got pissed about it, then tried to hit me up again out back a few nights ago, but he was alone. I punched him and told him to fuck off and not come back, and now this happens."

"Now he sends the rest of his posse over to jump you." Nitro shakes his head. "Dog move in my book."

"Do you know who any of them are?" Brock continues, rage in his eyes.

I shake my head.

A few moments later, Stevie comes running out, almost barreling into me. "Axton!" she cries.

When she gets to me, she touches my bloodied face, then my hands, like she's unsure which part of me is broken, if any. Little does she know, I fight well, even when hit with a fuckin' crowbar.

She winces when she sees my face and split lip. "Jesus, what happened?"

I glance at Brock, who shares a look with Nitro, and when his eyes lock on mine, he shakes his head subtly. *Club business.*

"Some guys tried to rob me. Didn't get away with much except a few sore heads."

She still has her hands on me, and I want her to fuckin' nurse me back to health, in my bed, all night. I don't even care she's still touching me and the boys are watching.

"You're bleeding," she says, her eyes worried.

I shrug. "It's all right, I've bled before."

She frowns, tears in her eyes, then looks to Brock. "Do you know who they were?"

He shakes his head. "No, but that's why we have the best surveillance money can buy."

A tear drips down her cheek as I reach out and wipe it away without thinking. I can feel Brock looking at me in my periphery.

If he's not curious by now about our interaction, then I'll eat my hat.

"Don't get upset, I'm still breathin'."

"Barely," she whispers, brushing her tears away. "I'm sorry, I just don't like violence."

"Might be wise to get checked out. Frankie's inside," Nitro says, giving me a chin lift. "I was about to buy her a drink."

"Sorry I ruined your plans."

"I think it's gonna take more than a drink to get her into my bed," he replies gravely.

"Who's Frankie again?" I mutter. I'm hopeless with names.

"Angel's baby doctor," Brock replies.

"How's she gonna fuckin' help?"

"She's a doctor, dipshit," Brock says.

"You've got the hots for Angel's baby doctor?" I don't know why I care; I think the blow to my head is starting to take effect.

"It's complicated, we go back a long way."

"Then go buy that drink before some other fucker does," I snort.

"No other fucker is gonna do shit," he replies, surprising me. "Frankie's mine, she just doesn't quite know it yet."

Brock gives him a side eye as I laugh. "How's the rest of you?" Brock asks ignoring him.

"Fuckin' sore," I reply. "Feels like a I got hit with a crowbar."

"Jesus!" Stevie says, stepping back and running her hands through her hair. "They hit you with that? This is crazy. We need to call the cops."

We all look at her sharply. "No cops," I say, before either of them can chime in.

She's visibly upset. "But you just got assaulted. They could've killed you, Ax."

"I'm fine. I survived a lot worse than that." Even if my body feels like it's been struck by a freight train.

"Maybe Nitro's right," Brock says. "Frankie could check you out…"

"I said I'm fine. I just need to go upstairs and clean up."

They all stand around me like I'm some invalid, before I shrug out of Brock's hold as he holds two hands up in surrender.

Stevie puts a hand on the small of my back and I know I'm gonna get questions about that later, too. I'm in too much pain to think of something too smart to say that he'll believe, and at this moment, I don't rightly care. As long as she's not hurt.

I can hear Brock saying something to Nitro and I know he's not gonna let this go.

Once inside, I feel Brock's hand on my shoulder. "Sure you're okay, brother?"

I turn and give him a chin lift. "I'll be fine. Gotta expect shit like this. Just didn't expect it so soon."

He points at me. "I'm gonna take care of this."

"You don't have to do anything. Not tonight," I say.

Then to Stevie, Brock says, "Don't want anyone goin' out there to the dumpster or otherwise until I work out what the fuck went on tonight and where they came from. Got me?" She nods.

Limping toward the stairs, I grimace at how much it's gonna hurt to climb them.

I hear Brock and Nitro's footsteps disappear back through to the bar.

As I start climbing, I know Stevie is still behind me. When I reach the landing, I feel her arm around my waist.

"You're hurt bad," she whispers.

I look down at her. "Like I said, I've been hurt a lot worse."

"Stop saying that."

"Why? It's true."

"Jesus Christ, Axton."

We reach the top stairs when I say, "You better get back downstairs. People are gonna talk."

"People? Or your brother and Nitro?"

I turn and look at her, and she says, "Why are you smirking?"

"You suck at playing the part of concerned boss."

"What? I *am* concerned!"

I reach to her face with one hand and stroke the side of it. "I meant; you play concerned lover a little too well."

Her eyes go slightly wide. "Lover?"

"Better than fuck buddy."

She shakes her head. "Do you think they noticed?" I shrug. "Don't give a fuck."

"Axton," she says after a moment. "You're being very cavalier."

I chuckle and my body pays the price as I wince. "I'm a lot of things, but I've never been called that before."

"Get inside my apartment now. I'm not taking no for an answer."

"You goin' all Nurse Nancy on me?"

"Something like that."

I don't disobey. Frankly, the thought of her taking care of me warms my insides.

She unlocks her door, then turns to me. "Listen, I'm sorry… about before. I was out of line."

I shake my head. "It's already forgotten."

I walk in after her.

"But I was a bitch, and I took it out on you."

"You were jealous. Admit it, and I might forgive you."

She puts her hands on her hips, the famous Hart temper slowly simmering. But she doesn't scare me.

"That's bribery."

"I'm wounded."

She jabs a finger in my chest. "You're gonna milk this, aren't you?"

"Only if I can," I muse. "Depends on how good a nurse you really are."

"I'm glad you think this is amusing. I'm freaking the fuck out."

I can't help but stare at her, enjoying having her freak because it proves she cares. I've not had that feeling for a very long time.

She doesn't wait for me to reply. Instead, she marches off to the other room and comes back a few moments later with a first aid kid.

I give her a chin lift. "What do you think you're gonna

do with that?"

"Bandage your hand, since it's bleeding. Your lips are split too, and your face is swollen, which is going to need an ice pack," she says. "Then give you some Advil since you won't go to the hospital. Park your ass."

I make a face that tells her I'm enjoying her bossiness.

She marches off again and comes back with an ice pack, holding it to the side of my face as she says, "Hold still and keep this on your cheek."

"You really are a pistol," I say as I lean my ass against the little dining table and raise the crook of my finger for her to come closer.

She stands between my legs. Her lips twitch, and I run a hand through my hair.

Fuck it.

I'll let her patch me up, then hopefully, she'll let me spin her around and fuck her against the table. Won't that be a nice end to a shitty night.

I give her the full force of my stare, letting her know exactly what I have on my mind.

"Don't look at me like that, Altman," she says, unzipping the first aid kit, avoiding my eyes.

"Like what?"

"I know what you're doing, and it's not going to work."

"Then why won't you look at me?"

"Because I'm busy fixing you."

I snort. "Gonna take more than some magic cream, an ice pack, and a bandage to fix me, babe."

I know there's a lot going on in that pretty head of hers. The least I can do is try to make light of it.

I cup her face with my other hand. "Talk to me, Stevie."

"I… I don't know what to say."

I frown. "Did I scare you tonight?"

I wait with anticipation for what she's going to say. I never, ever, want her to feel unsafe around me. In fact, it's a hard limit for me.

I hope to God I haven't fucked things up before it's even begun.

BRACKEN RIDGE
REBELS
ARIZONA
M · C

CHAPTER 10

STEVIE

HE WATCHES ME INTENTLY AS I CLEAN HIS SKIN, MY HANDS SHAKING.

After a moment, he stops me and holds both my hands in his. Our eyes meet.

"Stevie?"

"What?" I swallow hard.

"Take a breath."

I blow out a puff of air, looking down at my hands. "Are you sure you're okay?"

"Don't change the subject."

"Fine. I don't like the idea of you being hurt," I admit. "It… it frightens me."

"Do I frighten you?"

I frown, indignant. "No! That's not what I meant."

He looks relieved.

I feel the intensity coming off him, and when he lifts my chin with his finger so our eyes meet again, the look he gives me is like wildfire.

"You sayin' that as a boss, or somethin' else?"

Forced to look at him, I can't hide. "Ax…"

He frowns. "Don't say we're nothin'. We both know that's not true."

"I wasn't going to."

"So, you feel it too, or is it just me?"

He waits, wanting an answer.

I look down again, then he says, "Stevie, I've been away a long time. I spent a good number of years with a lot of time on my hands, a lot of time to think. And I know the difference between a one-night stand and somethin' more."

"That's just it," I say. "We can't be *something more*, not at the moment with the club, with you working here…"

"When, then?" he presses. He pulls me to him. "I can't explain this feeling, Stevie, and I know that makes me sound like a schmuck because I hardly know you and all you know about me is all the bad shit I've done."

"That's not true. I know that's just one part of your life."

"Yeah, and it's a big part," he says. "What happened tonight shouldn't have happened, but this shit follows you and it never goes away. It's part of who I am. It's always gonna be part of me, whether I like it or not."

I know he's not trying to purposely make me feel sorry for him, but I can't help it; he's so heartfelt.

"It's not your fault that you got attacked," I remind him. "That isn't on you, Ax. You did your time, and you're trying to make a life on the outside. I admire that. I think it's brave."

"Brave?" He snorts. "Babe, there ain't nothin' brave about it, but I gotta toe the line, no matter what. I don't ever wanna go back to that hellhole. That's not an option, not for me."

One side of his face is red and starting to bruise and he has a gash on his nose. I know he's hurting, but he acts like he's made of steel. I wish he wouldn't. He shouldn't hide.

I work silently as the tension between us simmers.

"I have to go back downstairs and close up," I say when I'm done.

He reaches for me. "Please don't go."

I know I'm playing with fire when I say, "Why don't you wait here? I'll get Rory to lock up. If neither one of us goes back down there, it'll look a little suspicious."

He drops his hand from my hip and nods. "All right."

"Show me your ribs."

"Is that your best pickup line?"

I give him an eyebrow raise and he chuckles, then winces, coughing.

I'm shocked when I see that he's heavily bruised on his arm and his ribs.

"Jesus, Ax, you need to go to –"

He holds one finger up to my lips. "No doctors or hospital."

"How about you rest on the couch, and I'll get you some Advil."

He nods. I know he's in pain.

"Are you sure you don't have a concussion?" I ask worriedly as I head off to the kitchen.

"I didn't hit my head."

"No, but you got punched and hit with a freaking crowbar."

I come back and hand him two Advil and a bottle of water.

He snorts. "Babe, go lock up and hurry back."

"Who's bossing who now?" He raises an eyebrow, and I hold up my hands. "I'll be back shortly. Just get some rest."

He rests back, and I head out the door. I end up being a little longer than expected as Colt and Gunner came over to secure the premises after the incident. I don't see Brock, but Nitro's still here.

"Can you stay at your sister's tonight?" Nitro asks me as I approach where they're congregated.

"Why?" I ask, confused.

Nitro's eyes meet Colt's and Gunner's before he says, "The club isn't happy with you bein' here while these freaks are on the loose. They may come back."

I shake my head. "Colt has installed the best security possible. Plus, I'm not here alone; Axton's right across from me." I don't add he may be underneath me as well, but I'm sure as shit thinking it.

"It didn't stop them scaling the gate," Colt says,

palming the back of his neck. "Or beatin' Axton up."

"He put up a good fight," Nitro puts in. "Considering there were three of them, and they had weapons."

"I don't think they're gonna break into the Crow. They came to send a message to Ax when they saw him as easy pickins," Gunner says. "Cowardly way to fight, but they obviously wanted to try and fuck him up."

My blood runs cold. I can't hear any more of this.

I turn my head away. "I'm gonna head up, check on him, make sure he's not concussed."

Nitro glances at me, and I know what he's thinking without saying anything. *Fuckety fuck.*

"Any issues, give any one of us a call," Colt says with a chin lift.

I smile weakly. "Will do."

I head over to Rory and briefly explain what happened, and he agrees to lock up, then, I'm heading back upstairs.

When I get inside my apartment, Axton's asleep on the couch. His massive frame takes up the whole two-seater and then some.

I stare at his beautiful face and his even more beautiful body, even though he's fully clothed.

His sandy blonde hair matches his beard, which is neatly trimmed and oh so sexy.

When I think about him going down on me, then telling me I was his first, it makes me tingle all over. I've never wanted any man like I do him.

The ice pack has fallen down onto the floor, and I bend down to retrieve it. I also grab the throw from the back of the couch and shake it out, laying it over him. I only hope when he wakes, he doesn't have neck ache because that angle and those cushions can't be comfy.

Still, I don't want to wake him now. I turn off the lights and walk over to my bedroom. Unlike Axton's place, mine is a little bigger and has a separate bedroom, and bathroom with a tub.

I'm tired, so I take a quick shower, tying my hair up on the top of my head so I don't get it wet. I let steam fill the bathroom as I wash myself, and I try not to let my mind wander to when I saw Axton getting beaten up… It worries me, though, that these thugs showed up with crowbars and weapons, clearly intending to hurt him, if not kill him.

I shut off the water and step out, drying myself off as I slap lotion all over my body and pull my pajamas on.

When I head back through my bedroom to grab a glass of water from the kitchen, Axton's still in the same place I left him.

I don't want to disturb him, so I don't even turn the TV on in my bedroom. Instead, I watch some YouTube videos in bed before falling asleep.

Hours later, I hear a noise as I'm startled awake. My iPad tumbling off the bed and onto the floor with a clatter.

Axton stands in the doorway of my bedroom and walks slowly toward my bed as I watch him, my heart racing because I'm not used to a man being in my apartment, much less my room.

"I'm sorry I woke you," he says. "I tripped over your shoes."

I bite my lip. "Shit, I must've kicked them off in the doorway."

His eyes; I can't get over how blue they are, even in the dark.

He moves closer. "Is it okay that I'm here?"

I pat the spare side of my bed. "Of course."

He chuckles, peeling back the duvet as I watch him, shirtless in just his boxer briefs, slide into my bed. I feel like rubbing my eyes to make sure I'm not still dreaming.

"What's so funny?" I ask.

He shakes his head.

"Tell me!"

"You have a side," he says simply.

"What?'

"You have a side of the bed."

I'm not one of those people who can sleep in the middle of the bed, it just feels kinda weird.

"Oh," I say, as if just realizing it.

He reaches for me as we face one another. He's so warm. His hands cup my face as he leans over and kisses me with such feeling that it takes my breath away. I clutch his biceps as we kiss in the dark. His tongue seeks entry into my mouth, and a groan leaves the back of my throat. One hand wanders down past his abs, and I rub his cock through his boxers.

"Fuck," he hisses.

"You're in pain," I say, knowing it's true. "Should we…"

"I'm fine."

"Ax, are you sure…"

He cuts me off, rubbing his thumb over my bottom lip as he inserts it into my mouth.

I suck, scraping his thumb with my teeth, and he growls low.

I bite the pad and he grips my hair with one hand. "Need your mouth on me."

Pushing him onto his back, I settle between his legs, pulling his boxers down to his knees as I free his cock.

It's big, hard, and fucking beautiful. I sheath him a couple of times as he watches me, his eyes burning as I lean down and take the tip into my mouth.

"Jesus," he mutters as I lap my tongue back and forth over his slit, tasting the saltiness of his pre-cum.

I take him farther into my mouth as I hollow my cheeks and suck him up and down, gripping his cock with my fist. Each time he hisses and curses softly under his breath, saying things like, *"so fucking good"* and *"damn, babe, fuuuuck."*

I can't get enough of his moans and what I do to him. I go deeper, jerking him as well as sucking him, enjoying every moment of making him come undone.

"Stevie…" he mutters. "I'm gonna come, babe..." He tries to pull out, but I don't let him. Instead, I suck harder, knowing that he's almost there, and I want to taste him. I want him to feel this as much as I do.

His hands go into my hair, and I don't even protest when he thrusts up into me. I almost gag as he hits the back of my throat, pumping hard, faster.

"Oh, babe… fuck…" he grunts as he shoots his load, and I swallow it all as his hips slow, circling. When he pulls out, I continue to clean him up with my tongue as he watches me in fascination.

When I'm done, I look up at him, and he has this look in his eyes that reads like pure possession.

"You like cleanin' me up?" His tone is dark, and I know we're far from done here.

I nod. "Love it."

"I need your pussy so fuckin' bad," he says, pushing the hair back off my face as I sit on him.

"Shouldn't we have, like a break or something?" I whisper as he sits up, wincing again as I notice he can't lift one of his arms properly.

"Axton, please let me take care of you."

"You already did."

I shake my head. "I don't mean like that. I mean, medical attention."

One hand cups my chin as he kisses me, not even caring he can taste himself on my mouth.

When he licks my lips, I just about convulse. Holy shit, he's kinky.

"No, I've got you right where I want you, *boss.*"

"Did anyone ever tell you you're good at changing the subject, too?"

He smirks. His poor lip is banged up pretty good, but he doesn't seem to care. "Did anyone ever tell you that you wear too many clothes to bed?"

He doesn't wait, reaching down and pulling my top over my head as I hastily shed the bottoms. He runs his hands up my body from my thighs, up to my breasts.

Cupping them, he rubs my nipples with his thumbs as I close my eyes. My body's so in tune with his, so desperate for him, that I let him touch me with wild abandon, and I don't fucking care if the whole neighborhood hears my cries.

One of his hands lowers as he cups my pussy. "This is mine," he mutters, his teeth sinking into my neck gently.

"This body belongs to me."

"Axton," I gasp when he pinches my clit.

I squirm on top of him as he continues to assault my body. "Yeah?"

I try to rub myself on his fingers. I want him so bad.

"I need it," I whisper.

He smirks again. "I wanna make you come like this."

"Keep rubbing me like that, and I will."

He does, and I'm so wet for him as I begin to move my hips, rubbing myself on him, not caring about anything except his touch. He's like a drug.

When he inserts two fingers into me, and says, "That's it, baby, ride my fingers, let me watch you," I start to slowly unravel.

He reaches down and sucks one nipple into his mouth while his fingers fuck me in and out as I ride him.

"Oh, God," I whisper. I need to release this tension, and every movement he makes has me one step closer.

I grip his shoulders, trying to impale myself, but he doesn't let me, holding my body as he sucks on my nipple. I throw my head back as I start to come, calling his name as he rides me through it and squeezing his fingers as I melt into his body.

"Condom," I gasp when he pulls his fingers out of me.

"Got any?"

I shake my head.

He reaches up and kisses me. "Good, keep it that way. Don't like the idea of you havin' a stash."

I shove him back into the pillows as he laughs.

"Axton, even if I did have a 'stash', there's nothing wrong with that. I'm a grown ass woman."

"Says she who got shitty because of me and –"

I hold a finger up to his lips. "Please don't say her name before I'm about to fuck you."

"*You* fuck *me*?" He snorts.

"You're the one on your back, bozo."

His eyes crinkle. "My pants are out by the couch if you really insist."

"Ax…" I groan as he continues to run his fingers through my dripping pussy.

"Wanna fuck you bareback," he whispers as our eyes meet. "You on birth control?"

"Ax," I gulp, knowing I want it too.

"Answer me."

"Yes."

"Fine. I'm clean, only ever used wraps. I'll pull out if you want me to."

Imagining him inside me without a rubber makes me shiver all over. I didn't realize up until this moment that I don't want anything between us, and this is only the second time we've been in bed together.

"I don't want you to pull out," I tell him, reaching down as our mouths collide. "Hurry, I need it."

He grins. "Think I like you on top, bein' bossy."

Before he can say any more, I grip his cock and lower myself down as he glances down to where we're joined, his face in awe as I revel in pleasing him. One large hand runs down my back, cupping my ass as he squeezes it, settling the other hand on my other cheek as I pull up and sink down again, just as slow.

"Fuck," he hisses. "Feels so fuckin' good. So tight, babe."

I begin to move a little faster, taking his thick cock all the way down. His strong hands grip my ass more firmly as he helps me. He rests back on the pillows, admiring me as I ride him.

"Cup your tits," he says. "Play with them."

I do as he says, pushing them together as he watches, and I move back and forth, changing the movement as his eyes heat when I pluck my nipples. He leans forward, and I hold one breast to his mouth as he suckles, his eyes flicking up to mine. He's so damn hot.

The sensation is too much as I move faster, grinding my clit down on him as I come again, harder this time, his hard, fat cock filling me so good that I scream as he moves my hips back and forth with vigor.

"Baby," he whispers, as I grip his hips so I don't collapse.

"You make me come so hard, Ax," I whisper back.

"Ride me harder," he says. "Ride me so fuckin' hard, boss. Wanna hear you scream again."

I do just that as he lifts me so I bounce up and down on him, feeling every single inch of his erect cock plowing in and out of me. I swear, I can't get enough of this man and what he does to me.

"Is this a first too?" I pant, my tits jiggling up and down as we fuck hard.

"A woman takin' charge, or no wrap?" he pants back.

"Both," I cry out as he reaches a hand between us and brushes one knuckle against my clit, and I explode. He pushes up into me as I ride him, and he empties himself on a mighty roar as I collapse on his chest.

He pulls me back down to the bed, and we both gasp for air for at least two full minutes. My body tingles everywhere; my need for him is off the charts. We're like a couple of animals.

"Now I've been inside you like that," he whispers, kissing the top of my head, "I may not wanna let you go."

I don't even answer. I just snuggle into the warmth of his body, and even though we're still attached, I don't care. I just want to be close to him.

He makes everything better.

He makes me feel alive, and I want to hang onto that for as long as I can. If that makes me a martyr, I don't care.

In this moment, it's just us, and for the first time in forever, I'm free to be me.

BRACKEN RIDGE
REBELS
ARIZONA
M · C

CHAPTER 19

AXTON

Going to the clubhouse to see Hutch is never easy. The man is as intimidating as fuck. And I've got a father who's right up there, where terrifying is concerned. However, with Hutch, at least he lets you speak, and he seems to be invested in your overall wellbeing. Yes, that benefits the club, but in turn, it also helps me get somewhere in life.

Everything has changed since I got out, technology being one of them. I can't keep up with it or even get with social media, but it's part of today's world. And so is being adaptable.

Something I've been realizing more and more in these last few weeks is just how much society has changed and how it'll leave you behind if you don't keep up with the Joneses.

One advantage I have is that I don't give a fuck about any of that shit.

I came here to settle down, make some money, set myself up, find a good woman, and start a family. I'm done with wishing for things that I wanna make a reality.

If Hutch tells me to grovel and shovel fuckin' cow manure, then I will, because I know that it'll also benefit me in the end. I'm past that stage of everyone's out to get me. When I got locked up, I was a kid with a chip on his shoulder, and nobody could tell me anything – I thought I knew it all. Of course, I fuckin' didn't, and I had to grow up fast. Too fast. I missed out on all of my twenties, going to college, having that whole new adult experience. I know they say that finding yourself is hard when you get out, but it's overwhelming. For me, I can't wait to get to my destination fast enough. I've been on the journey for ten fuckin' years. I'm done.

So, when I arrive at the clubhouse and I see all the bikes in the lot, I know that I'm not just having a meeting with Hutch; it's the whole damn club and probably all of the committee members.

I steel myself as I walk into the empty entryway and hear talking coming from the meeting room. This isn't somewhere I've ever been, since as a prospect, you don't get to sit in on the meetings or go anywhere near Hutch's private office, except to clean it.

I hover around outside, not wanting to go in until I'm invited.

After a few moments, Colt sticks his head out and asks, "You ready?"

I give him a nod. Though I'm only surmising that

I'm here because of what happened the other night, I say, "Ready as I'll ever be."

When I follow in behind him, everyone is around the long table.

Hutch at the helm, then Brock, Gunner, Colt – when he takes his seat – Bones, Rubble, and Steel.

I stand there, albeit a little awkwardly, as Hutch glances up at me.

His hair's out today, not something I've ever seen before, as usually it's tucked under a bandana. He looks younger somehow, his grey and white beard matching his hair as his piercing eyes look me over.

"Axton," he says, as if it's a surprise that I'm here. "Take a seat."

There's an empty space at the other end of the table, where I pull the chair out and take my position. My eyes glance to Brock as he watches me, giving nothing away. Fucker.

Not that you can ever get a read on him anyway; he's been the V.P. for far too long.

"I suppose you know why you're here?"

I link my fingers together in front of me on the table and say, "I guess it has something to do with the other night." While I'm sore, spending the night in Stevie's arms while we fucked each other's brains out has made me almost forget that I'm even in pain. That's what the love of a good woman can do for you, though I doubt love comes into the equation from her side of things.

I know for a fact I'm fuckin' nuts about her.

"Brock told me briefly what happened, but you're gonna need to fill us in on the rest."

I nod. "Well, you know about Little Mick. We did time. He was the go-to guy to get anything. I got cigarettes mainly, books, paper to write home, but I never did any drugs, not even weed. I was too shit-scared in the early years to fuck up and get caught. Fast forward ten years, Little Mick is out, and he's paying a visit to his former inmates, bribing them like he did me, if I don't get involved in his next scheme. Playin' on the fact most ex-cons who get out don't land on their feet like I did. I guess he wasn't exactly countin' on that."

"So you told him no," Hutch says. "Which is why he sent his bunch of goons to fuck you up."

"He's not countin' on the fact that I have an entire MC behind me."

"That you do, and I have to say, I'm not pleased."

"I'm sorry. There's nothing I could've –"

"Not with you, dipshit," Brock pipes up, my eyes flicking to his. "With the fuckers that jumped you."

"When someone attacks one of my own, no matter that you are a prospect, that's a direct insult to me and my club." Hutch goes on. "I didn't spend thirty years of my life bringin' this club into reputability, only to have one of my boys fucked over by some low-life scum. Colt's done some diggin' of his own and we've found out more."

I brace myself for whatever the hell they're about to say next.

"Like the fact that Little Mick is peddling drugs in Bracken Ridge," Colt affirms as I turn my head sideways.

"That son of a bitch has some balls."

"No shit," Brock adds. "Obviously, we don't take too kindly to anyone, much less an outsider comin' into our town and mixin' shit up. No fuckin' way."

I glance back at Hutch. "So, you know where he is?"

His lips twitch. "You're forgetting who owns this town."

That I am. "What did you have in mind?" I ask, knowing whatever it is, I'm all in.

"Simple. We wanna put an end to what he's doin', our way." Hutch goes on. "There's no use involvin' the cops at this point in time, as they'll only give him a slap on the wrist. He'll do some time, but be back on the streets before we know it."

I swallow hard. The intensity in this room just went up about seven hundred notches.

"That's pretty much how it works these days," I concede, knowing that they're gonna ask me to do something that I don't really want to, and there's nothing I can do about it. "So, you want me to get in with Little Mick?"

Brock's eyes look murderous. "That's not gonna be

happenin'," he grunts.

I ignore him and look straight at Hutch. "If that's what I gotta do, I gotta do it. Only thing is, I fucked him up pretty good the last time he cornered me, and I'm pretty sure I broke one of his goon's jaws. Might not exactly be flavor of the month."

"Little Mick might be good at gettin' shit on the inside," Steel puts in, his eyes flicking to mine as he points at me. "But he's got shit for brains in the real world. For one, we found his place pretty easily. We've had Gash watchin' him to see what's goin' on, and it seems like he's got an elaborate set up and every fuckin' finger in the pie."

"We're not sendin' Axton in," Brock reaffirms. Clearly, the raised voices I heard earlier were about this subject. I know what my brother's like, and he won't put me in any immediate danger. "I won't vote on it and if any one of you have any common decency inside you, you won't either. If things go south, which I imagine they will at some point, Axton's gonna be involved, and he's gonna go right back to prison with them."

"Which is why I vote we involve Jenkins," Gunner adds, giving me a chin lift. "He's always been half-way in our pockets."

I frown. "And Jenkins is?"

"Chief of Police," Rubble says. "We throw some work his way every now and again. Keeps him in a job and makes him look like he's runnin' this town, when we all know he ain't."

"No cops," Steel reiterates. "They only complicate things. Plus, we know how to deal with things our way, without gettin' caught."

"Only trouble with that plan is there's more than one person to bury," Bones says, which I have to admit, is the truth.

"Big ass desert," Steel grumbles. "Scum like that don't deserve to go back to prison. They'll be guaranteed a hot meal every night and a nice, clean bed to sleep in. Sick and tired of people comin' into this town and tryin' to fuck up what we've built. Whether the pigs like it or not, we keep this town clean, and they can't say any different."

Hutch nods. "That's true, but we can't get anyone on the inside other than Axton."

"Why not one of the prospects?" Colt offers. "Fuck knows they're always seekin' out new recruits."

"It's too risky," Brock says. "They get wind, we lose one of our own. Prospects may be low on the hierarchy; no offense, little brother, but I still don't want to see any of them six feet under."

"That won't happen," Hutch says, rubbing his chin like he's deep in thought. "We could send in Gash."

Gash is one of the newly patched-in members, keeps his head down, and doesn't cause trouble. He's been helping Nitro at the scrapyard, plus filling in here and there around the bar and at Rubble's.

"I don't know about that," Steel interjects. "Could've seen him around town already, put two and two together."

"He's been stuck at the yard most of the week," I put in. "Helpin' out Nitro. Doubt they've been staking out the club. They weren't even aware I was part of the MC until the night they jumped me."

"Still, I don't like the idea," Steel maintains. "Don't trust any of the motherfuckers. Puttin' anyone in the direct firing line is risky. I'd offer to do it myself, but I confronted the asshole you call Little Mick the night he came into the bar, so he knows my face."

"Kinda hard not to forget, with a mug like that," Gunner says across the table, earning him a middle finger from Steel.

"Steel makes a good point; it is risky, but I don't see how else we can get intel on their next move," Hutch continues. "Without one of us goin' in."

"Let me talk to Linc," Steel says, then turns to me. "He's my right-hand man when it comes to tappin' phones, gettin' info, and anything illegal under the noses of the feds."

"Pays to have friends in low places," I agree.

All the while, Brock continues to look at me across the table. I know that he's serious; he does not want me involved, but I feel like it's almost my duty to put myself in the firing line. I could easily say I've changed my mind and...

"Don't," Brock says as our eyes meet.

All eyes switch between the two of us.

"You readin' his mind now?" Rubble laughs.

Brock shifts his eyes to Rubble. "Somethin' like that. And I'm tellin' you whatever you're cookin' up, don't."

Hutch glances at Brock, then at me. "The V.P. has spoken, Axton."

Fuckin' brothers.

"Even if I know I'll be able to get the information faster?" I say.

Hutch points at me. "Even then."

"Don't you get to vote on it?"

Hutch shakes his head while I hear Gunner say, "Cocky little fucker."

I scratch the top of my head. "Well, if I hear anythin' else, I'll be sure to let you know. Am I free to go? I've got shit to do at the Crow."

Hutch regards me for a few moments, and I've no idea what the fuck he's thinking, but I don't think it's good.

"Go," he says.

I nod to the others.

When I get up to leave, I barely make it out the door, when I feel a hand on my shoulder.

"You good?" Brock asks as I turn.

"You don't have to babysit me," I throw back. "I am capable of fightin' my own battles now."

"You sure about that?"

"Positive."

"Those are tough words, but I know what you're like, Ax. You don't gotta go be a hero just because you think you gotta prove somethin'."

"Don't I?"

"Damn straight, not to me."

"But to the club, Brock. I'll never get in with any of the guys until I prove myself."

"And that's not by disregarding direct orders and goin' into danger, when you'll one hundred percent get caught."

I stare at him for a few long moments.

"You been practicin' that speech?"

"What's that supposed to mean?"

I run a hand through my hair, feeling the frustration. "Don't pretend that you don't think I'm gonna fuck up soon. It's written all over your face."

"Don't be a fuckin' smart mouth," he warns. "I've got your best interests at heart."

"You don't have to keep me safe. I'm a big boy now, I can fight my own fights."

He points at me. "You'll never fight them alone. I've waited ten fuckin' years to be with you, and I'm not gonna lose you again, so fuck me for givin' two shits about you. Fuck me for tryin' to keep you from makin' another stupid decision."

"Right," I mutter. "*Another* stupid decision, like that's all I do."

"It was a pretty fuckin' big one."

I shake my head as I see the regret in his face the minute the words leave his mouth.

"Axton…"

I shrug his arm away. "Yeah, and I'm glad I've got you around, big brother, to remind me every damn minute."

Stalking off, I leave him behind. I storm out to the lot, mount my bike, and fire her up, roaring from the parking lot in a blaze of fury.

What the fuck just happened?

I get on the 101 and keep going. I don't know how long I ride for, but when it turns to dusk, I turn around and head back.

Riding is the only time I really feel freedom. It gives me time to think, or in my case; more time to stew.

I had no idea that Brock was in the 'let's wait for Axton to fuck up' team as well as everyone else. What a fucktard. That's the thing when you fuck up once and do it good, you never get to live it down for the rest of your life.

I ride back to the Crow, knowing exactly what I need to douse this fire inside me.

And her name is Stevie.

She's cleaning the bar as I come through the back.

When she sees me, she smiles, then she sees my face

and frowns.

"Axton?"

"We alone?"

She nods.

"Good." I come toward her, cup her face, and kiss her rough, my tongue seeking entry into her mouth.

When she reciprocates, I sigh like a dying man as she grips my hair with her needy hands.

When we come up for air she asks, "Axton, are you okay?"

I grin against her mouth. "Never better."

I lift her and place her ass on the bar, reaching to cup her tits as I squeeze them, moving in between her legs.

"Fuck, I've dreamt of doing this," I growl, nipping her neck with my teeth as she gasps.

"Doing what?" she pants.

"This." I unbutton her jeans and pull her zipper down, then yank them off, and her panties are next.

"Axton!" she cries.

I turn and dim the lights down. If she prefers some moonlighting, then I'm her man.

"Spread your legs," I tell her.

To my astonishment, she does, her feet on the bar so she's bared to me. So fuckin' pretty. I get down on my haunches and start to eat her out as her pleading turns to moans that go straight to my dick. She arches her back, and I'd give anything for her top to come off so I could stare up at her tits, but time doesn't allow for that, and I'm fuckin' hungry.

I lick through her folds, opening her up with one hand as I keep her legs open with the other.

I don't relent. I give her exactly what she wants, and when she starts to come, I latch onto her clit and suck it into my mouth, fingering her deep as she calls out my name.

I don't give her time to recover. I replace my fingers with my tongue, fucking her tight little hole as she writhes, scraping at my back with her nails. I'm being rough with her, but fuck me if she doesn't like it as much as I do.

When she comes again, I groan as much as she does as I revel in her sweet taste, and I know that I'll never get enough of her. I could do this all fucking night.

"Ax…" she cries when our eyes meet, and I gently lick through her folds.

"I need it," I say. "I wanna be rough with you tonight."

"Come here," she breathes as I stand, reaching for her. I grasp her neck as we kiss. One hand squeezes my bicep, the other squeezes my cock.

"Get it out," I tell her.

She undoes my buckle and zipper as I pull her top off. I can't take her clothed anymore.

Pulling her bra down, I cup her tits, lowering my mouth to her erect nipples as one hand still fingers her wet pussy. I do it slowly this time, teasing her, keeping her right on the edge.

"Did you have a bad day or something?" she breathes.

I smile against her skin. "Not at all."

I lap, suck, and lick both nipples back and forth until she's fumbling with my jeans, trying to get them down. I help her out as my cock springs free, and she grips it hard in her fist.

"I want you so fuckin' bad," I say as I kiss her again, happy to find she's just as frantic as I am.

"Fuck me, Ax. I need it," she cries, pulling my dick as I just about blow my load all over her hand.

I pull her to me, her tits squashing up against my chest as I grin. "You're so fuckin' beautiful," I tell her. Then I place her on her feet, turn her around, and tell her to bend over, slapping her ass.

"Ouch!" she cries. I do it again.

"You're a horny little girl, aren't you, boss?" I growl in her ear, pulling my shirt over my head, my jeans pooling around my ankles. There's no time to kick them off, but I don't need to. I'm gonna blow fast.

"Y… yes," she sighs, pushing her ass against me.

"I want your ass," I whisper.

She stills. "Now?"

I nip her neck again. "No, but I will have it soon."

She reaches back, cupping my head as I grip her tits with both hands. "Watch me play with you while I fuck you," I say.

I don't give her any time to react; I pull her hips back farther, line her up, and push into her slick, tight pussy. She groans at the same time I do, and I begin to pound her in and out.

"Fuck," I moan, my head tilting back as I try to think of anything to distract me and make it last longer. I know I can't. My thrusts become harder as I grip her tits, pushing them together. Her hands rest on the bench, but I need to get deeper. I push her down farther, so her arms are flat and her head's now sideways on the bar.

"Oh, oh… Axton…" she cries, and I know she's about to spiral. "Oh, yes, yes…"

I keep thrusting as her moans get more and more intense, and then she lets go. Thank fuck, because a second later, I'm spurting my cum, jerking until I'm spent as I hold her up around the waist.

We're both panting hard.

I kiss the top of her hair, reveling in her smell, the way she tastes, fucking everything. I don't need drugs; she's my own personal brand of heroine. "I guess we skipped past the first date, huh, boss?" I say after a few moments.

She laughs, then I do too, it feels so good. The best thing of all is being in her arms. Nothing could top that.

"I'm not sure how many public health violations we just broke," she concedes. "But the bar definitely won't pass the next health inspection."

BRACKEN RIDGE
REBELS
ARIZONA
M · C
REBELS
ARIZONA

CHAPTER 20

STEVIE

I tiptoe out of bed when my cell rings late at night.

I'm in Axton's apartment, and it's three in the morning. Though, we only just got off to sleep. After our fuck session in the bar, we barely made it up the stairs when we fucked again on the edge of the bed, me riding him as he made me come over and over.

He was different tonight, when he first took me in the bar. Angry at first, the look in his eyes perilous for a moment, then it dissipated.

I don't know what happened, but his oral skills when he's mad get an A-plus.

He also likes to spoon.

Anyone that told me Axton Altman is a hardened criminal and a bad apple is so full of shit that I'd fight them on it.

He's sweet. Taking care of my needs, making it good for me. Even when he was rough in the bar, I wanted every second of it.

I can't say I was any better when I rode him. We were both so frantic to have another release, to just enjoy one another. Skin to skin, just the two of us, with no outside distractions.

It was like heaven on earth. Being in his arms always is.

I know he got back from the club because he went there earlier today. I hope everything's all right.

I don't exactly know why Lukas is calling me so late, or why I answer, but I slide the green button across.

"Hello?" I whisper.

"Stevie?"

Who else would it be?

"Lukas? What's wrong?"

The line feels fuzzy, like I can barely hear him. It sounds like he's in a bar.

"I miss you," he says.

"Are you drunk?" I whisper-shout.

"Yes, but that's not why I'm calling."

"Lukas, it's three in the morning," I moan. "You just woke me up."

"I'm coming to see you," he tells me as my eyes go wide.

Oh no.

"What?"

"You heard me," he slurs. "Me and you, we're not done."

I shut the lid on the toilet seat and sit down. "Lukas, you're not coming here. It's late, I'm tired, and I'm going to bed."

"I should never have let you go." He goes on. "I thought… I

thought I was doing the right thing, letting you spread your wings. I was wrong."

"Lukas, we'll talk about this when you're sober." I palm my forehead. "Now is not the time."

I hear movement at the doorway.

"Stevie?" Axton is standing in the shadows.

At the same time, Lukas asks, "Who's that?"

I put my hand over the phone. "Go back to bed," I whisper.

"Who is that?" Lukas shouts down the phone.

Axton rubs his eyes with the heel of his hands. He looks so sleepy and utterly delectable, standing there naked, his dick at half-mast, finally.

"I have to go," I say as Axton stares back at me and doesn't leave.

I hang up on Lukas.

"What are you doing?" He yawns.

I stand and go toward him. "Peeing."

"You were on the phone."

"It was my ex." I sigh, ducking under his arm as I head back to bed.

"Your ex?"

I flop back into bed and even though I feel like throwing my phone, I resist. He's not worth breaking it over.

When I don't answer, a few moments later, I hear him pee and then the toilet flushes.

When he slides back into bed, he pulls me against his front. Even though I've only been out of bed a few minutes, I'm freezing. Luckily, Axton is like an inferno as we spoon like we've done it forever.

"What did he want?" he asks, his voice low.

"Nothing. Go back to sleep."

He mumbles something, kissing the back of my head, and a few moments later, I hear the soft lull of his breathing. He falls asleep so freaking fast.

Me, however, I've always had issues sleeping, and I know that I'm unlikely to get back to the peaceful slumber I was in before I got woken up.

His call has rattled me.

Lukas barely drinks, for one. And calling me like that, out of nowhere. It's just so out of character for him.

My mind starts to kick up thoughts about us, how we were together. While yes, he was away in the military for the most part, the last six months together were no picnic.

Stop! I tell myself. I cannot think about one man while I'm in another man's bed.

The one thing that strikes me, which is blaringly obvious, is how much I'm enjoying being around Axton. In a short space of time, he's worked so hard, and I know it's to prove something to Brock, to his family, and the club. I should've known to trust my gut and not worry.

I'm falling for him.

It's not just the hot, rough, amazing sex we're having. When Axton talks to me, he really listens. He doesn't just pretend to. He's quiet but soulful when you least expect it.

What he did to me in the bar was so demanding. So rough.

I can't forget his eyes when he first stormed in the backdoor; they were furious as he sought me out. He needed me. But even with how much I loved that, a part of me doesn't like it when Axton comes home angry or upset. Even though I know he probably has other shit going on. We all do.

Home?

Is that what this is?

I wonder if he ran into Bambi while he was over there. Then again, he did tell me he didn't want her, and he didn't do to her what he did to me. That has to count for something, doesn't it?

I can't help but feel a small amount of satisfaction over that admission.

Any which way you look at it, Axton is an oddity. There is nothing about him that screams he's been to prison and done hard time. Aside from his rough good looks and his tattoos, he's like a cuddly bear, though I wouldn't ever admit that to him.

Nothing like this feels like it did with Lukas.

None of it.

That's not the problem at all. In fact, it's the least of my worries. But all I can think about until the wee hours of morning, is how much I don't want Lukas to come here and that makes me sad.

Time has moved on, even if it is a short space of time. I've changed.

I see clearly what I want now. Maybe it has something to do with the fact that Axton got hurt the other night. Panic went right through my veins, and I thought my chest might cave in when I saw him being beaten up. The only thing I could do was go get help, and lucky for me, Nitro and Brock had walked in only a few minutes earlier.

The memory of seeing him hurt makes my blood run cold. It makes me wonder what kind of stuff happened to him in prison. None of it can be good.

I can't even imagine how it would have been for him being locked up with hardened criminals at nineteen years old.

His grip tightens around me as I hear him mutter. I can't quite work out what he's saying, and I consider waking him up when he jerks suddenly, his grip around me tightening. When I try to move, I realize I'm pinned, but a moment later, his grip relaxes, and I can breathe again.

He likes being around me, I think suddenly.

It must be a far-cry from a freaking prison cell, sure. But the way he holds me, the way he protects me. It makes me feel… *loved.*

I shake it off.

It may be way beyond fucking for me, but I'm well aware Axton is just having a good time. A good time with his boss, no less. And I've no intention of telling him that I'm developing feelings for him… that somehow this thing between us has sparked something in me that I never knew I needed or wanted. But it's there.

I fall asleep feeling the most content and happy I've felt in years.

"What do you mean, he called you?" Kennedy asks when I call her the next day.

"Just that, he called me at three in the morning and said he missed me and was coming back to Bracken Ridge."

"What the hell?"

"I know," I say, shoveling toast into my mouth. I'm back in my apartment, getting ready for work, and I had to get this off my chest to someone. Since Cassidy wasn't answering, Kennedy is my next saving grace.

"What the hell does he want?"

"He sounded pretty miserable."

"Of course he is." She snorts. "He gave up the best thing he ever had. The guy's been having a good time for months, and now he's back home, he wants to see you?

Seems convenient."

Kennedy has never really been a fan of my relationship with Lukas. She always said we were too young to be so serious. I guess you could say they tolerated each other.

"I'm sure he's just feeling nostalgic or something. I mean, I was right there for seven years."

"Old habits die hard. It'd be strange for him coming home and you not being there."

"This is what he wanted, K." I sigh. "And if I'm honest, so did I. We'd grown apart, and it was blaringly obvious. I never wanted to admit it."

"I hope he's not serious about really coming here."

"Tell me about it," I moan. "That's going to be really awkward if he just shows up on my doorstep."

"Well, call me if he does."

"You're healing. You don't need to be involved in my love life."

"Fine, I can send Bones. He'll protect you."

I laugh. "I don't need protecting, K. It's Lukas, he's not going to do anything to me."

"Except tear out your heart again? He wasted seven years of your life; he doesn't get any more moments."

There she goes. My sister, the firecracker.

"I know that. I can only hope he just drunk dialed me and doesn't even remember what he said."

"He's got some nerve. He never even saw you in person

when he broke up with you," she hisses. "What kind of asshat does that?"

"A big one?"

There's a knock at my door, but because it's left ajar, Axton appears around it and calls out, "Hey, boss, you left your panties in my bed!"

I slap a hand over my mouth as Axton's eyes reach mine, and then sees I'm on the phone and stops in his tracks. He mouths, *oops*, as I clear my throat.

"Stevie? Who was that?"

"Uh, no one," I reply, throwing my shoe at him as he bites down on his lip, as he laughs.

Fucking laughs!

"Don't lie to me! Was that… oh my God, was that Axton?"

"I have to go," I say quickly. "I'll call you later, okay?"

"Stevie, don't you dare hang–"

I end the call and drop my phone on the cushions. "Axton!"

He does a very bad job of looking contrite. "Sorry, didn't know you were on the phone. Please tell me that wasn't someone we know."

"Worse, it was my sister."

"Fuck."

"Yeah."

"Did she know it was me?"

I run a hand through my hair. I don't need this

complication right now. I don't need my feisty, lawyer sister dragging me over the coals about it.

"I'd say she put two and two together."

"Fuck."

Our eyes meet.

"Ax, this complicates things."

"Will she tell Bones?"

"Not if I deny it."

"Are you that good a liar?" He frowns, clearly knowing I'm not.

"No, and I don't usually lie to my sister. We tell each other everything."

"If she finds out, she'll tell Bones, then I'm fucked."

"Shit," I mutter. "I really don't need this shit right now."

"I'm sorry." He twirls my panties around on his finger as he tries not to smile. "I was just being dutiful and bringing these back, though now I think I'll keep them as a souvenir."

He stuffs them back in his pocket as I shake my head.

"This isn't funny. "

"It's not, I could actually get kicked out of the MC."

I frown. "I know that."

"Club rules come before women."

"Because I'm associated with the club?" I snort. "It's ridiculous that it's up to Hutch who I bang."

"No, it's up to Hutch who *I* bang. He's just tryin' to keep you safe and keep me outa pussy that could potentially cause him grief, like if I piss you off."

"I'm a grown ass woman and you're a grown ass man. We should be able to bump uglies if we want to." I know I sound petulant.

He bursts out laughing. "What the fuck?"

I throw my other shoe at him. "You've never heard that expression?"

"Not since high school, no."

"Well, all jokes aside, it won't be a good look if we're seen together when we're not supposed to." God, it feels like high school all over again.

He rubs his chin, his gaze searing into mine. "What if I said I don't give a fuck?"

"You say that, but there are consequences. I'm not the club's property like they seem to think I am. I work for them; there's a difference but Hutch won't see it that way."

I don't want him to get into trouble, that's the bottom line.

He shakes his head. "It's worth the risk."

"No, it's not. Not for you to get kicked out and lose your place in the MC."

He won't admit it, but it's true.

"What are you sayin'? You don't wanna continue?"

Panic races through me. "I'm not saying that, Ax."

"We gonna fight over this, then?"

"No, because there's nothing to fight over. I know Hutch is protective and looks after everyone who's associated with the club, I respect that, but he shouldn't get to tell me who I can have warming my bed and who I can't."

His eyes darken. "I better be the only one warmin' it."

He's so sexy when he goes all alpha on me. "Or else what?"

He grins, and it's cheeky, like the look of a naughty schoolboy. "You might find out if you keep it up."
I think about what he did to me on the bar and blush as I look down at my empty plate.

He inhales deeply as his chest rises, watching my reaction. Then he asks, "Why are you blushing?"

"I'm not."

"Are you thinkin' about what I did to you?"

I rise from the chair as I dust crumbs off my shirt, avoiding looking anywhere except at him. "No." It doesn't sound very convincing.

He comes closer to me. "Why do you go all shy around me when it comes to talkin' about sex?"

"I don't do that," I stammer. "I just… last night you were intense."

"You liked it, didn't you?"

"Yes," I say, my eyes finally reaching his. "And it was totally amazing."

"So what's the problem?"

"There's no problem. You were just… different."

He cups one side of my face. "I like eatin' you out, so

sue me."

I wet my lips as I feel that throb between my legs. What this man does to me is insane. I may never be the same again after being in bed with him. Each time gets even more exciting and more intense.

"You seemed… agitated."

"I'd been at the club." As if that explains everything.

"Were you in trouble?"

His eyes dance with amusement as I stare up at him. Lost in the sea of his beautiful blue gaze.

"No, boss, I wasn't. But I'd like to be in trouble with you."

"You would, huh?"

He rubs his chin. "Yeah."

He leans in for a kiss and my phone chimes, making me jump. I glance at the table and see it's Kennedy calling back.

"See what you did?" I notion to the phone. "That's my nosy sister calling back because she knows you have my panties."

"Yeah, not too sure what to make of that." He doesn't look very sorry.

"So I'll just ignore her and hope she goes away."

He grabs me by the ass and pulls me to him. "Don't give a fuck. Like I said before; it's worth gettin' in the shit for. One thing I never planned on was comin' here and findin' someone I actually connect with, like I do with you."

I'm floored by his admission, blinking a couple of times to make sure I heard right.

"But, I don't like your ex-boyfriend calling all hours of the night, gettin' you out of my warm bed."

"Sorry, I had no idea he was going to drunk dial me."

Something crosses his eyes. "Like I said, I don't like it."

"Why?" I fire back. "It's not like we're dating."

He cups the other side of my face. "Don't even think about it."

"Think about what?"

"Goin' there."

"Where, exactly?" I know I'm challenging him, and I don't care.

He growls low. "You might think I'm a patient man, boss, but when it comes to you with another man, whether it be your ex or some other guy, I'm not gonna be okay with it. In fact, I'm not gonna stand for it."

His fiery words set my insides alight. "That's very alpha Dom of you."

"Mean it. He had you, he let you go. Stupid fuck. But then again, it's my gain."

"Ax, he said he was coming here, to see me."

He brushes the hair back off my face. "You want that?"

I shake my head. "No, I don't."

"Then I'll take care of it."

"That's not what I meant." I sigh. "You don't have to

take care of anything. He drunk dialed me, that's all it was. He won't come here."

He kisses my lips gently. "This mouth is mine," he whispers, cupping one breast. "So is this." He cups my ass with the other hand. "And this." He reaches down and cups my sex. "And this."

I swallow hard, my panties wet and my clit throbbing. "I want you," I whisper.

He reaches down to his dick and cups himself through his jeans. "Look what you did."

A small smile plays on my lips. "I think now is about the time I show you just how good my oral skills are. That's if you haven't had enough?"

We fucked for most of the night in various positions. One thing Axton isn't, is a selfish lover. He's in it to pleasure me first and that just makes everything that much sweeter.

I move my hand to his dick and squeeze him as I start to unclip his belt. One of his hands reaches into my hair, wrapping my ponytail around his fist as he watches me.

Oh, this should be good.

I slide down to my knees and unzip him, a smile on my face.

"What's so funny?" he asks when I look up at him, his eyes heated as I pull his dick out.

"This is so much better than coffee," I muse.

His eyes crinkle in the corners as I squeeze him, and he

hisses, bucking into my hand.

And I spend the morning repaying him in turn for what he did to me in the bar last night.

BRACKEN RIDGE
REBELS
ARIZONA
M · C

CHAPTER 27

AXTON

Saturday is manic.

I cracked a couple of skulls earlier in the night when the patrons became unruly, arriving already drunk from another bar. It's not often shit gets rough, but every bar has problems now and again.

One of the dicks slurred a brash comment at Stevie, and I wasted no time in jumping over the bar and slamming his head down on the wood before making him apologize.

Even though it's not my bar, I don't stand for that shit.

Can Stevie fight her own battles? Sure. But she doesn't have to put up with that. No woman should have to.

Some dicks, you just gotta put back in line, there's no two ways about it.

When she gave me a look that said I'd gone too far, I pointed at her and said, "You know what Hutch would say to that."

We both know he's pro-women and wouldn't hear of it, whether it was her or any other woman. She's turned this place around and he knows it. The Rebels look after their own.

I also notice a couple of things that strike me as odd tonight; most of the brothers are hanging here; Steel, who sits at the end of the bar, with Nitro and Gunner. Colt is also in the back on the security cameras with Bones. Gears and Jax are on security front and back.

My brothers also here, but he's stuffing his face in the kitchen, and I haven't seen him for most of the night.

One thing we can all agree on about the Stone Crow is we don't want people starting fights and brawling, or making lewd comments to females. Hutch spent over a hundred grand bringing this place up to scratch, and I'll be fucked if it's gonna go to shit.

Of course, my girl takes it all in her stride, but I ain't standing for her being called names.

Next time, I'll take him out and use him for a punching bag away from prying eyes.

Brock's also avoiding me. Fuck knows why.

He's been weird the last couple of days and I don't know why.

I know if it had anything to do with finding out about me and Stevie – which he'd only know through Bones via Kennedy – he'd already have my head in a vice, so it can't be that.

When I come back from taking the trash out, I stop by

Stevie's office and give Bones and Colt a chin lift, "Is it just me, or is something about to go down?"

I've grown pretty good at reading body language. Knowing Bones used to be military, he gives nothing away, like Steel and Brock, but Colt on the other hand looks sideways at Bones before speaking.

"Why'd you say that?" Colt asks.

"Everyone seems to be on high-alert," I say.

"Nothin' wrong with extra security on the busy nights," Bones pipes up. "After you got jumped, Hutch doesn't want any shit goin' down. There are women to consider, and if anything happened to Stevie, Emmaline, or Roxy, Hutch would never forgive himself."

"Nothin's gonna happen on my watch," I say. "I got it covered, got the prospects on the door."

"Good to hear it," says Bones.

"Just finishin' up installing this new update," says Colt.

Still. I don't buy it. They're hiding something, but as a prospect and a bottom-dweller, I don't get to know what the fuck's going on and that ain't gonna change any time soon.

I don't linger.

When I get back to the bar, I look around for Stevie. When I finally spot her, she's at the end of the bar, having a heated discussion with some guy.

From the way she's talking, it's like she knows him, but she's quite visibly upset.

I look at him for a fraction of a second before deciding that it's him. Her ex.

He fits the typical military description: tall, lanky, with a short buzz cut and a clean-shaven face.

I can't even control my feet as they start moving toward the restaurant to get closer.

I know she was anxious the other night after he called. She didn't seem one bit enthused about talking to him, and that provided me with some slight relief, but clearly, that's been shot to the wind.

I don't need him coming back here and disrupting what we have together, trying to rekindle things. He had his chance, and he let her go.

I don't know what that makes me and Stevie, but I know we're not just fuck buddies.

The jealousy I feel raging inside me is like nothing I've ever known before. And seeing her with him, I want to explode.

I didn't survive prison to be fucked over the millisecond I get out. He blew it. She's mine now.

"I don't know what to say," I hear Stevie's voice. "I told you I needed time to think."

What the fuck?

"I told you the other night I wanted to see you. I've come a long way," he says. "At least give me a chance to talk."

"Lukas, you've caught me off-guard."

"I didn't mean to do that," he says. "I just had to see you."

"I think you heard the lady," I bark as I approach.

They both turn to look at me, and I swear Stevie's face pales ever so slightly.

"Axton…" she says, but trails off when she sees my not so happy face.

"Everythin' okay here?" I ask, staring directly at him.

He's sizing me up, and while he might be military, he's got no fucking clue what I'm capable of when push comes to shove. Let's hope it doesn't. Plus, I'm bigger than him and have the scars to prove it.

He's suspicious of me, just as much as I am of him.

"Who's this guy?" He motions to me as he looks at Stevie.

Stevie takes a long breath. "This is Axton… my bar supervisor."

I wait for the rest, but it doesn't come.

I mean, what was I expecting her to say? Resident fuck buddy?

He stands a little taller as he takes me in, then says to Stevie, "Can we go somewhere and talk? Privately."

"She's working," I butt in before she has a chance to reply.

"Lucky she's the boss then, isn't it?" he fires back.

Oh yeah, I know a challenge when I see one.

We stare at each other, and I actually visualize ripping this guy's vocal cords from his throat.

He's been inside my woman before me, that's punishment enough.

"And you are?"

"Lukas, her boyfriend."

She closes her eyes and shakes her head, then says, "Ex-boyfriend." I can't help but feel a swell of pride in my chest at her admission.

Lukas frowns. "You don't have to answer to him. Let's go somewhere quieter."

He tries to put his arm around her, and I see red. I reach forward and throw his arm away, shoving him in the chest, one arm reaching back into a fist, ready to strike. Stevie steps between us. He goes to shove me back, but she's now standing in the way.

"Who the fuck is this jerk?" he spits. It doesn't do my resolve any good. It means he's here to get her back, otherwise he wouldn't be so worried about who I am.

"The guy who pumped her full of my cum earlier," I growl, pointing in his face.

Stevie's eyes go wide just about the same time as Brock steps out of the kitchen and stops in his tracks. She slaps a hand over her mouth as she mutters something that I can't decipher.

"And it doesn't look like she really wants to go with you, so do us all a favor and fuck off!"

"Axton, stop it!" Stevie cries.

My eyes fly to hers. "Well, let's hear it. Do you want to

go with him, or not?"

She looks to him, then back to me again, which just makes me all the angrier.

"Wait, *he's* the new guy?" Dickface asks in confusion.

"You got a problem with that?"

"Yeah, I do, actually. She's been my girlfriend since high school."

"And you broke up with her, so back the fuck up."

"Hold up, hold up!" Brock steps between us as Stevie steps out of his way. "What the fuck is going on here?"

"This dick is trying to lure Stevie away, when she clearly doesn't want to go with him. Do you, babe?"

I ignore Brock's frown as Stevie's eyes meet mine.

She lays a hand on my arm. "Axton, he's come a long way…"

The smug fucker smirks, and I lose it. I shove past Brock and sock him in the face.

Stevie shrieks and Brock pulls me off him the minute my fist makes contact with him, holding me by the shoulders.

"Cool it!" he barks, yanking me by the back of my shirt.

"Stevie doesn't want him here!" I bellow back as Brock holds me back.

"Is this true?" he asks her, looking right at Lukas. "Do you not want him here?"

She hugs herself as my heart feels like it's gonna rip out of my chest. "It's fine. We need to talk." She glances at me.

"I'm sorry, I have to do this."

Brock nods to Stevie as she stares at me with wide eyes, then turns to Lukas, who's now holding his jaw.

He came here with one objective and one only; to get her back.

Well, over my dead body is that happening.

The worst thing of all, is seeing the disappointment in her face toward me.

I don't know why; this is who I am. I make no apologies.

I'll protect what's mine, even if it is from her ex who means her no harm.

As Brock starts to walk me back toward the bar, I hear Lukas ask Stevie, "Is it true? What he said?"

I don't get time to hear her reply as I'm being shoved down to the back near Stevie's office, where Brock can interrogate me further.

Brock tells Colt and Bones to beat it before he turns to me and barks, "What the fuck was that?"

"What the fuck was what?" I fold my arms over my chest as we square off.

"Don't get cocky with me, Ax. Not now."

"Stevie doesn't want him here, she made it abundantly clear."

"Didn't seem that way to me, or are you just lightheaded from all the cum you pumped into her? Jesus Christ, Ax."

I swallow hard. *Shit.*

I hold up my hands and he shakes his head.

"Don't even bother lyin' to me, brother," he warns. "'Cause I don't wanna hear it."

I open my mouth to spurt some kind of lie, but swiftly close it again. He's right. I never was a good liar, and it would be in insult to him if I tried.

I run a hand through my hair. "Obviously, you weren't meant to hear that. It was just for his benefit."

"So it's true, then? You've been fuckin' her?"

"Don't say it like that."

He snorts. "I'm not sayin' it like anythin', that's the truth of it. You've been fuckin' Stevie on the side. Your boss, I might remind you."

"It's not like that."

"End it now," he says. "You've had your fun. It only puts the club in jeopardy, and not to mention, a prospect with a club girl…"

"No," reply. "I won't."

He frowns. "You won't end it?"

"Yeah, that's right, and I don't see how it puts the club in jeopardy."

"You wouldn't, Axton. Do you know how hard it was to find someone like Stevie who can run things properly? Who cares about the place as much as we do? Who the patrons all love and keep comin' back to see? That shit takes time and you fuckin' her every which way till Sunday doesn't help matters. It's all good three days in, but what happens when you decide you've had enough."

"Nice to see how concerned you are about your own flesh and blood, but I suppose bein' an ex-con and a prospect, I don't get the chance at bein' heard, right?"

Brock scoffs again. "I heard you all right, and from where I was standin', none of it sounded good."

"This isn't just about pussy." I go on, before he can cut me off again.

He puts his hands on his hips, his face stern, like I'm some child getting a telling off from the school principal. Except this is a lot worse.

I don't wanna be on the wrong side of the club or the bad side of Brock, but I also want a chance at being with Stevie, for real.

I can't explain how I feel or why I feel it, but it's there. It's the only real thing I probably do know right at this moment.

"No? Then what is it about?" Brock growls. "I know you're a grown man and you can do whatever the fuck you want, except with her or any club girl. I don't get how clear it has to be. There are rules for a fuckin' reason."

"You know how good I am with rules."

"Don't get smart, Ax."

"Don't treat me like a child, Brock. I'll work this out,

just like I worked out how to get through the last ten years." His eyes bore into mine as he stares at me for an enormously long time.

My brother is the toughest man I know, aside from my father.

"Don't let prison define you," he says, his tone shifting. "It's easy to fuck up and I'm tryin' to keep you here with me, where you belong, and you're brawlin' with some fuckturd who's military and could put you back in jail."

"Not gonna fuck up. Told you before, I know what I'm doin'. It's easy to say don't let it define me when all I do, every waking moment, is think about how much I don't ever wanna go back there."

Brock runs a hand through his hair. "Why her?"

"Why not her?"

"Be fuckin' serious."

I shrug. "I like her. She's sweet and kind, and I like bein' around her."

"Fuck, Ax."

"I didn't plan it like this."

"So you like her or are you just fuckin'?"

I look down at my boots.

"Jesus fuckin' Christ," Brock mutters.

I look back up at him. "That's all fucked now anyway. Her ex is back and the one thing I can't compete with is time. I never got to know her, so now he'll swoop back in because he's got the monopoly on bein' in every one of her memories. I can't compete with that."

"Ax, you barely know this girl."

"I know how I feel when I'm with her."

He looks uncertain. "You've never had a real relationship, that's what this… this nonsense is…"

I shake my head. "It's not nonsense. I haven't even been interested in another woman since we first…"

Brock shakes his head. "One thing you better get clear; this ends now, Ax, despite what you say. You can't be fuckin' around with her anymore. All it will do is come around and bite you in the ass."

"You know I can't do that."

"Well, then, you'd better think of a way to get your sorry ass outta this."

I pause for a moment. "You gonna tell Hutch?"

He rubs his beard. "You know I have to."

"No, you don't gotta do that."

"Does she feel the same way?"

I rub my eyes. Suddenly everything feels like a great big burden. "I doubt it."

He frowns. "You haven't even had the conversation?"

"I tried, couple of times, but I just couldn't find the right moment."

He points at me. "Find the moment, and don't fuckin' break her heart. She's had enough to deal with these last few months without this."

"Trust me, she was a willing participant when she chose to ride my dick."

Brock tries to shake the thought off, but I see a slight tug to his mouth. "You're a cocky little fucker, you know that?"

"I learned from the best."

"This isn't over with."

"I'd be sorely disappointed if it was."

Brock's phone begins to ring. "This is exactly why I should've given you an ass whoopin' when we were kids."

"Well, I'm always up for you to try, old man, but you're pushin' forty, bro. Probably not as quick on your feet as you'd like to think."

He slaps me upside the head before walking out while answering his phone.

I run a hand through my hair.

While I know Brock has my best interests at heart, I also know that he's the V.P. and he will tell Hutch what's been going on. I'm kinda hoping he'll let us work this out on our own. Stevie's a grown ass woman who can make her own decisions. If she wants me in her bed, then that's nobody's business.

It's a sobering thought, until barely an hour later, I get a text from Hutch, telling me to meet him at his place. He needs to talk to me urgently.

Fuckin' great.

I've a good mind to go find Brock and give him shit.

I know I could take him. Not that I wanna punch the old fucker out, but to get a hit in would be kinda neat.

I also can't find Stevie.

I rang her phone a couple of times, but she didn't pick up.

I have to try to tell myself that he didn't hurt her physically all the time she was with him, so safety isn't an issue, but to say I'm not jealous as fuck is an understatement. I may have even gone up to her place and banged the door down. Images of them having makeup sex just about curdled my blood.

It's that rage that I take with me when I jump on my motorcycle and race off into the dark of night to the address Hutch gave me, only, when I slow down entering the neighborhood, it doesn't look like the rich heartland of Bracken Ridge where Hutch resides. It actually looks like the wrong side of the tracks.

The buildings are old and some are barely standing. There are broken streetlights.

Still, I don't question it. If Hutch says jump, I'm obliged to say, "How high?"

Just when I think I've got the wrong end of town, I see Hutch's fat boy parked in the drive.

I pull onto the gravel and park next to him, shutting off the engine. I take off my helmet and pull out my phone. No messages.

Where the fuck is he?

I walk up to the porch, no lights on there, either.

When I knock and there's no answer, I palm the back of my neck and step off the porch to go around the back.

"Is anyone here?" I call out. The backyard has a large, open, rundown shed and weeds as high as my hips.

What the fuck is this place?

I hear movement behind me, and as I turn, I see Hutch.

Relief sweeps over me, followed by confusion.

I give him a chin lift. "Prez."

"Axton," he says, his eyes never leaving mine. "I'm glad you could make it."

It doesn't take a genius to realize something's goin' down, I just don't know what it is.

The feeling that Hutch would ever cross me doesn't even come into the equation, yet the way he's looking at me is a mixture of sympathy mixed with regret.

Maybe I really did fuck up?

"Listen, if this is about Stevie."

He narrows his eyes. "What about her?"

So Brock hasn't told him?

"Her ex came by the Crow. I punched him when he put his hands on her."

"He put his hands on her?"

"To steer her away, to talk."

He rubs his chin. "Always the fuckin' hothead, runs in the family."

His eyes dart over my shoulder, and I hear movement behind me. Just as I turn my head to look, I hear the clocking of a gun, then the cool metal pointed to my head.

"What the fuck?" I splutter, automatically holding my hands up.

I look to Hutch whose eyes are on the guy pointing the gun at me, and he shakes his head.

"He came alone," he says. "That was the deal. He isn't to be harmed."

What the fuck? Hutch double-crossed me?

"Fucker owes us," says another voice from my left side.

Then I hear Little Mick at my ear. "Looks like your biker friends aren't so loyal, after all."

My eyes go wide as I look to Hutch in disbelief. "You set this up?"

"Deal was too good to pass up," Hutch tells me as I gape at him. "You don't get rich workin', Axton. Rule number one, son."

Pain hits my chest like nothing I've felt since I got sentenced. Bile rises in my throat and I'm sure I'm gonna lose it.

I can't believe it. Everything Hutch has done for me, but more so for Brock over the years… I just can't comprehend why. It can't be just about the money, because Hutch is loaded. He owns half of this town.

Little Mick shoves me in the back as I turn around, but

it's not his eyes I stare into.

Looking back at me are the same sharp, ocean blue irises that run in the Altman family gene pool.

My father.

I stare at him in disbelief. *What the fuck is going on?*

"Hello, Axton," he says.

Ten fucking years.

My eyes go wide. "Pop?" I don't even know if I get the words out, before I feel a blow to the back of my head, and then everything goes black.

BRACKEN RIDGE
REBELS
ARIZONA
M · C

CHAPTER 22
STEVIE

I STARE AT LUKAS.

So many emotions run through me as I sip on the martini he bought me.

It's late, but there's a quiet table at the Zee bar. I didn't want to go back to my apartment. It's better on neutral ground.

I'm shocked to my core about him showing up here, even more shocked at Axton hitting him in the face.

I should be completely appalled, and I am, but I'm also extremely turned on, and that, I can't explain.

I know Lukas is a good man. He'd never hurt me physically, even though I cried for months after breaking up.

But, all I can think about is Axton.

I've only ever been with Lukas, but Axton is something else entirely.

He manages to shut my brain down at every turn.

Not only does he keep me fully occupied with his mere presence, but he keeps me coming back for more.

It makes me wonder if there's anything I wouldn't do to

be closer to him.

That thought doesn't rattle me nearly as much as it should.

I've given him enough power as it is.

Just remembering how he kissed me, how he took me in his arms, how I was wrapped around him in bed only this morning… holy smokes. I know I'm in too deep, too soon.

All I know is I feel the passion between us that started off as a slow burning ember, and now it's a full-blown inferno. I can't explain it. Maybe I don't need to. Maybe I'm tired of compartmentalizing everything in my life. With Axton, there're no rules.

And, I kinda like it.

Even after his crudeness earlier — something that was a total pissing contest and just the right amount of alpha to piss Lukas off.

I look up at him, the bruise on his face starting to show. "How's your face?"

He smirks. "Like gettin' slapped from my mother."

I roll my lips, knowing that's not true. His face is swelling.

"I'm sorry about that. Axton can be…" He stares at me as I try to find the words. "…a little intense."

He frowns a whole lot more. "You never answered me before."

"When?" Oh, I know what he's asking, but I'm avoiding the question.

"Have you been with him?"

I swallow hard. "Lukas, you've no right to ask me that."

"It's true, then."

I take a big sip of my drink, as I think I'm going to need it. "I don't answer to you. We broke up, remember? I've no right to ask you what's going on in your personal life. It was you who ended us. "

He runs a hand through his non-existent hair. "I needed time."

I snort. "Time? Come on, Lukas, you're away six to ten months of the year. How much time does a person need?"

"A person can't make a mistake?"

I look down as I hold the stem of my glass. "What's changed all of a sudden?"

He reaches out to cup my hand in his. "Can you look at me?"

Him being here, it's bringing everything back up again that I want to keep buried, but I suppose these things have to be brought to the surface at some point.

"It's hard, Lukas, I'm sorry," I say. "You didn't exactly make our breakup very easy. I didn't even get to break up with you in person, like normal people."

"I'm the one who's sorry for that. I thought a clean break would be better. I didn't want to hold you back, Stevie. It felt like the right time."

"Hold me back from what?" I feel a lump in my throat.

"From the things you really want."

I know right here, right now, I don't want to marry Lukas or have his children.

What does that make me?

Am I a fraud?

I still love him, deeply, but not passionately, not anymore.

I take a long time before I speak again. "Lukas, we can't get back together."

He stares at me. "What if I tell you things have changed?"

I shake my head. "In the space of a few months?"

"I want you back, Stevie," he says simply. "I'm not going to beat around the bush. I should have talked things through, worked it out, gone to therapy, like you said."

My heart feels like it may break when I reply, "But we didn't. And I've moved on, Lukas. I still love you, I always will. You've been a big part of my life, we've done so much together that I'm proud of, but this doesn't change the fact that a few months ago, we wanted completely different things. We were going in opposite directions."

"I can't stop thinking about you," he admits, his eyes dropping to our hands. "All this time without you has been torture… not hearing from you."

"Yet you waited until just now to pick up the phone?"

"I didn't know what to say. I thought about writing to you, but it seemed kinda lame."

"You could've tried. That's what I mean about all of this; everything's always on your terms."

"No, it's not."

"Yes, it is." *You showed up when I begged you not to.*

"After years together, I expected a little bit more."

"I thought it best if I give you some space."

"To grieve you? I did. Thanks for being so considerate."

He at least looks a little guilty. "Stevie…"

"What? Am I not allowed to be a little bit angry? I loved you, was loyal to you for all these years, and you dumped me. No matter how you look at it, it is pretty cold, Lukas. I was left to deal with the loss of you without anyone…" I trail off, tears stinging my eyes.

He clutches onto our joined hands.

"Please don't be angry with me."

"I'm not angry, I'm just disappointed."

After a long moment, he says, "Is this new guy serious?"

I don't want to talk about Axton with him.

"I don't know, it's new."

"He doesn't seem like your type." He pulls his hands away, sitting back in his chair.

"I don't have a type. All I've known since high school was you, Lukas. I've never really dated anyone else before."

"So now you've had a taste of the bad guy from the wrong side of the tracks, you like it?"

My eyes meet his. "Being like this doesn't suit you."

He folds his arms over his chest defensively. "What do we know about him? He looks like he just escaped from prison."

It takes everything I have not to snort my drink all over the table, though this is far from funny. Who the hell does he think he is anyway?

"That's very judgy. Just because he has tattoos and looks a little on the rough side."

"A little? The dude punched me."

"And you didn't provoke him?"

He shakes his head. "I don't like it, and I don't like him."

"I didn't ask for you to like it."

"Has he been violent with you?"

"No!"

I'm about two seconds from drowning him with the rest of my drink if he keeps it up.

"Just because we're separated, doesn't mean I don't still care for you or won't look out for you."

"That's not helping, Lukas. And being overbearing and asking questions you've no right to ask is more than looking out for me."

"Luckily, he had his brother there, that's all I can say. I never did like you working for those dirty ass bikers."

The heat starts to rise in the pit of my stomach and work its way upward.

"They're not dirty assed. Hutch has been very good to me. I live rent free, I have a very good salary, and just because they're bikers, it doesn't mean they're any different than you or I. You never got to know them like I did. They're family."

He snorts again. "Family?"

I hold my chin up. "Yes."

It's hitting me all over again how judgmental Lukas is. I'd kind of forgotten since I saw him last.

If he wants me to say anything bad about Hutch, then I won't. He's been like a father figure to me for this past year and a half. He's never treated me poorly, been a creep, or done anything to make me think that he's a dirty biker. I've had many employers over the years, men and women in business suits who live in high-rise apartments and ride around in flashy cars, and they've been absolute assholes.

"I don't see why it matters to you, anyhow." I go on, when he offers nothing more. He doesn't even look contrite for saying it. "Who I work for, what I do, or who I'm fucking."

His nostrils flair at that last part. "You've made your point, Stevie, and I'm willing to say I'll wait it out."

My eyes go wide as I try and comprehend what he just said.

I give up, and instead, I say, "What?"

"You heard me. I think this is just a phase you're going

through right now. As you said, you've only known me, you haven't dated anyone else since before we met in high school. If you need to… do what you need to do, then I'll wait."

I gape at him. "Are you actually serious right now?"

I've heard him say some dumb shit before, but this takes the cake.

He nods. "I can't say I'm happy about it. In fact, I want to go rip that guy's throat out. But in the end, I know he can't give you what I can. You'll tire of him eventually." I've always known Lukas wasn't a saint, but not until now did I realize what a pig he can be.

"What?" he asks when I don't respond.

He glances down at my hand, now placed over my chest as I grasp what he said.

"Lukas, that is the most… disgusting thing I've ever heard."

"Why is it? I love you, Stevie."

I balk. "So, let me get this straight, you'd be fine with me… being with another guy, while you wait in the wings? And then what? We ride off into the sunset together?"

"I forgot how dramatic you were," he says, like we're discussing the weather.

"Is this why you really came back?" I challenge. "Or was it just to see what I'm doing?"

"It's a long way to come just for that."

I snort. "Right, so you did just expect me to drop my life

and run off with you? Like that would solve any of our problems."

"That's not what I meant."

Why can't he get it? I don't want to try anymore.

Tears spring to my eyes, I forgot a lot of things since he's been away. His ability to undermine me being one of the many things I don't miss.

I'm not comparing him to Axton. I know they're two different people from two very different walks of life. But Axton never makes me feel like an errant child.

"Really? Then what did you mean?" I fire back, anger rising in my body.

"You couldn't be serious with a guy like that, and frankly, I'm surprised."

I stare at him as I let his words sink in. "You don't even know him," I spit out.

I feel awfully protective over anyone saying anything bad about Axton. All he's done since he got out is work his ass off, and when he's not doing that, he's running around doing shit jobs for the club like some errand boy.

"I know you're too good for him."

"That's not fair, he's a good person. And, for the record, I don't want you to wait."

"Stevie," he says, his tone exasperated. "While I wasn't expecting you to have found someone else so soon, I take responsibility for that, for what I did and how things ended, and I'm sorry, for all of it."

I shake my head. "It's not your responsibility Lukas, it's *mine*. I'm not making a rash decision, hoping that one day you'll come to your senses and come rescue me. It doesn't work like that. I've been doing fine by myself. I've learned to adapt."

He looks displeased. "I thought you'd be happy," he says, running a hand over his head. "I really thought we could go back to the way things were before. Give ourselves time to figure shit out."

"The way they were before wasn't great," I remind him. "It wasn't even good, even you can admit that. We weren't in a good place."

"I know that, but I was rash in ending things. I –I should never have done that the way I did. I thought I was doing the right thing."

"I do love you, Lukas, I always will…" I say quietly.

He looks confused, then says, "But?"

I look down at my martini glass. "But – I'm not in love with you anymore."

All the things I used to love about him now just seem like a distant memory. And I meant what I said. A part of me will care for him. I always will. But I'm also nobody's fool.

People don't change, not really. Maybe he likes the comfort of me. Of knowing I'll always be there when he gets home. Knowing that nothing has to change, and things can go back to what he calls *normal*, but everything has changed. Namely me.

I feel like I've turned a corner. I'm finally living life on my own terms.

And to be honest, this is a real dick move.

He looks astonished, like he knew my world did once revolve around him and only him, so it's a shock to find out it no longer holds power over me. He watches me as if trying to see the change. "You do seem different," he says after a moment. "Stronger."

I swallow hard. "I don't want us to bicker, Lukas. Sure, I was obviously pretty distraught when we broke up, but I get it now. There's someone out there for you who wants exactly what you want, and the same for me. I don't want it to end with us arguing and one of us storming out or worse."

He actually looks really upset. "I'm sorry I hurt you, that's the truth."

"I'm sorry too. And I don't want you to wait, Lukas. I'm finding my way through this maze called life all on my own, and I want to continue to do that."

And I'm falling in love with Axton Altman.

The thought hits me like a freight train.

"I'm such a fool," he mutters, covering his eyes for a moment with his hand. "I should never have let you go. That's on me. I'm a fucking idiot.'"

I stare at him, unable to cry, but inside I feel wrecked. He will always be a big part of my life, but I no longer want to be with him.

We're going in different directions.

"I don't know what I did," I say softly, "to make you suddenly wake up and realize all of this, but we both deserve a chance to find our true happiness. I don't think it's a good idea that we get back together."

He swallows hard as he watches me. It's like a sudden feeling comes over him when he realizes I'm serious. It has to be this way.

It feels sad, looking at this person you spent so much time with, someone you once admired and loved with every fiber of your being. Someone you planned a future with.

But time really does change things.

"I should never have come," he says, his voice low. "But I had to try."

I reach over and squeeze his hand. "We have to move on, and I'd like to do that as friends. You were such a big part of my life, but my life is here now. This is where I'm going to stay. This is where my family is."

I see the resolve in his eyes, as his anger disappears. It's better this way. If we really can go forward as friends, then that means we did something right.

"I'm sorry I said those things." He looks down at his shoes. "Seeing how protective he was – that should've been me."

My heart may actually break tonight. The one thing I'm holding on to is that Axton isn't getting his ass kicked by Brock because I'm pretty sure he heard Axton's comment about what we'd been up to.

While I should be appalled, the woman that I've become loves every second of her hot-headed man and how alpha he went. I'm not the sort of woman who enjoys two men fighting over her, but even I have to admit, he was pretty hot. The whole thing is surreal, my ex and my… *whatever we are,* getting into a scuffle.

In a way, I know this had to happen. I had to have closure.

"It gonna be okay, Lukas," I whisper.

His eyes meet mine. "What will you find, do you think?" he asks as I let go of his hand. He sits back in his chair as a genuine look of concern crosses his face.

This is really it.

This is life without Lukas.

"I don't know," I say, taking a deep breath. "But it's a chance that I know I have to take."

BRACKEN RIDGE
REBELS
ARIZONA
M · C

CHAPTER 23

AXTON

I wake up and the first thing I realize is my hands are bound and my mouth is taped. The back of my skull throbs like a bitch as I try to focus my eyes.

Everything happened so quickly. As I try to pull myself together and shake it off, my mind starts to recall what happened.

The rundown house.

Hutch.

Little Mick.

My father.

Wait. *My dad, really?*

I must be delusional or perhaps they hit me really good over the head this time. I could've sworn I saw his face.

As I try to move, I realize I'm secured to a pole, in some kind of abandoned building, and my feet are also tied together. I've no idea where the fuck we are, but there're people talking. As I try to listen, I also realize that this is about as fucked as a person can get.

How the fuck is Hutch going to explain this to Brock? And… why the fuck is my father involved? I know he hates me, and I brought shame on the family and all of that, but really?

Enough to kidnap me and tie me up… and then what? Hand me over to Little Mick so they can finish me off. My mind reels at the possibilities.

None of it makes any sense.

There was a time, not long ago, actually, when I thought that Hutch really had my back, but now I'm not so sure.

Since getting out, I've realized the world really is a different place. Nobody trusts anyone anymore. Everyone has their noses stuck in their phones and they're more concerned with what's going on with social media than actual talking.

I really have been living in a ten-year time warp.

My father, on the other hand, he's a different man all together.

Mom indicated he wanted to try and that I had to give it time. Ha, what a joke. I wonder what dear old Mom would think now, or how he'll explain his way out of this one.

One thing that's not happening is any chance of me dying tonight. I don't give a fuck.

I want my new life as badly as I suck in air every day. I've got too much to live for, too much at stake. Sure, without a weapon to try and get out of this, it seems pretty fruitless, especially with Mick pointing a gun to my head. But I do know that I'm a born fighter. I will find a way out of this.

Stevie.

The thought of never seeing her again, and the fact that I left her with her ex-dickface boyfriend makes me all the more determined.

Then, when I hear Hutch's voice, it snaps me out of my reverie, and I try to listen a little harder. I can only see the side of my father's and Hutch's backs. Mick is standing opposite them, but I can't see his face.

"…you want the kid so badly anyway?"

"He owes me," says Little Mick. "Setting him up ensures he gets back in the joint and that while he's getting arrested and fingerprinted again, we'll be on our way out of town. It's win-win. Someone has to pay, gentleman. This is how it works. Then we can continue to do business down the track. I'm no use to you locked up, but the pigs have been sniffin' around, and Axton is already on their radar. Seemed like a nice parting gift." He laughs like this is somehow hilarious.

"We had a deal," my father says. "You keep the drugs comin' through, but we take a cut. It's the only reason I've allowed you to even step foot in this town."

I frown. My father doesn't even live here. *What the fuck is he talking about?*

He's never been involved in dealing drugs in his life. If anything, he detests it, more than any other issue on the planet. When I got caught with a blunt when I was fifteen, my dad kicked my ass so hard that I couldn't sit down for few days. If he could get away with punching some sense into me, I'm sure he would have, but Mom would've noticed. I remember the lecture he gave me as plain as day, and I never touched drugs again, not until I was eighteen and out from under his nose, at least.

"And that deal remains. But it's not up to you what we do with him anyway. Why do you care so much?"

"We don't want blood on our hands," my father says. *What in the ever-living fuck? He wants me dead now?* "We wanna be sure this doesn't lead back to me, us, or the club."

"I told you. I've set it up so that nothin' leads back here, you have my word."

Hutch snorts. "Right, *your word*. Excuse me if that doesn't exactly fill me with confidence after your goons came onto my property."

"Well, like I said, an example had to be made of people who don't do what I ask the first time. Axton is just one in a long line of many. It's a pity I didn't get to use him as my mule. It would've been fun to see how he'd smuggle the next shipment. Fuck knows his ass got a pounding in prison. It'd fit nice in there without detection."

I hear my father growl low.

That's not true, of course. My ass is still a virgin, by some miracle.

And I don't know if Mick hears it, but if this is some kind of test for loyalty, then my father will fail. He should explode right about now if…

"We don't give a fuck," he barks, his voice echoing off the walls. He points a finger at Mick. I not only see, but also feel, the anger radiating off him. "This kid means nothin' to me; I need your assurance that every measure is being taken that this stays under wraps. You're known as being a slippery little fucker, Mick. You know if you double cross me or Hutch that you won't even know the world of pain you're gonna be in."

"You act like you work for the fuckin' mafia or something." Mick laughs again.

"Maybe I do," my father says. "Or maybe I work for men who will cut your balls off and leave you bleeding to death while sending your family the footage of the entire drawn-out process, before making you eat them."

I can hear Mick swallow hard even from here.

He might have been the Kingpin in prison, but out here, he's just another slimy fuck who doesn't know which side of the bed to piss on. At least that makes me feel slightly better.

"You don't have to get your panties all up in a twist," he says. "I told you the plan. We've already got the next shipment comin' into Phoenix. We plan on another drop in a couple of weeks, so be patient, and this will work out for all of us. You continue to push the shit south and maybe next time, we'll double the deal."

"Until then?" Hutch interrupts. "We just sit tight and trust that you'll come through?"

"You'll get contacted before the drop to test the product. I can assure you, this next shipment from Colombia is high-grade coke. This stuff is beautiful. With all of your contacts within the MC, we'll expand farther south and eventually across the border. My boss is very happy with how this has all gone down so far. It's the perfect ruse. Who'd have thought you boy scouts would actually be the worst criminals out there under all that pretense of bein' a legit club."

My heart races in my chest at accelerating heights.

I know this has to be some kind of sham. Hutch doesn't push drugs either. None of the MC do; the Rebels are not a 1% club… and from what I've established from Brock, Hutch isn't about to change his mind on that stance…

"Well, your boss should think himself lucky. I don't usually deal with bottom-dwellers," Hutch replies, sounding bored. "But this opportunity was too good to pass up."

"Where's the money?" Little Mick gives my father a chin lift, ready to seal the deal.

"You're forgetting we'd like the rest of the bricks," he replies, his stance rigid, one of his hands clenched tightly into a fist. "Before the rest is exchanged."

Mick rubs his chin for a few moments, then a grin spreads out across the asshole's face.

He's one ugly motherfucker. No wonder he has to delve into the world of crime, nobody would employ him otherwise. He'd scare any good law-abiding citizen away.

He gives the word to one of his soldiers behind. It's then I realize there are others flanked behind my father and Hutch too.

Patch. Dalton. And an old man I think could be Knuckles. Men that are part of the MC but not part of the committee. They're all holding guns.

If there's a fuckin' shoot out, it'll be hard to say who'll be leaving with their brains intact.

None of the other club members are here. Where is everyone else?

My father may hate me with a fiery passion, but is he really gonna give me over to this dick who's definitely gonna put a bullet in my brain? Just for the fun of it, because I defied him and wouldn't be a part of this. I guess some vendettas run deep.

Where have all the good people gone?

The thought makes me angry as I try to wriggle against my restraints. Some fuckin' asshole did them up good, because everything is tight as fuck. I also don't want to alert anyone to the fact that I'm awake. And I thought I was alone back here, until…

I glance up, and in the shadows, I see Bones. He's buried in the dark behind a huge pile of old boxes and crates to my left. He's in camouflage, holding a rifle on his shoulder.

When he makes eye contact with me, he moves one finger up to his lips to tell me to be quiet.

I didn't even know he was fuckin' there this entire time as I've been watching the scene unfold.

Whatever fucked up plan is going on, this just got even more interesting.

A few moments later, his soldiers come back with a wooden crate filled with bricks. Holy fuck, Little Mick isn't kidding around. Whoever he's caught up with is someone with a lot of power to have this much coke and more on the way. This is big-time.

"Very nice," my father says, inspecting the bricks as Hutch does the same.

"Beautiful," Hutch agrees. "I've waited thirty years for a shipment like this."

"As I said, we don't sell low-grade shit." Mick goes on, because as I know, he's always one to brag. "Your dealers and clients are gonna be houndin' you for more, trust me." *Yeah, trust you, like a hole in the head.*

My father turns around to Patch and gives him a nod of his own. Patch turns and Knuckles produces a briefcase and hands it to him.

This is really fuckin' going down…

As he turns back toward Mick, our eyes meet.

He looks at me like he's seeing me for the first time. Then he does a strange thing.

He touches his nose once with his fist.

I know what that means. Dad's been in the military since before I was born.

He's giving me a signal.

Duck.

The briefcase gets handed over and Hutch and my father shake hands with Little Mick as he hands the case to one of the soldiers behind him. "Pleasure doing business with you."

"Oh, trust me, pencil dick," my father says, "the pleasure's all mine."

A moment later, a huge bang jolts me and my ears begin ringing.

"What the fuck?" Mick cries out as a bullet scrapes the top of his shoulder.

"Fuckin' pigs!" Hutch yells when they all duck at the same time.

Not before my father reaches out and grabs Mick, taking him into a headlock, pounding into his face like a man possessed.

My eyes go wide when he screams, "That's my fuckin'

kid! You fuckin' piece of shit! I'll fuck you up so good. I'll fuck you up so fuckin' good!"

He throws him to the ground and starts kicking him in the head, face, his body…

I watch in fascination, then I see Patch pulling on a mask, and so does Dalton, then Knuckles, and as I turn to my left, Bones follows suit. He's also moving toward me as he pulls the tape off my mouth and secures my mask. A few moments later, smoke fills the entire building, and the men start to cough and splutter as they scatter.

Bones cuts through my ropes and unties me, then he works on the rope at my feet. His knife saws through it fairly easily as everyone in front of me disappears. He pulls me up and drags me with him, out back through a side door that leads outside into the open area.

All around me, chaos ensues. Men are calling out, bullets are flying, and then when I get behind Bones's truck as we duck for cover, I see police cars all over the place.

This was a sting.

But the one question I have is why is my father involved?

Bones pulls his mask up as I do the same.

"What the fuck, man?" I pant, crouching down, watching the commotion as Bones holds the gun, ready to shoot if need be.

"Long time in the making."

"Does Brock know?"

"I didn't know until a few hours ago."

"Why?"

"From what I heard, the cops set it up with Hutch in exchange for your immunity."

"And my father?"

He just shrugs. "You better take it up with him."

I shake my head, trying to make sense of everything. The pain in the back of my head still pounds like a bitch, and this isn't helping.

"I need to check on my dad," I say after a few moments of watching men being dragged out by the swat team. "And Hutch."

"Don't worry about them. I'm pretty sure your father can handle his own."

He's not wrong about that.

My father is one tough son of a bitch. I never disputed where myself and Brock got our strong roots from. He made us this way.

"Fuckin' tear gas?" I shake my head, as we watch the scene unfolding. "This is some serious shit."

"No fuckin' kiddin'."

"This is so fucked."

"Be thankful it wasn't the alternative; I know there's a cactus out in the desert that had your name on it. It's why

Hutch took the deal."

"What deal?"

"The deal that kept you safe," Hutch says as I spin around to face him.

I stare at him in disbelief. "You fuckin' knocked me out?"

"Had to, son. It was the only way."

"I've got a feeling there's a lot more to it than just Mick gettin' even with me."

He comes to me and whacks me on the shoulder. "No hard feelin's now, prospect. Your father will explain."

Behind him, my dad steps out of the shadows. He's almost as big as me, looks the same too, only he's older than I remember and has gray and white in his hair. He's also keeping a short beard, which I find astonishing. In all the years I've known him, he's detested facial hair.

"We'll give you a minute," Hutch says, giving Bones a nod as they head closer to the first cop car, but still stay out of the line of sight.

"Dad?" I say when he doesn't say anything. He just stares at me with those big blue eyes that once used to frighten me, but now he just looks sad.

"Axton."

He swallows hard as I try to understand what he's thinking.

Before I can do anything or demand answers, he comes

toward me and throws his arms around me.

Never in my twenty-nine years of being alive do I remember my dad hugging me. Maybe he did when I was a small child. The photographs of us always show him holding us, propped on his knee or in his arms, but never like this. He's not an affectionate man.

He squeezes the fuckin' life out of me as I stand, stunned, wondering when the penny will drop.

"Is that all you've got for me, Axton?" He smirks when he pulls back, clutching my shoulders as he assesses my reaction. His hands cup my face as if he's making sure I really am his son, then he steps back.

"I'm a little in shock right now, Dad," I reply. "If it's all the same to you, I might need a moment."

I see tears in his eyes. Fuckin' tears. I open my mouth, then lose it again.

"I've dreamed of this day," he tells me, his voice gruff. I know this is hard for him. He's never shown me his feelings like what he's doing now. Never. "You wouldn't believe how many times I've wished that I could be standing here with you, my son, to say that I'm sorry."

I shake my head. "I'm the one who's sorry, I let you down…"

"You were a kid, Ax, and I was too set in my ways and disappointed in you to see that I was the one who let you down. I should've been around more, paid more attention to you, seen that you were falling behind, getting in with the wrong crowd. I know that what you did has been paid for, and I'll never know how hard it was for you doing time like that. It's my shame, son, not yours."

A lump wells in my throat. So much so, I rub my eyes. Dad snorts.

"Sorry, just checkin' to make sure I'm not dreamin'," I say.

"This is all very real, and I'm sorry that it had to go down like this, but I've been workin' this case for a long time. When the Colombians made contact with our mark in Phoenix and knowin' they wanted to spread their wings, it was the perfect opportunity to go undercover."

"Undercover?" I splutter. "Dad, weren't you in the army?"

He gives me a grin. "I did undercover work for the army, the navy, the police, you name it. I've been working undercover since you started high school, Ax. Due to the nature of the job, I had to keep up the pretense that I was being deployed."

"You work for the feds?"

"I work all kinds of cases, mainly drugs and guns. The only way to stop the violence in this country is to halt the operations of the underworld figures. And I wouldn't want it any other way."

"I thought you hated me enough to turn me in," I say as

he flicks his eyes down to mine.

"Axton, I've never hated you. Never. I was too pig-headed to see that I was being an ass. I had that heart attack last year, and it brought everything back to the forefront. I even retired for a year, then when this sting was presented and ultimately you became inadvertently involved, I knew I'd made the right decision."

"So Mick really was going to put a bullet in me?"

"One less mess for him to deal with," he says. "And it cleans everything up nicely without the cops having to investigate fully. When Jenkins, the Police Chief here in Bracken Ridge, contacted me about involving you, I didn't want that happening. I would never put you at risk like that, so, unfortunately, this was the only way."

"Fuck," I mutter.

"I don't expect you to forgive me right away. I know I should've come and seen you at Stradbroke…"

"Dad, that's on me. I'm sorry I let you down. I made mistakes, but I've changed. I'm not the same person I was back then."

He nods, gripping my shoulder with one hand. "I know, I can see it. And I'm proud of you. For not gettin' involved with Mick, for stickin' to your guns. That's when I knew that you really have changed, that you're gonna be okay."

I let out a deep breath, one I feel like I've been holding for ten years. "You don't know what this means to me,

Pop. I've also dreamed of the day we'd be like this, and in truth… I never thought it would happen."

He nods, pride in his eyes, and I feel like for the first time in my life, he sees me as a man and not a wayward child.

"I know, son, and I know we've got a lot to catch up on, but…"

We both turn as Brock's truck screeches to a halt right behind us. Dust flies everywhere as we both stare at him through the windshield. He looks fucking pissed.

Then, when he sees Dad with his hand on my shoulder, instead of his hands around my neck, he frowns. It's clear that he had no idea any of this was going down. That's going to be fun at the table. Not only did Hutch have to go against the committee members and keep them in the dark, he also had to lie to his V.P.

"I've got a feelin' that's gonna have to wait," Dad finishes.

I turn to him and pat him on the back. "I look forward to it, Dad," I say as our eyes meet. "Not before time."

"Welcome home, son."

BRACKEN RIDGE
REBELS
ARIZONA
M · C

CHAPTER 24

STEVIE

When I hear the news, panic hits me.

When Kennedy was kidnapped and I thought I'd lost her for those few hours, my life turned upside down. I reconsidered everything I knew about being involved with this MC

Then I saw how loving Bones is with her, how he lets her be herself. She's flourishing like she never has before and there's so much love between them.

When Kennedy phoned me to say Axton had been caught up in some kind of heist, I didn't know what to think.

My first thought wasn't that he might have gotten himself into trouble by doing the wrong thing, more like being in the wrong place at the wrong time.

I don't even remember getting to the clubhouse. I just floored it until I was skidding into the parking lot and racing inside as fast as my legs would carry me.

The place is bustling with activity as I search the room for him. When I catch Ginger's eye behind the bar, she nods over to the couch where Axton is seated. Some chick is passing him an ice pack, and when I look closer, it's Bambi. Freaking typical, can't leave him alone for five minutes.

Now isn't the time to probably charge over there and shove her off his lap, where she's basically sitting, but that doesn't stop my feet from moving in that direction.

When Axton sees me coming toward him, he tries to stand, but I'm there, in front of him as I push him back down and throw myself into his arms.

"Ax," I say, though my words sound jumbled. "I was so worried about you."

He wraps his arms around me as I hear Bambi gasp, but choosing to ignore her, I hold on tighter.

"I thought you were…."

"Don't say it, it's bad luck." He chuckles, and it's a lovely, rumbling sound. I don't want to let him go, but eventually I know I have to.

I sit in his lap as he holds me, our eyes meeting. I run both hands across his face, feeling his beard under my fingertips. "I'm so glad you're okay, Ax."

"I told you, I'm one tough cookie," he says, a glint in his eyes. He really is the toughest guy I know, and I try not to remember why that is, because the thought of him in prison is upsetting.

He looks like he's been dragged through a hedge backwards, though. His hair's disheveled, and there's a mean looking gash on the side of his forehead.

"What happened to your head?" I say, touching the bruise.

"Apparently when I got knocked out, I fell fuckin' hard. Nobody thought to maybe catch me before I landed."

I stare at him, horrified, looking for any sign of jest.

"Is this how you greet all your employees?" Bambi gives me a look of disdain when our eyes meet. I forgot she was even there.

"I can take it from here," I say, grabbing the ice pack from her. "Thanks."

"Hey!" she spits. "What the fuck?"

I shake my head. "He's taken, get it? I'm his woman. So I'll be icing him up from now on."

Bambi's eyes go wide as she wisely flounders off the couch and stalks away. I turn back to Axton, and before I know it, he pulls me in so I'm flush against him, and his mouth finds mine.

The kiss starts off slow, then it intensifies. The feeling spreads from low in my stomach, tingling every nerve as it works its way through my body.

My heart races as his tongue touches mine, every nerve in my body on fire as I sink my hands into his hair and his hands grip my butt.

My senses don't know themselves anymore, not when he's around.

His mouth is perfect, his beard soft and sexy, just like everything else about him that turns me on.

I grip him harder, and I'm sure a moan leaves my mouth, as I keep kissing him with everything I have to give him. I want him. I want him and only him. I grind farther into his body as I feel his dick push against my stomach. He might be injured and sore, but I still want to climb him like a tree.

"Fuck," Axton growls when we pull away, both panting.

I don't need to turn around to know that there will be eyes on us, and I don't care. I'm tired of giving a shit.

I love this man.

He's mine, and I want the whole world to know it.

"Don't ever do that to me again," I whisper.

"How much do you know?" he asks me, quirking one eyebrow.

"Enough to know that you were tied up and something went down with that guy from the bar that night. And now, apparently, someone knocked you out and you've got a gash on your head."

He gives me a nod, then his eyes flick over the top of my head as I hear someone clear their throat.

Shit.

As I turn, I see Hutch's massive form standing over us. When his eyes flick to mine, he arches an eyebrow in question.

I swallow hard. *Whoops.*

I start to climb off Axton's knee, but he holds me firm, not letting go.

"I see the two of you are still gettin' along," he says, a small smirk on his lips. "Though I'm not sure how this is gonna go down with Kennedy."

"Kennedy?" I question, confused. It's the last thing I'd expect him to say.

He rubs his hand through his beard. "We all know she's the real ballbuster around here. All I can say is, good luck, Ax. I think you're gonna need it."

"Listen, Hutch…" I begin to protest. "It didn't happen straight away… I mean, we didn't mean it to happen… it just sorta happened, you know?"

I hope he doesn't fire me, but for Axton, it would be worth it.

He shakes his head. "I don't fuckin' know how this is gonna work with you bein' his boss," he says, his eyes now on Axton. "But all I can say is that you better make sure you do what she says. Just because you're now dippin' your nib in the office ink, doesn't mean you're gonna get special treatment. Right, Stevie?"

Oh God, I would love the ground to swallow me whole right about now.

On the flip side; it seems I'm off the hook, and so is Axton. "I'd be sorely disappointed if you expected anything less," I say as a big grin spreads across my face. "Don't worry, Hutch, I've got some really nice jobs planned for him when he's better."

"Better?" Hutch scoffs. "Hardly came out with a scratch."

He gives me an eye roll before moving off, only a few moments later, another man approaches. I can tell straight away, before he even says anything, that this must be Axton's dad. They look exactly the same.

He's tall. Large in stature, with that no-nonsense stare. And the same piercing blue eyes. The only difference is Mr. Altman Senior is obviously older and a little grayer.

This time, I do climb off Axton's knee and perch on the arm where Bambi just was. I feel Axton move his arm around me, pulling me closer to him.

"Son," he says, his eyes assessing me, not Axton. "Aren't you going to introduce us?"

Axton turns to me, his lips twitching as I look at him in surprise. This is a turn out for the books. And why is his dad wearing a bulletproof vest?

"Dad, this is Stevie, my girl."

It warms my heart and makes my body tingle when he says my name like that and calls me his girl. All thoughts of what happened earlier in the night with Lukas have fled the building.

I feel better for it, and I truly hope that he moves on and finds his happiness.

He holds out his hand as we shake. "Pleased to meet you, Stevie. I'm Jim."

"Nice to meet you too." I don't know what else to say because I know their relationship is strained, but I never expected his father to show up here like this. I don't know what happened, but I go along with it. "It seems like you Altman men are full of surprises."

He gives me a smile that reaches his eyes as Axton holds me close to his side, his arm around me squeezing tighter.

"I can see my son didn't take long to set his sights upon the prettiest woman in town," Jim says. "It seems the apple doesn't fall from the tree, after all."

I do know his parents are still married, after some bumps in the road last year. Then Brock and his father made up after he had a heart attack. It's not like you don't hear the ins and outs of everyone's life in a small club like the Rebels, and a small town to boot.

"Cool it, Dad, we don't wanna scare her away just yet." Axton laughs, then holds his ribs like he's in pain.

"You need to see a doctor," I tell him, running my hand down his chest toward his ribs. "Something could be broken."

"No doctors," he says, pecking me quickly on the lips. "Just sore."

I can't get enough of him like this. He's so soft, sweet

and tender, making me his and not giving a shit who sees or what they think or say. It feels so right, I feel exactly the same; I don't give two shits what anyone thinks either.

I just wish he wasn't so beat up. I hope to God this is over now.

"Axton never did like takin' any help from anyone, even as a child," his father says as my eyes move back to him.

"He was as stubborn as a mule, infuriated the hell outta me. I'd like to say he takes after his momma, but we know differently. Unfortunately, he inherited my temper too."

"Yes, I've kinda gathered that," I muse. "When he banged a customer's head against the bar for mouthing off at me."

His dad grins. "That's my boy."

Axton covers his eyes with his hand like he's embarrassed.

His dad grips him on the shoulder. "I've gotta talk to Hutch, so I'll leave you in peace for now." Then he looks up at me. "And we'd love to have you both for dinner. In fact, his mother insisted. Taco Tuesday is always a winner."

"Consider it a date," I say as his dad squeezes my shoulder softly on his way by.

"I'm sorry about that," Axton begins as I shut him up with another kiss. When we break free, he adds, "What was that for?"

"Being you." I shrug. "I was so worried when they told

me you'd been taken and then nobody knew what was going on, but the cops did a raid and people were getting arrested. I still don't really understand all of what happened or why your dad's suddenly here and wearing a bulletproof vest, but I guess we can get to that."

He cups my face with his hand. "So much fuckin' happened since I saw you last. Speakin' of which, I'm not gonna apologize for hittin' your ex, so don't expect me to."

"Ax…"

He tightens his grip on the back of my head. "You are mine, Stevie. If he comes around here again, I won't hesitate to –"

"Shh," I tell him. "We're over, babe, we always were, but I needed time to explain it to him, to get closure, for both our sakes. It's well and truly done. I was never going to get back with Lukas."

He swallows hard, resting his forehead against mine. "I was so worried we were over, that he'd come to woo you back."

"He did try."

He pulls back a little. "What happened?"

I smile. "I'm here, aren't I?"

He cups my face, kisses my forehead, then my nose, then both my eyes, then finally, my mouth. Gripping me harder, we kiss for what feels like an eternity. That spark in my body is lit only for him. Every single inch of him.

My body knows what it needs, it always has, but my head needed a little time to catch up.

"I fuckin' love you, boss lady," he whispers against my lips. "Nobody and nothin' are gonna keep me from you. Got me?"

I push his hair back from his face as I study his beautiful features. "Let them try," I whisper. "I think I've loved you from the first moment I set eyes on you."

His eyes sparkle. "I've loved you ever since I first saw you checkin' me out that day in the bar."

"Ax…"

"Wait, you *think?*"

"No, I *know.*"

"Doesn't sound convincin'."

I laugh. "Okay, you got me. It was when you ripped your shirt off on the first day and I saw your body and your tattoos."

"You wanted me then, babe?"

"Yes."

He grins. I know we're probably making a scene, but I don't care.

"I wanted to rip those jeans down and have my fill of you against the bar," he whispers in my ear. "I wanted to taste you so fuckin' bad."

I swallow hard. "Axton…"

"Yeah, you'll be sayin' my name all night when you're

ridin' me, babe."

"We need to leave. Now," I say, looking around for the nearest exit.

He pulls me back into his lap. "Never heard such sweeter words, baby."

He kisses me again, and I help him up. Swinging his arm around me, we move toward the door at the same time Brock is coming in.

He eyes Axton's arm around my shoulders. "Shoulda known the two of you couldn't keep your hands off one another," he grumbles. "So much for fuckin' club rules."

"What can I say? Opposites attract," I reply, giving him a big grin. "And I'm not a club sister, or a club girl, I'm an employee."

"With a smart mouth," he quips, his lips twitching. He points at Axton. "Gotta talk to you, bro."

"Later."

"What's so pressin' we can't talk now? Got a fuckin' bone to pick with Hutch, and our father…"

"I've got my girl with me, you figure it out."

He frowns some more. "This isn't finished with."

"Thought you'd be happy to know me and Dad are gonna be okay."

"What the fuck happened?"

"Undercover Ops."

"I know that much, what else? This is some fucked up

shit."

"Dad isn't exactly who we think he is," Axton says. "And Hutch had to make a deal with the feds to keep me out of trouble."

"Jesus fuckin' Christ."

"I'll see you at Taco Tuesday," Axton replies, pulling me along with him.

"Hey!" Brock says as he pushes the door open.

Axton turns.

"I'm glad you're okay, little brother."

He nods. "Know it."

I lie in ecstasy, gripping Axton's head, as he rides me through another earth-shattering orgasm, courtesy of his tongue.

"I take it you approve?" He smiles up at me as I gaze down at him in awe.

"Let's just say your oral skills improve every time you do it, which is why practice makes perfect."

He runs a finger through my folds and slides into my soaking wet pussy. "Fuck," he growls. "I want this pussy on my cock, now."

He crawls up my body and grabs his very hard, very fuck-worthy cock, sliding the tip over my clit as I groan out loud. "You're such a tease, Altman."

"And you're beautiful when you come."

"Put it in me," I cry. "Hurry!"

He teases me some more, not penetrating as I grip his shoulders and pull him down to my mouth. I taste myself on his lips and I so badly want to return the favor, but I need him inside me before I die.

I reach down and grab his cock and position it at my entrance as he grins down at me. "Pushy little thing, aren't you?"

"Get to work, Altman, or I'll have no choice but to keep you captive in here."

He kisses me hard. "Doesn't sound like much punishment to me."

"What if I tie you up?"

"Fuck," he mutters. "Like the sound of that."

"You do?" I tease, wrapping my legs around his waist, trying to impale myself.

"I'm up for anythin' where your sweet pussy is concerned."

"Such a sweet talker."

He chuckles, lines himself up, and then finally slides into me. We both sigh at the same time as he fills me.

"Jesus, Ax…"

"Don't pretend like you can't take it," he says through gritted teeth.

"Are you holdin' back?"

He slides out, then slams back into me again. "If I fuck you like I want to, I'll break the goddamn bed."

"Faster!" I tell him, reaching around and slapping his ass.

He pushes his face into my neck and bites down on my skin as he begins to move his hips faster and faster, his body pressing into mine.

"Drive me fuckin' nuts, woman," he grunts as I clutch his ass with both hands and squeeze.

His whole body is God's gift to women.

I close my eyes, unable to form words, as his pounding continues, and he's right; he doesn't let up. Soon, I'm cascading into an orgasm that hits me like a hurricane, so intense I see freaking stars. He follows right behind me, shooting his load as he slows down and then collapses on top of me.

"Only trouble with goin' fast," he growls. "Is it's over too soon."

He lifts up when I protest that he's suffocating me, and I cup his face as he looks down at me.

"I couldn't agree more, but that just means you get to do it all over again."

He grins as he kisses me chastely, then flips me over so I'm on top.

I settle my hands on his chest as I sit up.

"Fuck, you're so goddamn beautiful," he says as I run my hands over his pecs, feeling every muscle of his fine body.

"Did anyone ever tell you you're not so bad yourself?"

"For an ex-con?"

"For a man who never gives himself enough credit."

He smirks. "Workin' on it."

I run a hand through his hair. "I think the world of you, Axton," I say as his eyes soften.

"The moment I saw you, I knew you were gonna get me in a whole world of trouble."

He runs a palm over my cheek, his eyes flashing with that boyish charm I love so much.

"You're the one who's in trouble here, boss. Remember, you might be the boss of me downstairs, but up here, you're all mine."

"Is that right?" I laugh. "Because it seems to me that I might have you right where I want you."

He sits up so we're face to face. "Don't count on it." He kisses me hard, rough, just how I like it, and I don't know how long we kiss for. It could be seconds, minutes, days. I lose track of time whenever we're here together. That's how I know that this feels right.

Despite the obstacles we may face, I can't help how I feel. I can only go with it, and gravitating to him feels like the most natural thing in the world.

It's like we were just meant to come together, no matter what.

It feels nice in his arms.

Safe.

Nothing else really comes close.

In such a short space of time, he's turned my world upside down.

And that's all I need to know right now; we'll work the rest out as it happens.

I can't wait to see what the future holds, but with Axton by my side, it's sure to be one hell of a ride.

BRACKEN RIDGE
REBELS
ARIZONA
M · C

CHAPTER 25

AXTON
ONE WEEK LATER

"F ine turn out," Hutch says across the bar. He's at his usual spot at the very end, where he can see everything.

Tonight is the snobby art society dinner and charity auction. Stevie's been busy, prepping all week, giving us little time to get reacquainted. Lucky for me that she lives right across the hall…

"Roxy's been prepping for days like a madwoman," I reply, handing him another Scotch. "And Stevie's been running all over, makin' sure everything's perfect."

"Glad Roxy's finally got some decent help in the kitchen; the woman practically lives here. Stevie's done a fine job tonight. Everyone seems to be happy." He gives me a chin lift. "You all good?"

I nod. "I'm fine."

"And your pop?"

"You'd know more than me."

"I'd like to say I feel bad about knockin' you out." He goes on.

"I feel a 'but' coming on?"

A slow grin spreads across his face. "I'm also kinda glad an old man like me can take a man half his age."

"Watch it, I'm not that old. And jumpin' someone by surprise isn't exactly a fair fight."

He shakes his head. "You know that old sayin'; flattery will get you everywhere? Load of shit, just give me the best Scotch."

"Touché." I turn and reach for the top shelf to top off his glass.

After the raid on the warehouse, everything changed.

Little Mick got taken out from gunfire. Nobody knows if it were Bones or the cops, not that it really matters. He's six feet under. Much to Hutch's dismay, since unlike my father, who still follows the rules, Hutch likes to deal with vermin his own way.

More arrests were made, and what followed suit was one of the biggest drug busts that Arizona has ever seen. So big, that it made the nightly news as it was the collapse of the drug syndicate that Mick's bosses had been working to build and push through the smaller towns throughout Arizona.

My father had been undercover for almost a year. This was one of the biggest busts of his career.

What was even more shocking, was that we've actually found some common ground.

I had dinner there last week, and while I wanted to take Stevie along and introduce her to Mom, she insisted that I have this time with my parents alone.

Things will probably never be perfect with my dad, but he's changed a lot. I'll never stop being sorry for the wrongs I did, but I know that I'll never do anything to harm the ones I love in my life ever again. They deserve better, and so do I.

For the first time in my life, I have to believe in myself. I know I can overcome any obstacle that I'm facing, as long as I keep my focus on the things I want.

I know I've got a long way to go, but you gotta start somewhere.

And as I look out at Stevie, who's hosting the annual fundraiser, I realize just what a lucky son of a bitch I am to have found someone like her.

"She's a good woman," Hutch says, as if reading my mind.

"Not wrong there."

"Even though you should get the shit kicked out of you, I can't say I blame you. Sometimes the temptation of a beautiful woman, who's intelligent to boot, just gets the better of you. I would know, and I'm still married to the woman."

"Same wife?" I chuckle.

He eyes me. "Same one. I was lucky enough to get it right the first time. I was fucked up once too, on the path of the self-destruction, then I made a choice, and it set in motion everything good that I have in my life. Can't say it was easy, but you know right from wrong, that's all there is to it. And if you find a good woman, learn all the ways you can keep her, don't be fuckin' around and messin' with her if she's yours. A man is only worth so much without the love and support of a good woman by his side. You can only get so far with a pretty face, kid."

I stare at him and wonder if I'll have good things in my life too.

Then I say, "You think I'm pretty?"

"I was referring to myself, fuckface." Then he chuckles.

"Though, long as the ol' lady still thinks I'm good enough to snag, then we're good."

"I'm serious about her," I say after a while, leaning against the bar taps as I watch her.

She's so effortless. Everyone loves her. She's like California sunshine.

"I can tell."

"Do you just know?"

"When it's the one?"

I nod. "Yeah."

"Yeah, son, you know."

I know I'll get the gist of it, like how weak at the knees I feel whenever we're alone together.

"I've never had these feelings before; possessiveness, jealousy, it's all new to me."

He snorts. "Get used to it. I almost blew a couple of heads off when Kirsty was younger. Can't say my temper has gotten any better over the years; not when it comes to other men lookin' at my woman. But your job is to protect her, not smother her. Remember that."

It's no wonder all the club members look up to Hutch. He's not only a decent human being, but he actually knows his shit.

Brock appears out of nowhere and sits down noisily next to Hutch as he gives me a chin lift. "What are you two grinnin' about?"

Hutch gives him a slap on the back. "Just talkin' politics and pussies."

He gives Hutch a side-eye before I hand him a beer.

"Should disown the lot of you," Brock grumbles.

Hutch side-eyes him right back. "Havin' you involved from the get-go would've spelled disaster. You do know your temper is legendary."

"Tellin' me I'm worse than Steel?" He snorts.

Hutch makes a face. "You got me there. Nobody is as bad as Steel. Least I can reason with you, most of the time."

He balks. "Most of the time? Fuckin' boy scout

compared to that fucker."

"You know I wasn't excited about it in the first place, but when the feds come callin', gotta try and make it seem like I wanna fuckin' help." Hutch goes on. "When it started to involve Ax, that's when your father came to me, told me what was goin' on. We both agreed havin' him go undercover was too risky."

Brock just shakes his head. "The old bastard can still keep us on our toes, I'll say that much."

"Glad to hear that I'm not just a shit kicker after all." I laugh.

Hutch eyes me. "Not like I'm gonna fuckin' argue with Jim. He drives a hard bargain, and trust me, he gives a shit."

I try not to feel the lump in my throat, but it's hard.

Everything is coming into fruition, and not for the first time, I realize how lucky I am.

"What about you and Stevie?" Brock gives me a nod.

"Not you too," I complain. "Prez has already given me the third degree."

"Had to fuckin' bone the boss." He runs a hand through his long hair. "Mom's already gettin' the church booked. The woman can't be contained."

"Kinda runs in the family," I say, giving Nitro a chin lift as he sits down.

"Who pissed in your cereal?" Brock asks when he lets out a heavy sigh.

The dude is pretty quiet most of the time, but we've had a couple of good conversations. I tend to think he's one of those guys who takes everything in and doesn't say a lot, but he knows exactly what's going on.

"Wouldn't be a woman, would it?" Hutch can't hide his grin.

"When is it ever not a fuckin' woman?" he grunts when I settle a whiskey down in front of him.

"I made it a double," I say as he gives me a grateful nod.

"So?" Brock goes on. "Don't leave us hangin'."

"Wouldn't have anything to do with a certain baby doctor, would it?" I've been observant; call it a habit I can't break. Plus, Nitro did admit that Frankie was 'his' that night I got jumped. I've been meaning to ask him a little more on the subject.

He looks up at me after taking a big draw from his glass. "Am I that transparent?"

I wince. "A little."

He runs a hand through his hair, avoiding looking toward the bustle down the far end of the bar that's been extended to fit everyone in at makeshift tables.

It's then I see Frankie about the same time he does.

"Trouble with small towns," he mutters. "Can't get away from the only fuckin' woman who haunts my life." I frown, and Brock and Hutch share a look.

"Deep, brother," Brock says. "What she do to you anyway?"

"It's what she didn't do that's the problem," he grumbles.

"What, she didn't jump on your dick the second you laid eyes so her?" I jibe. "Some chicks take a little more hard work."

"Like you'd know," Brock says. "What are you, five minutes in?"

I shake my head, ignoring him. Ain't nobody raining on my parade.

Like a siren's call, Frankie turns her head and looks right over, her eyes meeting his.

"Is it just me?" I say, as we all look at her at the same time. "Or has she got the devil in her eyes?"

Nitro shakes his head. "No, that's just how she looks all the time. Sweet as pie to everyone else, but a pain in the ass to me."

"You must've done somethin'," Brock insists. "She's a good girl, too wholesome for you, though. Probably gotta get past her lawyer, gardener, and her tennis coach before you even think about suckin' on that pussy."

"I might've done somethin'…" He stops.

"For fuck's sake." Hutch slams his glass down on the bar. "Gettin' fuckin' old here."

He sighs. "She might've… she just found out we kinda

know each other."

I give him a chin lift. "From Phoenix?"

He nods. "Yeah, long story… won't go into it now but, I sorta… stalked her."

Brock spurts his drink out all over the bar as Hutch proceeds to laugh and pat Brock on the back at the same time.

I lean down closer to the bar. "What the fuck, bro? You know that's illegal, right?"

He rolls his eyes. "Course I fuckin' know, but it's not what you think or how it sounds."

"Which is it, you stalked her, or not?" Hutch can't keep the humor out of his tone. "Either way, it doesn't sound good."

He rubs his chin, still looking over there, even though she's turned back around.

"I did, but she saved my life. Doubt she even remembers… it was a long time ago. To repay her the favor, I watched out for her, protected her, and made sure she was safe, that kinda thing."

"Doesn't sound so bad to me," I say. "But I'm guessin' she doesn't see it like that."

"Not exactly, and she won't let me explain."

I'm kinda getting the notion that Nitro has feelings for this chick that go beyond trying to apologize for stalking her.

"Just use some of that southern charm," Hutch says,

then rebuffs. "On second thought, maybe you'd better brush up on your skills a little. A woman like that, a fuckin' doctor, she's smart, she's one step ahead of you in her sleep."

He doesn't deny that he wants her. "Thanks for the vote of confidence," he says.

"Must've made an impression," Brock puts in. "For all the wrong reasons."

"Can say that again. Think she'd be fuckin' grateful. I'm not a weirdo like some of the fuckers out there," he says, exasperated. "She'd leave the hospital late at night, and any fucker could've been lurking around up to no good when it's dark. Didn't wanna see anythin' bad happen to her."

He's fuckin' serious.

"Ain't nobody in my bad books for shit like that," Hutch says. "Should be more like it."

Brock slaps him on the back. "It's the one you can't have that always gets you the most, learned that the hard way."

"Can say that again," he grumbles.

I catch sight of Stevie again as she works the tables, handing out little cards for people to bid at the art auction, which is about to commence.

There are three paintings to be unveiled, all the proceeds going to charity.

I know that she's excited about tonight, and so far, everything's gone off without a hitch.

I move closer to the fray, leaving the boys to their brews.

Her eyes meet mine across the bar, and I give her a chin lift.

She smiles like the bright ray of sunshine that she is. My eyes graze down her body. Her tight-fitting jeans and tank that hangs a little too low for my liking, both hug her curves. Her hair's styled long and half tied up, and I'd like nothing more than to run my hands through it while she rides me. All kinds of salacious thoughts run through my mind as I stare at her.

She rolls her lips as if she can read my mind as I eye fuck her. Blushing just a little, she looks down, then back up at me. I know she feels it too, there's no fighting it.

The announcer unveils the first painting; a beautiful landscape of the peaks and dips of the desert. The colors are amazing, changing from light to dark. Painting number two is of birds in the sky, the backdrop a mix of clouds, blues, and grays.

Then they reveal painting number three.

At first, it catches me by surprise because the first thing I see is a giant Harley Davidson.

It's surrounded by the scenery of the Canyon and the mountain ridges, and over the top, swoops a giant eagle, just like the eagle on my chest. In fact, it's the exact same one.

I stare at it a little harder. It's all in black and white, like a sketch, but it's so detailed, even from where I'm standing. The only flash of color is through the body of the bike, a light blue… the same color as my eyes.

I knew Stevie enjoyed artwork, but I didn't know she could do this shit… *Did she really do this?*

My head turns to look at her, but she's disappeared.

I know she's kinda shy about her artwork. Heck, I didn't even know she was entering anything or what she was sketching. I've been so caught up in getting to know her body that her interests have fallen by the wayside. That's something I'll have to remedy.

Now I know I have to have it, and I have to wait until the other auctions have finished before I can bid and then go hunt her down. The wait is agonizing.

It goes for five hundred, because that's how much I call out after someone almost snags it for three hundred.

Then I stalk off from the bar, satisfied with my purchase. It doesn't take long; I find her in the back office.

I lean on the doorjamb. "I knew you were talented, boss, but I didn't know you were quite that talented."
She turns and gives me a timid smile. "I almost chickened out, but Cassidy and a couple of the girls convinced me to do it."

"It's beautiful, but not as beautiful as you," I say, my eyes searching for hers. I don't like it when she's all shy and coy like this, though I like her vulnerable side, but I love her confidence.

"You didn't have to buy it…"

"I wanted to."

"It's just a silly thing…"

I walk toward her as I bend down onto my haunches and rub my hands up her thighs. "There's nothing silly about it. I've never seen anything like that before. Where did you learn to draw?"

She shrugs. "I got into it when I was a teenager. Mom moved around a lot when we were kids, and I needed an outlet. Since we were dirt poor, I started to sketch, since pencils and paper were pretty cheap."

I push back the hair from her face. "When did you sketch this?"

"A few days after…" She bites her lip.

"A few days after?"

"You started work," she finishes.

I can't help the shit-eating grin that spreads across my face.

"You really did have your sights set on me from the get-go, huh?"

She runs her hands through my hair. I'll never grow tired of her beautiful face.

"Something like that."

"I guess sometimes things are just meant to be. Like kickin' that asshole Lukas to the curb."

"Are you still going on about that?"

"I've just recently realized I have a jealous side," I admit.

She smirks. "Are you saying it was me who brought it out in you?"

"Definitely, and now that you are mine, expect more of it."

She reaches down to cup my face as we kiss lightly. "You didn't have to buy my artwork."

I shake my head. "You're wrong. It is my tattoo after all, and my bike, and just for the record, I only had my shirt off for a few seconds that first day. Talk about creepy."

She chuckles. "You're lucky you're cute, Altman, that's all I'm gonna say."

"Ditto."

I pull her closer, invading her mouth with mine as my tongue seeks entry, and she throws her arms around me. I don't know how long we kiss for, but when I pull back, we're both panting.

"I want it to always be like this," I whisper, pressing my forehead against hers. "Promise me."

"I promise, Axton. I'm yours."

I kiss her on the nose.

"Now, let's go get my art so I can mount it above the bed before I mount you."

"Spoken like a true romantic."

BRACKEN RIDGE
REBELS
ARIZONA
M · C

EPILOGUE

STEVIE
SIX MONTHS LATER

I stare at myself in the mirror, unable to fathom how my life got to this point.

If someone had told me six months ago that this would be how everything turned out, I'd tell them to take a running jump. It's funny how life works.

Kennedy fusses around me on one side, fluffing a brush over my face, and Lily is on the other side, curling my hair. Cassidy is my main bridesmaid, and she's running around trying to make sure everything's in place before we start. Amelia has agreed to film the entire ceremony, in fact, I couldn't stop her.

I didn't want a fanfare, just a small, quiet, personal wedding.

When Axton asked me to marry him three months ago, I knew that I wanted to spend the rest of my life with him. After being in such a long relationship previously, Axton thought it best if we slow things down, get to know each other. He even took me out on dates and for long rides up to the Canyon; his favorite place. That didn't last long, though.

As cliché as it sounds, we're simply in love. And Axton is a man who knows what he wants.

No matter how many times I bugged him about if he was sure he was doing the right thing, he has made it clear he's all in. After all, being out of prison for a short period, most guys would surely spend that time boning anything that moves. Not Axton. Then again, he's not like anybody else.

And honestly, I've never been this happy. He's the reason.

I'm sure a lot of people will think we're rushing it, taking things too fast, but when you know, you know.

I look back at myself and I can't do anything except smile.

I chose a long, flowy dress with very few embellishments. I'm not a bling kinda girl like my sister. And with it being summer now, I wanted something loose-fitting.

The only thing Axton insisted on was the dress being white.

"I think I've got everything all set up, but I want some candid moments of you before you walk up the aisle," Amelia says, looking down at the video camera.

"As long as you don't stick it in my face, we're all

good," I say, letting out a slow breath.

She smiles. "I'm so glad Axton found his happiness, and now I have a new sister too!"

"I'm so lucky to have all of you," I say as Amelia gives me a big hug.

"You're going to be fine," she whispers.

"Hey, don't ruin your makeup!" Kennedy scolds.

Amelia dashes off to get set up.

I take another deep breath.

"Nervous?" Lily asks when she catches my eye in the mirror.

I shake my head. "No bridezilla here." I laugh.

She smiles back. "He's going to be so blown away. You really do have that whole glowy bride thing going on."

I bite my lip, excitement bubbling up inside of me. I can't wait to be his wife. I can't wait to start our new life together.

"That's because the two of them go at it night and day like no other," Kennedy pipes up as I look at her with wide eyes.

"Kennedy!"

"What? Like it's not true?"

"You can talk. Bones barricaded you in your apartment when you got released from hospital. I had to leave food parcels outside and book an appointment to see my own sister," I kindly remind her.

Her lips twitch. Gotcha, sis.

"Well, Bones is a very persuasive man," she concedes as I chuckle. "That can't be helped."

"You two are hopeless," Lily says. "Though, love does make you do the strangest things, I'll say that much."

Lily sets the curling wand down and begins to fluff my hair around, spraying a little hair spray here and there. I wanted my hair in loose, long waves, growing it longer for the wedding and adding some highlights. Axton loves my long hair.

Kennedy has tears in her eyes. "Wait till Mom sees you, she's gonna flip."

There's a knock on the door, as we all turn to see who it is.

"Boss lady?" I hear Axton's voice.

The second he calls out, Lily and Kennedy squeal and run in front, blocking me from view. A few moments later, Summer and Deanna come running in.

"Hey! You're not supposed to be in here," Deanna tells him. "So if you know what's good for you, beat it!"

"Fine watchmen you are!" Lily huffs. "You had one job to do and that was to keep the groom away."

"We got distracted," Summer says. "And she's right, it's bad luck to see the bride before the wedding."

"I just wanted to make sure she's still comin," he says, exasperation in his tone.

I shake my head as Kennedy turns to look at me in the mirror, the look on her face softening.

"I love you, Altman!" I call out. "But if you don't get out of here now, it's not just my wrath you're gonna face, it's the entire crew of club girls."

Yep, I'm not just a club girl now, I'm an ol' lady. God help me.

I'm marrying Axton, and that means I'm also marrying the club.

"I'd love you a lot more if we could hurry this up a bit!" he calls back as Deanna and Summer begin to unceremoniously usher him out the door.

I can't help but laugh. "Keep your hair on, a girl can't get married in flannel!"

"He was literally two seconds away from seeing you," Lily scorns when he's gone. "Men are so fucking infuriating!"

I shake my head. "Tell me about it, if it were up to Axton, we would have had more of a fanfare than what we have now. I said a small, quiet wedding for family only."

"Hey, what was Axton just doing in here?" Cassidy says, appearing a few moments later.

"Being annoying," I laugh.

Cassidy gives me a great big smile. She's been a godsend. While everyone has helped us and gone above and beyond to get this wedding organized, Cass has been my tower of strength. Whenever I started to even remotely get stressed, she'd talk me down and remind me that we're having a low-key wedding and there's nothing to worry about.

The entire club is out there, plus some of my family and all of Axton's.

"It's so sweet, though." Kennedy goes on. "He really does love you, sis. I'm happy for you."

She squeezes my hand. "Thanks, sis. I'm a kept woman now, according to Ax."

"Is that because he works two jobs, or because he's over-protective and doesn't want you working?" Lily rolls her eyes, like she's had the same conversation herself.

"Both," I concede. "But he knows I love working and just because he's my husband now doesn't mean I'm going to change who I am, nor does he expect that. But, he does get a little heavy-handed if a guy gets fresh at the bar."

"Understandable," Kennedy says. "We're involved with alpha men to the extreme, so what did we expect?"

"You can say that again," Cassidy agrees, then assesses me. "You look amazing, Stevie. Axton will be blown away."

"Thank you, but I had a lot of help," I say, smiling up at the girls.

"She ready yet?" I hear Hutch's voice boom, making me jump.

"Jesus," Kennedy says, clutching her chest with one hand. "You scared me half to death."

Hutch approaches with caution as I stand, and when he sees me, he gives me a wide smile.

He's wearing a nice pair of tailored pants, and a crisp white shirt with his cut over the top. His hair's tied back neatly, and he's trimmed his beard.

I guess you can't really take the biker out of the man after all…

"You look beautiful, darlin'," he says. "Axton's one lucky son of a gun."

We asked Hutch to give me away, along with my mom. Since he's the closest thing I've had to a father, it seemed fitting, and Hutch was really touched.

"You don't look so bad yourself," I say, smiling.

He pulls on the lapels of his cut. "Wife made me brush my hair and have a shave." He gives me a wink.

"Any words of wisdom before I take my last steps as a single woman?"

He takes my hand and gives it a squeeze. "Be happy, that's really all there is to it. It's the little things, Stevie. Don't get caught up in all the big shit, as you'll miss out on all the fun along the way."

I try not to cry as he nods in understanding.

"Thank you, Hutch, for everything," I whisper.

"We're family now," he says. "And that means you get permission to kick his ass any time you want. Perks of bein' an ol' lady."

I laugh as we get to the door. Mom appears as I step out.

She's wearing a sky-blue skirt suit and a wide-brimmed hat. Trust my mother to go all out.

She starts to cry when she sees me. I didn't want a veil, but Lily insisted I have a small headband of flowers. It's subtle and elegant and matches my dress.

"My baby girl," mom says as we hug. "You look stunning. I'm so proud of you!"

"Thanks, mom."

"Now, now enough of that," Hutch scolds. "You'll both ruin your makeup, and then we'll never get this show on the road."

We're getting married on Brock's property. Axton is turning one of the old stables into our house. It's a slow process and we're nowhere near ready to move in, but we both love it out here with the horses and the landscape. I can't wait until it's finished.

Mom dabs her eyes and puts her handkerchief in the pocket of her jacket. "You look so beautiful, a vision," she whispers. "I'm so happy, for both of you."

I smile. "I am too, mom. I love that color on you."

"We ready?" Hutch asks, eyeing Kennedy, Cassidy and Lily behind us.

"Ready," they chime.

Kennedy and Lily move ahead of us to go take their places, while Cassidy comes to stand in front of me and starts fussing with my hair. I swat her away.

Hutch looks down at me. "What about you, Mrs. Altman-to-be?"

A grin spreads across my face. "I've never been more ready."

He nods and we walk out of Brock's house toward the ceremony.

The girls have set up a marquee and there are white chairs on either side of the makeshift altar. They're adorned with sky-blue bows and someone has sprinkled rose petals all over the pathway.

Rawlings, Angel and Brock's daughter, comes running up to me in her flower girl outfit, holding an empty basket.

"Hey, kid." I smile.

She gasps. "You look just like a fairy princess!" she squeals.

Angel comes running up behind her. "Rawlings," she whisper-shouts. "You weren't supposed to use all the petals just yet!"

Rawlings slaps a hand over her mouth. "Oops!"

"I have more!" Kirsty calls, rushing over as I try to peek around the hedge to try and see my groom, but I can't. People are blocking.

I wait impatiently as Kirsty fills Rawlings's basket again, kisses me on the cheek, and then kisses Hutch before dashing off in her sky-high heels.

"Okay, just like we practiced, all right?" Angel says to Rawlings before giving me a thumbs up.

"I know, Mom! Jeez!" she says, slapping her forehead. "Go!"

Angel takes off, not before straightening out Rawlings's dress.

Hutch pats me on the arm. "Without further ado," he says. "Let's get you married."

Cassidy takes Rawlings' hand and they proceed to walk in front of us as the music begins. Rawlings begins throwing more petals down as she walks.

As we round the corner, I don't see anything else over the sea of people, just him.

Axton.

He's standing at the altar in a white suit.

My groom.

My beautiful groom.

He smiles when he sees me, shaking his head in disbelief, then he wipes his eyes as I realize I've brought him to tears.

I love you, I mouth.

I love you too, boss.

This is the best moment of my entire life.

I've waited so long for him to come along.

And now he's here.

We're here, together.

My forever is waiting.

AXTON

Stevie walks toward me as I stare at her beautiful face. Her skin is flawless, her eyes sparkling, her dress perfect. I can't believe how fuckin' lucky I am.

This woman is going to be my wife.

Some kinda fuckin' miracle happened when this all lined up, and I'll never stop being grateful for every damn moment.

I turn to Brock as he squeezes my shoulder. "Deep breaths, little brother."

I nod. "She's stunning."

"That she is. I knew you'd do good, bro, but I never thought you'd do this good."

I chuckle. "Thanks."

"You two are gonna be fine, I know it."

I can't take my eyes off her as she walks slowly toward me, too slow. I want her in my arms.

Hutch grins at me as I give him a chin lift, and I smile at Stevie's mom as she tries her hardest not to cry while she walks her daughter toward me.

A few stray tears leak, and I don't fuckin' care how that makes me look. It's our day, and it's gonna be one to remember.

The moms did all the cooking and we've set up the stable for the reception. There'll be a buffet, speeches, and then we'll get the music cranked.

No matter how many times I imagined this in my head, I never expected it to be this perfect.

My ray of sunshine reaches me, and her mom pats my hand before sitting down in the front row.

Hutch shakes my hand, then loud enough for everyone to hear, he says, "Just remember what I said about kneecaps only bendin' one way."

I grin. "Got it."

He pats me on the shoulder, gives Stevie a kiss on the cheek, and then takes his seat next to Kirsty.

I catch sight of my parents in the front row, too. Mom's blowing her nose, tears streaming down her face, and Amelia isn't much better. Dad bounces little Ethan Wolf, Brock and Angel's baby, on his knee as he watches on, giving me a thumbs up.

We're like the fuckin' Brady Bunch. Another thing I'm grateful for is the relationship I now have with my parents. It's been a long time in the making, but it's better late than never.

I take Stevie's hands in mine, as she looks up at me.

I bend down and kiss her nose. "You look so beautiful."

"So do you," she whispers back.

"Ahem," Knuckles says, clearing his throat. "Can we

kindly leave manhandling until after the ceremony, please?"

Another turn out for the books is that Knuckles is a marriage celebrant. Who would've thought?

"Oops," I say with a grin as I look at him. "Sorry."

Murmurs of laughter ring through the crowd and the proceedings begin.

As we say our vows, the tightening in my chest gets more intense when she speaks to me and only me.

"…and I'll love you forever, Axton John Altman."

I squeeze her hands and can't wait for the last part.

"With the powers vested in me, I bless this union, and I now pronounce you man and wife. You may kiss your bride."

I waste no time. I move in, clutching the side of her face as our lips meet. I don't care for half-assed "wedding friendly" kisses, I go all in. My tongue seeks entry as she throws her arms around me, and I lift her off the ground.

Cheers and wolf whistles ring out as well as "get a room" from probably Gunner — it's the type of thing he'd shout out. As I set her down on her feet, I wipe her tears with my thumbs.

"Don't cry, Mrs. Altman," I say, kissing them away. "I never want to make you cry."

"They're good tears," she replies as our fingers link. "Always."

"Ready?"

"I'm ready."

We walk down the aisle as everyone claps and then they throw confetti at us, drowning us in the stuff as Deanna takes pictures and Amelia holds out a video camera as she films us. Sneaky little things; we said low key and that meant low budget, but one thing about this MC is that everyone bands together.

The food was all donated, as were the flowers, and the tables and chairs, we borrowed from work. Stevie's hair and makeup was a gift. I got my suit second-hand, as did Stevie with her dress.

The rings I saved for. Nothing but the best for my baby.

I'm also building us a house on the property, so between that and my shifts at the Stone Crow and setting up my van for my electrical business, things are tight. When the house is done, I'll be an electrician full-time. My first job is to rewire the downstairs office, bar, and kitchen for the Crow.

As we walk toward the barn, I squeeze her hand tight.

This is the happiest day of my life. I've no idea how I could get any happier.

Everything just feels so right with her by my side.

I really do have two left feet, but I try to dance for Stevie because she can move really well. She and the girls have been dancing up a storm for most of the night.

Hutch and Kirsty's wedding present was a professional singer and guitarist, playing all of our favorite songs.

"Can I have this dance?" my father interrupts as I turn Stevie in my arms.

"She's only been my wife for a few hours, dad," I complain. "Give it a minute."

He grins. "Yes, and you've got the rest of your life to dance with her. Hand her over and take your mother for a spin."

Mom reaches for me as I lean forward and kiss Stevie before dad whisks her away.

"Hey, mom," I say as she looks up at me proudly.

"Oh, Axton," she says, trying and failing not to cry again. "I'm so proud of you, honey. You look so handsome, and Stevie makes such a beautiful bride."

"Thanks, mom."

We spin around the room, hoping I won't crash into anyone.

"It was a gorgeous ceremony. I can't wait to watch it back on video."

"I'm sure you've taken enough happy snaps to fill an entire house," I say, knowing my mom well.

Then out of nowhere, she says, "Your father and I wanted to wait until tonight before letting you know that as your wedding present, we'd like to help contribute with the rest of the build for the house."

My eyes go wide. "What? Mom, you can't do that."

She nods her head. "Yes, we can, Axton John Altman, and we want to. We want you to make a home for your new bride and all those grandbabies you're going to have. Anyway, it's the least we could do to help make it a home and get you in there as fast as possible."

"Mom, we've been married for two hours. No babies yet."

"Yes, I know that, but a mom can dream."

I lean down and kiss her cheek. "Thanks, you don't have to do that, but I'm really grateful."

Dad gives me a nod on the way by as Stevie and him tear up the dance floor. "I think I might go get my wife back," I mutter. "Dad's gonna hurt himself if he's not careful."

"Indulge your mother for a few more minutes. You're still my baby."

I smile, shaking my head. "You're the best. I knew I was always the favorite."

She laughs happily. It's all I've ever wanted; to make both of them proud. It was just a little longer in the making.

When I eventually get my wife back, it's time to cut the cake.

Stevie's mom baked and decorated it, and it's absolutely amazing. White chocolate with lemon sponge.

Stevie already warned me not to smash cake in her face, not that I would ever disrespect her like that, but we do eat off each other's forks while Deanna takes more pictures, shouting orders at us to face this way and that. It only infuriates her more when I don't do as she says.

Amelia has been busy videoing not only the whole ceremony but also the night, capturing dancing, speeches and the embarrassing sight of me dancing.

When we're seated again, Stevie turns to me. "How soon can we sneak away?"

I pull her to me. "Cock's been hard ever since I saw you walkin' toward me."

"Last of the romantics." She sighs as I kiss her gently.

"Was it all you hoped it'd be?" I prod when we pull back.

She stares at me with those beautiful big eyes. "I just wanted you, Axton, that's it."

"Well, you got me, now and forever."

"So, let's sneak away."

I grin. "I think I like keepin' you waitin' for a change. Though, the idea of puttin' a baby in there does make me wanna throw you over my shoulder and run off with you."

She bites her lip. "Speaking of which, I do have a little surprise of my own."

I run a knuckle over her cheek. "You're gonna let me take care of you?"

She snorts. "No, it's much bigger than that."

"Now you've got me intrigued."

She looks down at her hands, and when she looks back up at me, she has tears in her eyes.

"Well, I wanted you to be the first to know… and I know that we didn't plan this…"

I stare at her, waiting for whatever the hell she's babbling about.

"…but it just kinda happened, as these things do, sometimes."

"Stevie," I say, kissing her on the forehead, "spit it out. I'm gettin' gray already."

She takes a deep breath as my heart races, waiting for the news that I know is gonna change my life for the second time tonight. "Axton, you're going to be a father." She runs her free hand to her belly.

"What?"

"I'm pregnant, Ax."

I stare down at her stomach for a moment while I register.

"You know how I've had swollen boobs and put on a little bit of weight… well, I skipped a period and took a test. The doctor confirmed it, and I'm almost eight weeks."

I run my hand over her flat stomach, unable to speak.

"Ax? Are you okay?"

I glance back up at her and bury my head in her neck, unable to face her. "I'm so fuckin' happy," I choke out.

"My baby… *our* baby." Never in my wildest dreams did I imagine this.

"Yes, you dear sweet man," she whispers as she runs a hand through the back of my hair. "I'm having your kid. I'm going to be big and fat and gross and you're gonna love it."

"I love you," I say simply, bringing my hands to her face as I kiss her hard. "I fuckin' love you so much."

"Good surprise, then?" She laughs when we break free.

"Fuck yeah."

I turn to face the room and ding the wine glass with a fork. "Hey, everyone!" I yell out as Stevie gasps, holding on to my arm as she giggles. "My beautiful wife has an announcement to make!"

Everyone stops and turns to face the head table.

I pull her up to stand, because my queen needs to be seen.

"Tell them, baby," I say in her ear, pulling her to my side.

"We're having a baby!" she calls out, as gasps followed by claps ensue.

I catch sight of my parents who have halted on the dance floor. My mom's jaw is practically on the ground.

Hutch and Kirsty look on proudly. Stevie's mom claps and dabs her eyes. Brock gives me a slap on the back as he comes to stand next to me, and Angel hugs Stevie.

"Welcome to the family," Angel says as she turns to hug me too. "And congratulations, you deserve it."

I pull Stevie into my arms and kiss her again as

everyone wolf whistles.

"Too late to get a room!" Gunner calls out. I flip him the bird, even though I'm still kissing Stevie.

"Proud of you, bro," I hear Brock say as I stare at my wife. She's crying again.

I've so much to do to prepare for my new family, but I wouldn't want it any other way.

I found her. I found my reason for being.

I'm finally home.

And I'm gonna spend the rest of my life making sure we're like this.

Forever.

THE END

429

ACKNOWLEDGMENTS

Thank you to my amazing team, Savannah and Brianna at Peachy Keen Author Services (peachykeenas) for all your help pushing my books out to the world

Thank you to my sister D @kikiedits for being my proofreader and reminding me of when I repeat myself fifty times! Whoops sorry!

Thank you to my Alpha reader Michelle (the outgoing bookworm) and my Beta girls Kerri and Alana for your suggestions and funny notes, much appreciated!

Thank you to my ARC readers, I hope you enjoy Axton. He really made me so emotional out of all the book boys I've written, he's right up there with Gunner

A big shout out to my blogger, author and reader friends for sharing my posts, graphics and sending me messages that make me smile. I'm so honored. I love hearing from you so don't be afraid to drop me a line!

Special thanks to my editor Mackenzie @ nicegirlnaughtyedits for your patience

A big OMG to Golden Czermak at FuriosFotog for this AMAZING exclusive and very hot cover picture of the beautiful Dylan Horsch – you're both awesome!

Thanks LJ from Mayhem Cover Creations for the cover design

As always, thank you to my reader family who may have been following along with the series, or you may be a new reader to my books - I hope you enjoy getting swept up in the characters as much as I do writing them. There are plenty more bad biker boys coming your way, I just never want this series to end LOL but while the end isn't in sight just yet, I do have other spin-off MC books already planned.

If you can spare the time to leave a review on GR and/or Amazon if you loved Axton or any of my books that would be greatly appreciated and helps me so much as an indie author. Links are on the following pages.

I can't wait for you to meet the next character in this series (hint…hint…keep reading)

Be sure to check out my private facebook group (links below) as I update this page regularly before anything gets released on other social media channels.

Love from Australia, MF xx

FIND ME AT

Facebook: https://www.facebook.com/mackenzy.
foxauthor.5

Instagram: https://www.instagram.com/mackenzyfoxbooks/

Tiktok: https://www.tiktok.com/@mackenzyfoxauthor

Linktree: https://linktr.ee/mackenzyfox

Goodreads: https://bit.ly/2TKp7ck

https://books2read.com/Steel-BRR

Website: https://mackenzyfox.com

Join my private Facebook group for all the juicy gossip, giveaways and spicy reveals first at The Den - A Mackenzy Fox Reader Group - https://bit.ly/3dgQfKk

ABOUT THE AUTHOR

Mackenzy Fox is an author of contemporary, romantic and erotic themed romance novels. When she's not writing she loves vegan cooking, walking her beloved pooch's, reading books and is an expert on online shopping.

She's slightly obsessed with drinking tea, testing bubbly Moscato, watching home decorating shows and has a black belt in origami. She strives to live a quiet and introverted life in Western Australia's North West with her hubby, twin sister and her dogs.

ALSO BY MACKENZY FOX

Bracken Ridge Rebels MC:
Steel
Gunner
Brock
Colt
Rubble
Bones
Axton
Nitro
Gears
Knox

Medici Mafia:
Fortress of the King
Fortress of the Queen
Fortress of the Heart
Fortress of the Soul
Fortress of the Damned
Fortress of the Brave

Bad Boys of New York:
Jaxon

Standalone:
Broken Wings